WARDEN OF WATER

REIGN OF DRAGONS

BOOK THREE

D.N. HOXA

Also by D.N. Hoxa

The Hidden Realm Series (Completed)

Savage Ax

Damsel in Distress

Deadly Match

Pixie Pink Series (Completed)

Werewolves Like Pink Too

Pixies Might Like Claws

Silly Sealed Fates

The New York Shade Series (Completed)

Magic Thief

Stolen Magic

Immoral Magic

Alpha Magic

The New Orleans Shade Series (Completed)

Pain Seeker

Death Spell

Twisted Fate

Battle of Light

The Dark Shade Series (Completed)

Shadow Born

Broken Magic

Dark Shade

Smoke & Ashes Series (Completed)

Firestorm

Ghost City

Witchy Business

Wings of Fire

Winter Wayne Series (Completed)

Bone Witch

· Bone Coven

Bone Magic

Bone Spell

Bone Prison

Bone Fairy

Scarlet Jones Series (Completed)

Storm Witch

Storm Power

Storm Legacy

Storm Secrets

Storm Vengeance

Storm Dragon

Victoria Brigham Series (Completed)

Wolf Witch

Wolf Uncovered

Wolf Unleashed

· Wolf's Rise

The Marked Series (Completed)

Blood and Fire

Deadly Secrets

Death Marked

Starlight Series (Completed)

Assassin

Villain

Sinner

Savior

Morta Fox Series (Completed)

Heartbeat

Reclaimed

Unchanged

Dear reader,

I'll be the first to say it: Ella's relationship with her father is fucked up. Beyond fucked up. I realize that some events in this book might seem senseless to some people, and I understand that, but please try to keep on open mind, especially at the end of the book. Try not to judge Ella too harshly. And do try not to hate me (too much).

I hope you enjoy the story!

D.N. Hoxa

ONE

FIRE BURNED SOMEWHERE FAR AWAY. I HEARD THE sound of the flames dancing and saw the weak orange light getting sucked by the darkness around me. I felt it calling to me, calling to my blood—the element was brimming with magic, same way that I was, but I couldn't see it. It was still so far away. Too far out of reach.

But even so, I searched for it.

A little light would help me see better. A little warmth would melt the ice around my heart—I wasn't even sure where it had come from. A little strength would make putting one foot in front of the other a bit easier. I was walking without direction, without aim, but I still had a tiny bit of hope in my chest that I'd get there...wherever I was going. Wherever the fire was.

It was a long time before I saw his silhouette.

He was just as dark as the empty space around me, but the orange light still revealed the shape of his shoulders. And I knew who he was. I knew it in my bones, even though I'd only ever seen him once before.

John.

The name echoed in my head. I tried to hurry, tried to get to him, tried to shorten the distance between us, but no matter how fast I moved I couldn't get closer. I couldn't see his face, only make out the shape of his limbs and head.

"You see me," he said, and his whisper made the air in my throat catch, and my limbs lock down, and my eyes freeze open. "Finally, you see me..."

I heard him as if he were standing behind me, but he wasn't. He was right there, his shadow barely ten feet away from me.

"John," I tried to call, but only a whisper fell from my lips.

"We're close, Estella," he told me, and his voice was strange —so much like Jack's, but so different, too. Lighter. More breathless.

"Close to what?" I dared to ask, even though I thought I might already know the answer.

"*You have to find the wyrm.*"

John disappeared before he finished speaking. His shadow fell away and whatever nightmare I was trapped in this time made so little sense. My other nightmares were always vivid—I saw clearly in them, heard in them, felt in them. This one was so secretive. So dark.

"John!" I cried out, desperate to see him again, to talk to him, to understand...

"Find the wyrm, Estella. We don't have much time."

His voice came from the left. I turned, but the darkness was too dark, and I could barely make out the shape of his shoulders.

"There is no wyrm!" I thought I shouted. "Won't you come closer? Let me see you. Let me—"

"*Find the wyrm.*"

The voices came from everywhere all at once, like a tornado of sounds, different people spinning around me saying the same thing: *find the wyrm.*

Find the wyrm.
Find the wyrm.

I WAS SPINNING, falling, being pulled to the sides, so that when my eyes opened, my mind didn't catch up to the image in front of me for a long time. It was still stuck in that nightmare, searching for John.

How strange was it that I knew him but didn't. How strange was it that I knew his brother.

How strange was it that every set of twins I'd ever known was something...unique.

Izet, my kidnapper, and his twin sister Izma who was born a fox. Jack, my guard and attempted kidnapper, and John, his brother who visited my nightmares but refused to show me his face.

My mother...and her sister, half her face ruined, her blue eye looking down at me now as if she had never been more disgusted by anyone in her entire life.

The world picked up on the spinning, and my lungs expanded, filling up with air. I moved, sat upright, and she fell back a couple of steps, looking down at me, trying to make up her mind about what to do with me.

Tears in my eyes. They snuck out without my permission. I just felt their wetness on my cheeks as I took in my surroundings.

We were near a forest somewhere. Trees around us, big green leaves over my head. She'd laid me down on the ground near a large trunk, and her navy-colored van was just behind her. She was still looking at me like that—disgusted and uncertain. Confused and uncomfortable, like she would rather be anywhere else in the world.

"Hi," I choked, somehow finding my voice, desperate to

chase away that awful silence between us. "Hi, I'm...I-I'm Estella."

I don't know why I said that when it was apparent she knew.

"You're out of your damned mind is what you are," she told me, then turned to her van and slid the door open. That same door she'd opened before she threw me inside, then knocked me out cold. The sound of it grabbed me and put me back there all over again. I lost track of reality instantly.

Memories rushed to me, some fast and some slow. My father, half shifted, holding Lucien up by the neck.

Chains around my wrists.

Lucien hugging me to his chest tightly...

I told the moon about you...

I cried harder.

Because I remembered Alexandra, too.

What have I done?

I looked down at the baby blue robe I wore over my pajamas, my initials sewn in a silver white thread over the pockets. I reached for them, my hands shaking so much I barely had any control over my fingers.

The mirror was not there.

The small golden mirror with the dragon head at the edge of the handle was not in my pocket.

I jumped to my feet, overestimating my strength. The view in front of me shifted, and I fell back against the rough bark of the trunk, reminding myself to breathe.

Just breathe. Everything will make sense soon.

As if I'd already forgotten the absurdity that was my life.

The woman turned her head to me for just one second, then said, "How did you find me?"

Her voice hung in the air, making my heart skip a long beat. I realized it was nothing like my mother's.

"I-I-I—"

I couldn't speak because I couldn't tell her what I didn't know.

How had I found her? How had I made it here?

Where was here?

The tears had stopped coming. The panic was threatening to turn my skin inside out. I pushed myself off the trunk, and my legs somehow held me though they were numb.

"My name is Estella Azarius. My mother was Antonette Moore. I—"

Her sharp laughter cut me off. She slowly turned around, pulling her shawl down around her shoulders, revealing her light blonde hair, streaked with grey here and there. She also revealed the scar tissue that zig-zagged on the right side of her face, like the skin had been clawed off her. Like my father had done to Jack with his talons.

"I know who you are, Estella. I know who your mother was, too," she told me, looking me up and down with her one eye, and she still hadn't figured out exactly what to feel about me. "You look just like her." The last words left her lips as if by accident.

"You're..." My voice kept failing me, shaking. "You're...are you my aunt?"

She flinched. She actually flinched as if the word disgusted her that much.

Falling back, she sat down on the floor of the van and rested her hand on the handle of the open door. With the other she rubbed her face a couple of times.

"I am Annabelle Moore, and yes—technically speaking, I am your aunt." She didn't look happy about that at all.

The tears were already back.

Aunt. My actual *family* that had nothing to do with my father. Not an Azarius, but still my family.

And she could barely stand to look at me.

I sat on the ground again—my legs were shaking too

much. I wrapped my arms around them and rested my chin on my knees. Just for a second. Just until it stopped feeling so... strange. Painful and joyful and so unbelievably strange to look at her.

"How did you find me, girl?"

I shook my head, trying to swallow the lump in my throat. "I don't know."

Her brow shot up. "You don't know."

Again, I shook my head. I could try to explain it to her—the...*shadow*? of my descendant, Alexandra Azarius brought me here. I summoned her through a golden mirror and asked for her help. I woke up here—without Lucien. Without Jack.

Why?

I didn't think Annabelle would take kindly to that.

Or believe me.

"Where are we?" All I could see were trees and a road with half-broken asphalt a few feet away. More trees on the other side of it, though not as many as in Aither. Not as many as on my father's estate.

"You think this is funny?" the woman asked me.

My eyes widened and I leaned back. "No, I—"

"I don't have time for silly jokes, girl. Why don't you tell me what you want and be on your way?"

The venom in her voice nearly killed me.

I shook my head again and again—it was the only thing I seemed to know how to do. Hold onto my knees and shake my head.

Gods, I just wanted to find Lucien...

"This is not a joke," I finally told her, and once I started speaking, I couldn't stop. "I don't know how I got here. I don't know where I am. All I know is that I found out—*today* —that my mother had a twin sister, and now you're her, and I don't know what to think. I don't know what to make of any of this. I don't..." Her face blurred completely from the tears. "I don't know who my mother was."

And that, out of everything else, was what crushed me. *I don't know who my mother was.*

So hard to breathe. So little air out here in the world.

"By the Wind, wipe your face," she suddenly said, leaning down to rest her elbows on her knees. I didn't—what was the point? The tears weren't going anywhere. "Figures. My gods, Annie. *Figures!*" she muttered to herself.

"Figures what?" I asked in half a voice.

"That she didn't tell you about me." Again, she rubbed her face. She was right there, maybe six feet away sitting in her van, and she was *mine*. My family, my flesh and blood, yet I felt nothing for her. Nothing at all except this desperate need to see my mother, to talk to her.

"Is it true?" I found myself saying. "That...that..." I touched my right cheek with my shaking fingers. I couldn't say the words out loud.

Too much. All of this was too much.

"Is it true that your mother ripped half my face off?"

Knives in my chest, in my stomach.

Annabelle smiled coldly. "Why, yes, it is. Right down there, in that forest." And she nodded her head to the road, to the trees on the other side of it.

I was shaking so badly I was afraid to open my mouth because I knew I'd scream.

"She wanted to go to that godsdamn tournament, so she did."

"Why?" I choked. Why, why, *why* would my mother—why would *anyone* do such a thing?

She raised a brow. "Because she decided she was going to save the world."

My eyes closed and tears fell down my cheeks like waterfalls. So many of them, all at once.

"Oh, yes. That's Annie for ya. She said she'd carefully analyzed the situation, deemed that I would *never* be able to beat anyone in that tournament, and she came to terms with the fact that she had to *sacrifice* herself for me, take my place, win—and then save everyone." She laughed. "She was very unhappy about it, too. Her plans had been different—she wanted to see the world, my sister. She wanted to explore. She wanted to be free. But she was willing to give all of that up because the world needed saving."

I opened my eyes, but I no longer saw her.

"She said that she was going to marry the dragon prince, and then she was going to give birth to the *next* dragon prince, and raise him herself, prepare him to be a *true king* after his father died. He was going to save everyone because she was going to teach him *how!*"

Such a cruel sound, her laughter.

"I imagine she was pissed off when she gave birth to you, wasn't she? She hated girls!"

Needles on my skin. A hammer slamming against the center of my mind.

"I said *no,* naturally. My parents had chosen me to go to the tournament for a reason. But Annie never did know how to take no for an answer." As if she just remembered what her face looked like, Annabelle pulled her shawl over her head again. "This one time, we were eleven years old, I think. Dad had to go pick some horenias two towns away. Said he would only need one of us to help him carry it back, and he chose me. But Annie wanted to go. She *had* to go, and so we woke up to half the herbs in Mom's pantry burned to ashes. No more utheria or tillies. And no way could Dad and I carry them back by ourselves, so Annie had to come along. She...she just had to."

She smiled so bitterly my soul withered.

"I used to admire that about her. She saw something she

wanted, and she went for it. Nobody was ever going to stop her. I loved her for it, until... until she turned on me, too."

"No," I think I whispered and again shook my head so many times I was dizzy.

"Nobody was *ever* going to stop her..." she said, looking down at her own hands.

"That was not my mom." It just wasn't—I remembered her easy smile and sparkling eyes. I remembered the way she spoke, the way she read to me, the way she *held* me.

These were lies, all of them, because she *never,* not once in her life said a bad thing to me about my father, about his reign. She never once told me that she wanted me to be *different* when I became queen.

"Maybe..." Annabelle said. "But that was my sister." The pain that suddenly flashed in her blue eye startled me. "I don't know why you found me, Estella, but you have no friends here. You have no family here."

You don't have me, she said with her eye.

"Everybody in this place will recognize you when they see your face, so I suggest you don't stay long."

She stood up. I stood up, too.

"They're not a big fan of the late queen and the way she pretended this place doesn't exist once she won that tournament." Turning to her van again, she grabbed two large sacks filled to the brim, but I couldn't see with what. "But you can stay here for a little while if you want. I can give you clothes if you don't have any." She threw a pointed look at my dirty, bloody robe.

I couldn't stop crying.

"Come. Help me out. It's going to get dark soon."

She threw those sacks to the ground before she turned to pick up another two. Then, she slid the van door closed and turned toward the trees at my back, never looking to see if I followed.

Two

WE'D BEEN NEAR THE SMALL WOODS AT THE BACK OF a wide one-story house that had seen better days. It was atop a steep hill, with another twelve houses to its sides before the town stretched below it. The low fence was made out of thick grey stone blocks, and the grass in the wide yard grew in unhealthy looking patches. An old red truck and two cars were parked in the front.

"Where are we?" I asked, dragging the two sacks full of leaves behind me, just like Annabelle was doing.

But before we reached the fence gate, and before she could answer me, the door of the house opened. The woman who walked out seemed to be in a hurry—or drunk.

Annabelle stopped just in front of the gate with a deep sigh and dropped the sacks she'd been carrying.

"Not again," she muttered as the woman came toward us, her eyes on Annabelle, her step faltering every few feet.

She was at least three inches taller than me, her dark curly hair touching her shoulders, her eyes a strange green that looked like it wished it could be blue instead. Her skin was pale, the bags under her eyes dark—*black* instead of blue.

I was wrong. She wasn't drunk. She looked exhausted.

"For gods' sake, Mikhaila," Annabelle said, grabbing her hips.

"I'm fine," the woman insisted. "I'm perfectly okay—and I'm leaving." Her big eyes could startle you in the dark. She looked pissed and tired and *desperate* at the same time somehow.

I said nothing, only watched.

"You're *not* okay! You can barely stand," Annabelle said, raising her voice. "You need more rest. You need medicine—you *can't drive* in this condition!"

And the woman—Mikhaila—finally made it to the gate, breathing as if she'd walked a hundred steps, not fifteen. She put her hands on the stone fence to catch her breath and looked Annabelle dead in the eye.

"*Watch me,*" she breathed, then pulled the gate open and stumbled out.

Annabelle raised both hands up in surrender and stepped aside to let her through. The woman dragged her feet toward the three vehicles parked to the side of the fence.

"Three," Annabelle said, raising three fingers in the air.

"*Fuck you!*" Mikhaila shouted without turning her head.

"Two..." Two fingers...

Mikhaila was barely three feet away from the faded red truck.

"One."

Annabelle held up one finger. Mikhaila collapsed to the ground like someone had cut all her strings.

My heart skipped a long beat. I dropped the sacks, unsure whether to move while Annabelle sighed deeply.

"See how far stubbornness gets you?" she asked, but she wasn't talking to me. When she turned and saw me standing there, she actually looked a bit surprised.

"Come on. Help me carry her back inside," she said.

"Who is she?"

"The most stubborn person in the universe is who she is," Annabelle muttered. "Grab her ankles." And once she put Mikhaila on her back, she grabbed her wrists.

The woman seemed so peaceful now, like she was just asleep. Her lips, so big they looked like they were drawn, not real, were almost blue. She had a makeshift bag strapped to her shoulder, her nails once painted red now completely chipped, her clothes as dirty as mine.

We carried her through the open gate without trouble—she was on the skinny side.

"Slowly," Annabelle instructed as she took the lead and moved us toward the door of the house.

"What is this place?" I asked in wonder.

"My place," she said without even looking at me.

"What about...what about my grandparents?" Her mom and dad, her cousins...

And I realized just how much Mikhaila had distracted me from my own questions, my own misery. I was almost thankful.

"Dead," she said. "They died a long time ago. I came back after they did, took over this place."

My heart beat so loudly I heard it in my ears. "Is this...is this where you grew up?" *Is this where Mom grew up?*

"It is. I left for a while. Then came back," she simply said, pushing the entrance door back with her foot. "Careful with the walls now."

And I entered the house where my mother had actually grown up.

I don't know why I was so emotional. Too much, all of it, and I still had to make sense of everything. I still had to take these feelings and put them in order and decide what I wanted to think because, right now, I could have sworn I could see my mother as a little girl walking down the narrow hallway that went both ways. I could see her small hands touching the yellowed walls, her small feet leaving imprints on the dark wooden floor. I could see her dancing as she went, blonde hair bouncing in the air, her smile big, her blue eyes sparkling...

And it just broke my heart.

"Last door. Keep moving," Annabelle said, and my tears fell down my chin and onto Mikhaila's boots. I hoped she wouldn't mind as I went, deeper and deeper down the hallway lined with doors. No dragons. No paintings. Nothing but wood and empty walls and memories that weren't even mine. Memories I would do anything to see.

The last door down the left hallway led to a large room with five beds in it. The first one across from the door, right below two big windows, was the only one with sheets on it.

"There," said Annabelle, and that's where we laid Mikhaila.

I still hadn't stopped crying.

"She's going to be fine," she said, putting her hand over Mikhaila's forehead. "She's going to be just fine."

Annabelle looked at me, then flinched again.

"You hungry?" she muttered, then turned around and walked out of the room without waiting for an answer.

OHIO.

We were in a small town just outside Akron, Ohio.

Where the hell was Akron, Ohio?

"Plenty of miles between here and your home," Annabelle said as she mixed the soup she was making, throwing a fistful of dried leaves in the pot. "So...how did you get here?"

I looked at the back of her head, her hair as blonde as mine. Hers was shorter, reaching just below her shoulders. Mom kept it long. It's the reason why I kept mine long, too, almost touching the small of my back. I'd always wanted to be like her. I'd always wanted to be *more* like her and less like my father.

I was starting to realize that I didn't understand what that even meant.

I was starting to realize that maybe...just maybe, I was better off trying to be more like me. It was safer that way because I knew myself. At least, I liked to think that I did.

Closing my eyes, I took in a deep breath, then exhaled slowly. The table I sat at was old, cracked, the brown of it faded. The kitchen was big, and maybe that's why it looked so empty. A large dining table, a few chairs, all different from one another—so different you'd wonder if Annabelle had collected them because of that reason alone. The wooden cupboards looked like they were barely holding onto the walls, and the curtains on the two large windows had once been white. Now, they were yellow.

But they were clean. Every corner, every old chair, every stained surface was perfectly clean, and the soup smelled so good, my limbs were weak. When was the last time I had eaten?

I'd drank that orange juice Malda made me while the team was preparing me for...

My wedding.

If there had been food inside me, it would have come out of me right now. I gripped the edge of the table tightly and focused on the air going down my throat.

So close. I'd been *hours* away from actually marrying another man. Gabriel St Revent. I'd been hours away from ruining everything...

Or maybe *fixing* it would be the better word.

"You don't have to tell me. I don't really care," Annabelle said after a moment, thinking I didn't want to answer her. I did—I just didn't think she'd appreciate the truth for what it was.

Magic had brought me here—except that's not how magic works, is it?

My ancestor, a queen who lived in the eighteen hundreds and is now dead, did a spell and somehow saved me—except that's not how death works. It isn't.

So, how could I even begin to explain to her things I didn't understand myself?

Nothing—I understood nothing. But I'd been about to get married, and I'd told Lucien that I loved him, and he'd told the moon about me.

I also told my father that I loved Lucien and that I'd seen him breaking apart in the library, just like I was breaking apart now at this dining table. The same table where my mother had probably eaten her meals when she was a girl.

Crack, crack, crack went my chest, and I was holding onto the table so tightly my fingers were numb. Too much, way too many questions and not enough answers.

I could have been home right now. I could have been *mated*—to another man, not Lucien. I could have been summoning the Ether right now.

Slowly, I slipped a hand in the pocket of my robe again, not that I expected to find anything. But my fingers touched the piece of paper I'd torn from that book anyway. It was there. The mirror was gone, but the spell to summon the Ether was still there.

A hand over mine.

My eyes popped open to Annabelle's face looking down at me, brow narrowed, eye concerned.

All that scar tissue...why hadn't she healed? *How* had my mother wounded her?

"If you collapse in my kitchen, I'm not going to carry you

back to the room alone," she told me. Then she turned her back to me and went to the stove. She put the soup in a white plastic bowl—clean. She grabbed a spoon from the drawer—clean. She brought them both to me, together with a piece of bread.

"Eat now. Cry later."

The soup smelled like heaven. My mouth watered but my stomach protested. It didn't want food.

"Was that...was that all?" I asked, too cowardly to look her in the eye.

She dragged the green armchair to the side of me and sat down.

"Is that everything she was? Just some...some evil twin who did what she wanted, when she wanted..." My voice broke. "Was that all?"

Annabelle sucked in a deep breath and didn't speak for a moment.

"She was not evil," she finally said, shaking her head. "She was just...different. Annie was my shield my entire life. She always took our father's beatings for me. She always fought with the other kids in town when they picked on me. She knew how to love." Her voice trailed off. "But then she grew up. Had wants of her own. Had herself to take care of. A world to save..." She laughed. "I imagine all that luxury and that bowing got in the way of that, though."

I flinched, my stomach turning again. My mother never cared about luxury or bowing. She always told the help back home to carry on when she passed by, not stop their work to curtsy. They still did it, but she told them not to. I remembered it.

"You never spoke to her again?" It just seemed so absurd. I had no siblings—all I had was Greta. And to go a lifetime without speaking to her? The mere idea of it suffocated me.

Not Annabelle, though.

"Never. I didn't even come back here until my parents

died." She didn't sound remorseful of that. In fact, she sounded a bit irritated.

I'd never known a grandfather or grandmother, not in any of my lives. All Azariuses tended to die young, and my mother always said that she couldn't take me to meet her parents, that she wasn't allowed.

Now...I wasn't so sure anymore. Realizing just how much my father had loved her made it very difficult to believe that he'd forbid her from doing anything. Made it very difficult not to think that she simply *didn't want* to bring me here to meet my family.

Until I was twelve, and she informed me her mother had died. Until I was thirteen, and she said her father had passed away, too.

Both times, she'd had silent tears in her eyes, a smile on her face. I'd never seen my mother upset, or screaming, or crying. She always had a smile on her face when I looked at her, no matter the situation.

But she never told me anything about them. She never told me anything about her father beating her, either. Or that she protected her twin sister from bullies.

Or that she *had* a twin sister.

"Hey."

My eyes snapped open. Fresh tears spilled out as my mind wandered, too fast, too far.

In how many more ways could I break?

"Eat your food. Sleep. Stay here—there are beds," Annabelle said, pointing her thumb back toward the door. "But when you're ready..." Slowly, she stood up. "You have to leave, Estella. Before anybody in town sees your face."

She turned her back to me and walked out of the kitchen.

Too many words in my mouth but no energy to pick a thought or to say it out loud, so I just watched her until she closed the door.

The soup was ice-cold by the time I forced myself to eat.

The realization was even colder when I left the kitchen: I was not welcome here. Annabelle might have been my mother's sister, but she was not my family.

And I needed to find my way to Aither asap.

THREE

YOU SEE ME.

THE WHISPER PULLED ME AWAKE—IN a dream, not the real world. But just because I knew it was a dream didn't mean that my mind accepted it wasn't real. Somehow, it was. To me, John was really here, in front of me, talking to me.

"You see me," he said again, his voice louder.

"I do," I said. "Tell me where you are. Tell me where—" *Lucien is,* I was going to say, but he beat me to it.

"Have you found her?"

I blinked. "What?"

"Have you found the wyrm?"

I shook my head and tried to get closer. My legs moved, but I stayed in the same place. There was no ground underneath my feet, just darkness. Darkness and the orange light of the fire I could hear but couldn't see.

"No, I—"

"You have to find her, Estella. Start searching—there's not much time," John said, and try as I might to see his face, I couldn't. I could make out the shape of him, just like before, but that's it.

"Won't you come closer?" I said, frustrated. "I can't see you. I *need* to see you." If only to convince myself that he was really who I thought he was.

Did he look like Jack? Did he wear the same color in his eyes, the same smile on his lips?

"Find her first. Find her now," John said instead, and he was starting to blend into the darkness behind him, too.

"I don't know how to find her! I don't know how!" I'd only realized that a wyrm might exist last night—how was I to find them out here, all by myself?

"The Water trick. Use the Water trick. It will guide you," John said. "Do it fast, Estella. Do it now."

"But I—"

Light exploded, chasing away the dark, melting the shape of him out of existence. I couldn't breathe, couldn't blink, too shocked to even scream as I looked up, at the white color dripping all around me like paint, and the shape of the dragon coming into view right over my head.

My father.

I knew his eyes. I knew his teeth. I knew the spikes on his dragon's head. I knew the Fire burning in the back of his throat.

His roar shook me to my core.

My eyes snapped open, this time in the real world. I was breathing so heavily it hurt. My hair was wet, sticking to my cheeks uncomfortably. My body buzzed, the food I'd eaten climbing up my throat to get out of me.

I squeezed my eyes. I closed my mouth with both hands. I breathed.

It took a while for my surroundings to come into focus. It was dark outside, I could see the moon through the window over the first bed across the room—where the woman,

Mikhaila, was still sleeping. No lights were on anywhere—no lamps in the room, just the main one overhead.

Earlier, after I ate, I'd found Annabelle in the hallway, waving for me to follow. She took me to her bathroom. Turned on the shower. Left me alone.

I felt like a different person now, wearing jeans and a black shirt, socks and worn tennis shoes, panties too big for me and a bra too small, but they were clean. *I* was clean.

And I needed to move before the voices in my head got the best of me.

I don't know why I slept with the shoes on, but now I was thankful I didn't have to waste time with them. Walking on my tiptoes, I made my way between the beds, stopping only for a second in front of Mikhaila's. I hadn't asked Annabelle about her again, but she seemed to be very uncomfortable. Gods, her sleep was so restless. She kept moving her head from one side to the other, pulling up the cover to her neck, then pushing it off her completely. It was like she was *fighting* some imaginary monster. Maybe she was fighting them in her dreams, just like me.

The image of my father's dragon over my head, red against the completely white background, made all the hair on my body stand at attention. Mikhaila said something I couldn't understand as she whipped her head to the sides fast a few times. It felt like I was *breathing* too loudly and she could hear me, so I turned around and walked out of the room as silently as I could.

Quiet. Too quiet in the hallway.

All of it seemed so surreal to me. I couldn't believe that I was here yet—how ridiculous to imagine that twenty-four hours ago I was in my father's manor, surrounded by guards, engaged, about to get married. How ridiculous to think that I'd been chained to a wall, too, and had told Lucien the truth.

The whole truth.

All of it.

And he'd believe me.

I barely made it to the front door of the house, opened it and stepped outside before the tears came. Before my legs gave and I hit the grass on my knees, hands over my mouth to keep from making a sound.

He'd believed me, just like that. Hadn't doubted my words even for a second.

I looked at the moon—not full, but not half either, like it had been about to turn and hide but didn't have the heart to do it yet. Like it knew I needed the light.

I broke under the moonlight, all alone, sitting on the ground, for as long as I needed. And when I was as light as the cold air going down my throat, I gathered myself under the same silver light again.

I had no idea how much time had passed since I'd slept—the sun had just set then, and I'd collapsed as soon as I lay down. There were no lights anywhere around me, not in the house or outside, and I was thankful for that. I didn't want the company of other people right now. I had the moon and the air. It was more than enough.

Eventually, I even put some semblance of an *order* to my thoughts, too. Not everything was lost yet. I knew where I was going—Aither. And tomorrow, I'd figure out a way to get to Vermont. I'd figure out the Water trick, too, just like John said, if that had even been real. And I'd find the...the *wyrm*.

The drawing I'd seen in Lucien's house came alive before my eyes. Blue scales, gorgeous blue eyes—four of them—no limbs and no wings, just a serpentine body that was as beautiful as it was deadly. I kept seeing it in the river, half of it hiding under the surface of the water, the shape of it mimicking the twists and turns of the riverbed.

It was real. That creature was real, not fiction. As real as my dragoness. As real as Lucien's wyvern. As real as the two-headed drake that Jack and John should shift into.

...Do they?

What if we got it all wrong? What if it was just wishful thinking? What if Lucien and I just *wanted* to believe that there was a drake out there? Because Jack had no clue what we were even talking about. He simply had come to find me so I could heal his brother, so John would stop taking so much of Jack's energy—that was it. That was all.

What if none of it was true, and what if the other kind of draca don't really exist at all?

What if my dreams with John are only that—*dreams*?

Lucien. I needed to find Lucien first. Together, we could figure out a solution to all of this.

The moon felt sorry for me. I felt it in its soft glow. It felt sorry for me because it knew my mind, and it knew what I was thinking—Lyran and the Pathmaker and Leanve and their Ether...

Beware of the man who takes your life, they'd said.

Beware of Lucien.

So many things had changed in this life. So many things were going on in this life that I kept forgetting that I'd lived six others. I kept forgetting that I'd died six deaths. That Lucien had killed me.

It was different in this life, and I believed him when he said that he hadn't intended to kill me all this time he'd been looking for me. He'd simply wanted to turn me against the king, convince me to help him *kill* my own father.

The moon wept for me now. Because it knew how terrified I was to think that maybe I'd have been convinced to do just that a few days ago. Maybe I'd have agreed before I saw what my father hid behind the mask of his face. Before I saw the man he used to be.

It didn't matter now, anyway. Because even if Lucien

hadn't intended to kill me, he would have. In two years, he would have come just like always. And no amount of my wishing it wasn't him was going to change the fact that it was. I knew him. Among a million faces, a million shoulders—I knew his.

Eventually, I was tired again, in desperate need of some sleep. Eventually, I opened the door of the house and walked inside, searched the hallways with my eyes, tried to listen to something, but there was nothing there.

I don't know what got into me, but I started opening doors before I realized I was doing it. And the one across from the main entrance led me to another hallway, this one wider, with big windows and thick drapes, with old rugs all over the wooden floors. I walked ahead as if hypnotized, feeling like I wasn't really here—I couldn't exist if I didn't know in what part of the world I was, if I didn't know what time it was, or if I was asleep or awake.

The doors started halfway to the other side of the hallway. I opened the first one without thinking. The large room was full of furniture, all of it covered in white sheets. I walked in anyway. My new old shoes left marks in the thick layer of dust on the floor. The moonlight followed me, coming through the dirty windows as if it wanted me to see the secrets this house was trying to hide.

But there was really nothing to see there except a mantle, tables, a dresser, vases—all empty, scattered all over, covered in white. Ghosts of what they once were, suspended in time.

So, I walked out the door and into another, to meet more ghosts. More sheets. More dust.

Behind the third door, I found ghosts that whispered back to me.

A big room. Two beds, two dressers, two small worktables in between. Two windows, two chairs, two lamps, two pillows, two rugs.

Two lives covered in white sheets that I slowly pulled to the floor.

I sat in the middle of the room, between the beds, and I tried to guess where my mother had slept. On the left, where one pillar of the twin bed was broken in half, and there were lines engraved on the headboard, and the nightstand table was a bit farther away, and the lamp with no bulb in it was at the very corner?

Or the right—where the moonlight fell on the old stained pillow without a case?

Right, I decided. Mom had slept on the right because back home, she'd slept on the left with my father. And somehow, that made sense to me.

I wanted to hate the universe for bringing me here. I wanted to hate my father, and Alexandra, and *myself* for searching for this very room without really knowing it, but I couldn't. Because as much as it hurt to be here, I needed to see it. I needed to know what the place my mother grew up in looked like. I needed to know so that when I became braver, and I faced all the questions gathered in my chest about her, I'd understand her better.

Or at least I'd try to.

"I haven't been in here in at least four years."

The voice that came from behind me wanted to startle me, but my body was too heavy. The tears that kept streaming from my eyes weighed me down. Was there such a thing as running out of them? Because it felt like I should have by now, yet here they were, big and warm and as eager as always to rush out of me.

"Gods, do you ever stop crying?"

The whisper shocked me, and I laughed without really meaning to.

Yes, I wanted to say, *yes—I do stop crying. In fact, I don't cry all that much. Not normally.*

But the words were stuck in my throat once more, so all I could do was laugh and cry and laugh some more.

"She slept on the right," Annabelle said after a minute.

Yes, I wanted to say, *yes—I know. The moon told me.*

"She used to sneak into my bed all the time, though. As brave as she was, a little rain against the window glass scared her shitless. She never liked to sleep alone."

That I did not know. Mom used to be *my* shield during storms.

Annabelle sighed. "I don't know your story, Estella. And you don't know mine."

It felt like half a sentence. It felt like there was *more* to that thought. Like there should be so much more to it.

But that's all she said.

And for a while, I just focused on slowing down the tears until I could speak properly.

"I want to know your story, though," I said, my whisper so low she probably didn't even hear it.

But...

"Maybe someday," she said.

I nodded. *Maybe someday,* I thought.

"Stay as long as you like. Do put the sheets back over the furniture when you're done. I won't be coming back to this room," she said almost reluctantly.

The soft click of the door when it closed let me know I was all alone.

I lay down on the dust-covered floor, knees to my chest. I looked out the window and tried not to want to be a little girl in my mother's arms again. I tried not to remember all those nights I'd snuck into her bedroom during thunderstorms.

It was useless.

She had Father, though. As twisted as it was, for that, I was thankful. She never slept alone again until the day she died.

FOUR

"WHAT'S THE WATER TRICK?"

Annabelle stopped squeezing ketchup into her sandwich to look at me, leaning against the kitchen door frame.

"Good morning to you, too," she said, nodding back at the dining table. "Sit."

I did so in silence. Even my bones hurt from sleeping on the floor all night, but it had been worth it. My soul had rested.

I'd put the sheets back over the beds, the dressers, the nightstands. And I'd come out of that part of the house, back to the main hallway, and the other rooms. I'd heard Annabelle in the kitchen right away. She looked worse than yesterday. I doubted she'd gotten much sleep, and somehow, I felt guilty.

I felt guilty for everything that had happened to her, as if my shoulders weren't heavy enough.

She put a plate in front of me on the table—empty. She grabbed a glass near the sink and filled it with a bit of water, brought it to me and spilled it onto the plate. Then she put the glass over it, upside down.

"Eat," she ordered, putting down another plate—this one with a sandwich on it. She had another two on the counter.

"What's that?" I asked, watching the glass on the plate filled with water.

"The Water trick," she said, grabbing one of the other sandwiches. "It's a myth, doesn't work. I'm gonna see if Mikhaila is awake." She spoke fast, then *ran* out of the kitchen like she was being chased by lions.

I tried not to take it personally. I failed.

Pushing the sandwich away for a moment, even though my stomach was playing a symphony of hunger, I brought the other plate closer, careful not to spill the water. I looked at it—at the glass upside down, the rim of it dipped in the water. It looked like nothing at all.

I grabbed it, pulled it up, put it back down again. How in the hell did this work?

"Nope."

I jumped at the sound of Annabelle's voice when she came through the door again, the sandwich still on the plate.

"She'll probably be out of it the whole day. Can't even wake up," she muttered, putting the plate down on the table. She was talking about Mikhaila.

"Do you have any idea how this works?" I asked, and she whipped around, her own sandwich halfway to her mouth.

With an irritated sigh, she came closer to the table. She definitely looked more tired, but also the blue of her eyes looked more alive somehow. Or maybe it was just the bright blue shirt she had on today.

"The tricks don't work. They're just silly stories," she said, then grabbed the glass and spun it around a couple times. "You give it your energy, keep the person you're trying to find in mind, then wait for the water to point you in the right direction."

I shook my head, brows narrowed. "Energy? Does that

mean *magic*?" Because I didn't have my powers yet. I wasn't mated.

"No, just energy. You have to feel the water as an element and let it sort of tune in with you," she said. "Useless. This does not work anymore than Air or Earth does. Or Fire, for that matter." And she threw me a pointed look. "Now eat."

I brought the sandwich closer to me again, my mind buzzing because...

The Fire trick worked.

I ate while my mind traveled to Aither, to Izet, the drunk man who'd kidnapped me, what he'd said to Lucien in the woods the first time I saw him.

I did the old Fire trick and it led me straight to her. That's what he said.

And he was right. Even though nobody believed him that day, Izet had been right. The Fire trick had led him straight to me.

"Do you mind if I keep that and try, anyway?" I asked Annabelle. I could take the plate and the glass back to the room with the beds and try it. It probably wouldn't hurt.

She shook her head. "Knock yourself out."

I ate in silence until I finished my sandwich. My stomach no longer sang and I felt stronger already.

"So, what is it that you do here?" I asked.

"I'm a healer," Annabelle said, biting into the sandwich she'd made for Mikhaila, too, after she ate hers. "I heal. I make potions. Family business. I don't suppose you'd know anything about that, though."

"Nothing." My mother had never told me what her family did. And as much as it terrified me, I never thought to even ask.

"Not to rush you or anything, but people will be coming here during the day. Right now, only Mikhaila is staying in, and she's not from around here so I doubt she recognized you,

but people from the town can't see you at all until you leave."
She met my eyes, hers hard and almost colorless now. "I don't
want any trouble." It was a warning.

I swallowed hard and nodded. "I will stay in the room
until I come up with a plan. Then, I'll get out of your hair for
good."

Annabelle looked relieved. I don't know why that made
my stomach twist, but I took my plate and brought it to the
sink to wash it, at least.

"Thank you for the clothes and the food. I appreciate it."

She nodded but didn't even turn to look at me when I
grabbed the other plate with the glass and the water, and left
the kitchen, feeling like I might suffocate before I reached the
room.

Mikhaila was still asleep. I tried to be as silent as possible as
I moved to the bed I'd used the night before at the far left
corner. I sat on the floor, back against the wall, and I reminded
myself that it wasn't Annabelle's fault that she hated me. It
wasn't her fault that she didn't want to have anything to do
with me.

But gods, I wished I'd woken up on the other side of the
world instead of here.

I understood why Alexandra brought me to this place—
Annabelle was probably my only living relative other than my
Father right now, but how was she to know that my own aunt
wouldn't want to even see me? She *couldn't wait* for me to be
out of her house, and that terrified me more than anything else
right now.

How was I going to get from Ohio to Vermont without a
dollar in my pocket, without a car—or even a horse? Theft was
the only thing that came to mind, and the thought of it made
me shiver.

Later. Right now, I had to focus on the plate and the
water and the glass in front of me.

I put my hand on the bottom of the glass turned upside down and I tried to give it my energy, just like Annabelle said. I had no clue what that meant or how to do it, but I tried anyway. I closed my eyes and I breathed in deeply and I tried to *feel* the water, tried to *will* it into moving, pointing me in the direction of a creature that probably didn't exist at all.

Won't you tell me where I can find a wingless, limbless draca with four eyes?

What a joke.

But to my surprise, the water did move. A single drop floated up inside the glass and suspended right there. I watched, mesmerized, heart barely beating.

I don't know what I expected it to do, but as the minutes passed, the water didn't turn into an arrow to point me in the right direction. The drop just hovered there under the glass innocently.

"*Do something,*" I whispered to it, trying to shake the glass a little bit. The drop didn't move.

When the door opened and Annabelle walked in with a small bowl in her hand, I didn't speak at all or even raise my head. Knowing how much she looked forward to my leaving here made me feel like I was the heaviest burden in the world. And despite the fear of what was out there, I couldn't wait to get going already.

"Well?"

She'd stopped in front of Mikhaila's bed and was looking at me like she was actually curious.

Surprised, I shook my head. "I don't know. It's not doing anything." I raised my hand to show her.

She nodded. "It's supposed to move. The drop is supposed to be your guide, and it's not moving," she said. "I told you, it doesn't work." And she went around Mikhaila's bed to give her whatever she had in that bowl.

I looked at the drop again, confused. It definitely wasn't moving, just hovering in place.

"Why do you need the Water trick, anyway? Who're you trying to find?"

Bringing my hands to my lap, I leaned back on the wall and sighed. The drop of water immediately fell down on the plate, as if it *disconnected* from me.

"Just...someone." A fictional creature. A draca that hadn't existed in centuries.

What a fucking joke.

The headache developing behind my eyes seemed to be laughing at me.

"Try a phone. Or a Google search. Way more helpful than that," she said, holding Mikhaila up by the shoulders and trying to get her to drink from the bowl.

I stood up. "Need help with that?"

"Actually, yes. Hold her up for me?"

I went closer and held Mikhaila up by the shoulders as she fed her the green liquid slowly.

"What are you giving her?"

"Just a concoction of calming herbs. The best I can do for her is to ensure she sleeps well," Annabelle said.

"What happened to her?" Mikhaila's face looked better than yesterday, her skin more alive, the bags under her eyes less visible. Her thick lips weren't blue anymore but a dark pink. Even her brown hair seemed to be shinier. Or maybe it was just the sunlight streaming through the windows.

"Fuck if I know," Annabelle muttered. "A young man dropped her at my door four nights ago, paid for her care, and left. No names, no nothing. And she won't say a word, either. Won't even tell me if she's a polar bear or a tiger. She just wants to get in her car and leave. Won't listen when I tell her that she needs time."

"But what's wrong with her?" Did she have wounds on her body or something? Because she just looked tired to me.

"I don't know. I can't figure it out," Annabelle said with a flinch, and it was obvious that it bothered her. "My magic barely works, and I've searched her body with what I have, but it doesn't find anything wrong."

That made me curious. "Why does your magic barely work?"

She raised a brow as if she was sure she'd heard me wrong. As if that was an absurd question.

"Same reason anybody's magic barely works," she said after a minute.

I shook my head. "What...what do you mean?"

Annabelle looked at me in silence for a long second, trying to figure out if I was joking. I really wasn't.

"What world have you been living in?" she finally asked me—and she expected an answer.

"This same world. This same *country*," I reminded her. "But where I'm from, magic works just fine." Everybody back home had magic. All of my father's guards and staff. Everybody in Aither had had plenty of magic to wield, too—I'd seen it myself. I'd seen Water shifters playing with the lake, and Air and Earth...

Annabelle smiled bitterly. "Well, aren't you a lucky girl," she said, taking a step back. "Out here, in the rest of the world, our elements are failing us. Some have boosts, incredible bursts of energy they can't even control, while most can barely access the elements. It changes with years, but it never goes away."

The words were at the tip of my tongue—*no way, that is not possible. I would have known. I would have seen it!*

Except I wouldn't. I hadn't seen anything out here in the rest of the world, just like she said. A thought took over my mind, one I had never really understood since I first heard about it in Lyran, but it felt like I was beginning to: there is no balance between the elements without the Ether.

For a moment, the face of Hector, the drunk who filled up crosswords with strange symbols in a stinky bar, who told me that the Ether was a man, came before my eyes.

We all belong to Fire here, he'd told me. I hadn't really thought much of it. Maybe I should have.

"How...how long has it been like that?" I asked, but Annabelle was back to checking Mikhaila's pulse and temperature, and she just shrugged.

"Always," she told me, then shook her head. "I don't get it. Physically she should be perfectly fine. Except..."

"She's not." Mikhaila was definitely not fine. And neither was I.

"I'll figure it out, though," Annabelle said, and when she heard the knock on her door, she jumped to her feet, instantly.

Panicked, she put the empty bowl on the bedside table. "Stay here," she said in a whisper, and again, it was a warning.

I didn't dare move until she was out the door.

Laying Mikhaila back on the pillow, I went to the end of the room again, mind full of questions, just like always.

So many things I wanted to talk to Annabelle about. How did her healing work? Why did some people have bursts of energy, and others couldn't control the elements at all? How did her Air search a body? Was it like Lucien, who searched *rooms* and hallways and always knew when someone was coming—or close?

Had both her parents done the same thing?

Could my mother do it, too?

Why had she *never* talked about it to me?

"Why, Mom?" I whispered, and only after I heard my own voice did I realize I'd spoken out loud.

Closing my eyes, I rested my head against the wall. It didn't matter *why*. What was done was already done and I couldn't take back the past. Right now, I just needed to figure out a way to leave this place, leave Annabelle alone, and find my way to Aither. My best bet was to ask her for a phone or a laptop, somewhere I could search for a map to know where I was and where I was going. It wouldn't be easy, but I was willing to do whatever it took. I'd come so far in this life, and I was *not* going to let it all go to waste. I would steal and lie if I had to, but I would find my way to Aither.

And once I found Lucien, I could stop to think and plan again.

FIVE

"You know that doesn't actually work, right?"

I sat upright so fast, I knocked the glass off the plate. The sound of it rolling on the wooden floor was like a drill to my brain until I grabbed it.

Until I looked up and saw that the woman was sitting up on the bed, eyes open, a curious look on her face as she watched me. Her hair was all over the place, her skin pale and glistening with sweat, but she looked perfectly alert.

"Oh," I breathed, looking around me as if I was realizing just now that I was still sitting on the floor, back against the wall. That I was still trying to get the stupid Water trick to work, and it refused.

"Yeah, it's just a myth. Pretty disappointing, isn't it?" She pushed off the covers and brought her legs out the bed, then stopped and sighed. "Here goes nothing." And she stood up.

A split second later, she fell back on the bed again.

"Maybe you should take it easy," I said, not really meaning anything by it, but...

"Maybe you should mind your own damn business," she snapped, her eyes suddenly furious.

I flinched, biting my tongue—she was just sick. I probably would have been in a shitty mood, too, if I couldn't even stand on my own.

Knowing I would say something if she was rude to me again, I just raised my hands and didn't speak. It really was none of my business.

I went back to the plate. I pressed my heel to the bottom of the glass and tried to *feel* the Water, just like I'd done the whole damn day. That's all I'd done—I'd sat here and tried to get the water to point me in the right direction. It just kept hovering aimlessly in the air instead.

Stupid water.

"Look, I'm sorry, okay?"

I raised my head again to find Mikhaila still sitting on the bed five minutes later.

"Not your fault. I'm sorry. I'm just pissed, that's all," she said, rubbing her face raw before she ran her fingers through her curls to try to tame them back. It was useless—they bounced right back to the sides.

"I imagine I'd be, too," I said with a shrug.

"You don't look sick." Her wide eyes scrolled down the length of me curiously.

"I'm not." Unless you counted the way I missed Lucien...

Unless you counted the way I worried about *my father,* which was definitely a disease. I had no business worrying about that man at all. So, why was I?

"So, why are you at the healer's?"

I raised my brows, biting back a smile. She was awfully curious for someone who just told me to mind my own business.

She must have realized the same thing because she smiled, lowering her head. "Right," she whispered.

And it made me feel a bit awful.

"Just visiting, actually. I'm leaving tonight," I said despite my better judgment.

And I meant it—as soon as people stopped coming to Annabelle's door, I'd leave, sneak into the town down the hill, try to steal a horse or a car or something. Not something I looked forward to, but it was my only choice. Nobody knew where I was. I couldn't just call them and tell them—I had no numbers, no emails, no nothing. My father had made sure I'd remain completely isolated in case I ever left his manor.

"Me, too," Mikhaila said with a nod. "You're family, right? Same hair, same eyes." She flinched. "Same *eye.*"

I smiled. "Something like that." There was no hiding the resemblance between Annabelle and me. Mikhaila was definitely not from this town; otherwise, she'd have known who Annabelle was.

We fell into a comfortable silence after that. I didn't want to pry, and she finally made it to her feet. She made her bed, found a tie to pull back her hair, then grabbed the makeshift bag she'd had with her yesterday and left the room for a little while.

I needed to use the bathroom, too. How much longer until the sun set? How much longer until Annabelle kicked me out of here herself?

The ache in my chest kept on intensifying because the things I still refused to think about were growing the size of a monster in the back of my head.

How much longer until my father found me?

Mikhaila came back no time, dropped her bag on her bed and came closer, her curious eyes on the plate in front of me.

"The way that's supposed to work is that it connects your energy to the biggest one out there—and the biggest energy out there depends entirely on *you.*" She wasn't shaking that I could see. In fact, she looked just fine. "May I?"

"Sure," I muttered, pushing the plate towards her, and just like that, she came and sat on the floor in front of me.

I watched her pale face, her skin clean—she must have washed it. Her eyes didn't look as tired. The way she analyzed the glass and the water on the plate for a moment, she really did look completely okay.

Maybe Annabelle's concoctions worked better than she thought.

"It's much like when you have a good opinion about a person. They can appear so...*big* to you, you know?" She looked up at me, pressing her palm on the bottom of the upside-down glass. A drop of water rose inside it instantly. "That's how you single them out. That's how your energy, connected with the water, figures out who you're looking for. That's how it pulls you in that direction."

She raised the glass and put it on the floor. I watched, mesmerized, as she held out her palm and the drop of water floated right over the center of it.

"And *this*," she said, raising her brows at me with a sneaky grin. "...this is why it *doesn't* work."

I shook my head at the drop of water simply hovering over her palm. "Maybe we're doing it wrong. Maybe, if I focus harder..." Because the Fire trick had worked, hadn't it? Izet had found me with it.

Unless he'd just gotten lucky.

Maybe those dreams, John's silhouette, his voice, were nothing more than a figment of my imagination, my mind's attempt to sort this mess out before I lost it completely. My attempt at giving sense to the senseless reality I seemed to live in.

Maybe.

Mikhaila slapped her other hand over the drop of water that had been hovering over her palm, making me jump back until I hit the wall.

"Oh, trust me, girl, I am *focused*. I am more focused than I have ever been in my life. I couldn't be more focused if I tried," she said in a rush, and now she seemed pissed—but not at the fact that she wasn't well. She seemed pissed at someone else entirely, when she smiled an ice-cold smile, pushing the plate toward me. "It's okay, though. I don't need this water to tell me how to find who I'm looking for. Lucky for me, I know just where he lives." She pushed herself up, somehow making it to her feet without even wobbling to the sides.

"You're looking for someone, too?"

"Yes, I am. I'm not only looking for him—I'm going to *find* him as well." She walked backward to her bed with a devilish grin.

"Something tells me he's not going to like that at all." Mostly the look on her face, her smile that was drawing out my own.

She sat down on the bed, crossing her arms in front of her. "I will make sure of that even if it's the last thing I do on this earth." It was a damn promise.

Shaking my head, I laughed. She was not how I imagined at all.

Turning back to my Water trick, I put the glass upside down, pressed my palm to the bottom of it, and I went back to praying that that drop of water did something else other than hover in the air. Praying it would move, point me in the right direction, do *something* to tell me I had a way out of this.

But the water didn't care.

~

THE HUNGER GNAWED at my stomach, searching for something to eat. Night had fallen just after Mikhaila left the room, and I was trying to gather up the courage to leave, too. It had been at least half an hour since anybody had come knocking on the door, so I would be free to go. The dark of the night would shield me on the way to town, hopefully. Then, I could steal something, and...be on my way.

So simple, yet perfectly impossible.

Closing my eyes, I took in a deep breath and stood up. The plate and the water and the glass were still there. Still just as useless.

The man in my dreams was nothing but a figment of my imagination.

That didn't mean I was going to let the fear paralyze me the way it had done all day. I still had a plan. I still had a safe place I could get to. Aither. I was going to Aither. I just needed Annabelle to show me the map, so I knew in which part of Ohio I was.

I'd take it from there.

And I wouldn't allow myself to think about my father at all.

When I left the room and was out in the narrow hallway, I realized I hadn't felt so completely helpless since my last life, the morning Lucien came and killed me. I saw no way out as I dragged my feet to the kitchen. Empty. Annabelle wasn't there. As much as I wanted to search for something to eat, I didn't. I'd already overstayed the cold welcome she'd given me.

So, I just opened the door and walked out of the house, feeling so strange at leaving it behind that I almost missed Annabelle and Mikhaila, sitting on the grass, looking up at the sky.

"There she is. I thought you were asleep," Annabelle said. "Come. Sit."

A wave of tears rose in my chest, threatening to spill out of me with a loud sob. I bit my tongue and did my best to pretend I didn't care that she'd invited me to sit with her. That I didn't care there were apples and bananas in a bowl in front of them—and they were both eating.

"Sorry I don't have anything better," Annabelle said, pushing the bowl toward me. "It's not just the lack of magic, but hospitals and modern medicine have made people lose their faith in herbs. Not to mention the king has made pretty much every powerful potion illegal." And she smiled sneakily. My empty stomach turned.

"It's fine. I'm not hungry anyway," I lied, suddenly feeling stupid for not stuffing my pockets full of gold back home. I would have left everything with her. She wouldn't need to eat fruit for dinner ever again.

But how was I to know that Jack was planning to kidnap me and that I'd barely get out of the manor with my life?

"Liar," Mikhaila said, biting her apple. "These are delicious, though."

My hand shook as I reached for a banana in the wooden bowl. How pathetic was it that I couldn't wait to sink my teeth in it? Gods, it felt like I hadn't eaten in ages.

"Why?" I found myself asking. "Why did he make powerful potions illegal?" I never knew that there even were healers who could make potions out here, but at this point I wasn't surprised. *Nothing* was ever going to surprise me anymore—of that I was sure.

And I was just really, really hungry.

"Because," Annabelle said with a shrug.

"Why would the king need reasons for doing what he does?" Mikhaila said. "He's the king."

"Yes. Sucking the life out of their people seems to be what kings do," said Annabelle, and the look in her eyes said the comment was intentional.

The banana in my mouth lost taste.

"Queens, too," Mikhaila said. "His daughter is going to be even worse than him—you just watch."

My appetite was completely gone.

Annabelle looked at me. "You think so?" she asked Mikhaila.

"Definitely. I mean, she was raised by a monster—what more can you expect from her?"

And it sucked because Mikhaila genuinely meant what she said. I looked away into the sky, the moon, almost identical as the night before, laughing at me now. But I doubted they could see the tears pooled in my eyes. I would just have to keep from blinking until they dried.

"Tell me more," I said, my voice small, a whisper. I was starting to really think I had a thing for pain—what other explanation was there? "About the king. About the kind of monster that he is."

Mikhaila laughed. "Where have you been living, girl?" The same thing Annabelle had asked me, too.

I forced a smile. "Behind a really large rock." One that stretched for miles and miles all around the manor.

Mikhaila thought I was joking, so she laughed again. "Is she your daughter or something?" she asked Annabelle, and the both of us said *no!* so fast, she leaned back with her arms raised. "Okay, okay. Fine," she muttered.

"We're just...relatives," Annabelle said. "Distant relatives." She was too kind. We were nothing but strangers.

"Well, let's see," Mikhaila said, biting her apple again. "His idea of *keeping the peace* somehow means to put everyone in jail for doing anything at all, and then starve them until he's pleased. Upholding the law, too—doesn't matter if we're talking 'bout kids or teenagers or grown ass men—*beat* em, arrest them, and make sure to leave enough bruises to serve as reminders that the law is always above them—and don't even get me started on the law itself!" she said.

"Don't get me started on the people, the multi-million-dollar companies that control every aspect of our lives because he allows it. They inflate prices and make it impossible for shifters to be able to afford working for them—who cares how many families are actually starving out there? And if, gods forbid, someone dares to even speak about it, what does our king do? Throws them in jail—or worse." She shook her head, suddenly exhausted.

"The people are losing themselves, losing their animals, their elements, and they're expected to live with no support system, no back up, no jobs, nothing to guide them or ensure their safety or the safety of others. Shifter orphans are being thrown into human orphanages—did you know that? And what happens when they shift, and they don't know how to control their animals, and they hurt someone by accident— what then? A bullet to their head or rot in jail for the rest of their lives, that's what...

"The school system is wack. Most shifters are sending their kids to human schools, forced to *disguise* as humans just to be able to survive while our king grows more powerful and richer by the day..."

Mikhaila went on and on and on.

With every new word she spoke, I became heavier. I'd always known that my father was a bad man. I found out recently that my entire family for the past eight centuries were cruel psychopaths, but it still hurt. It still cut me right through the heart to hear those words.

Because despite everything, he was my father. And try as I might, I just couldn't get myself away from that.

"Eat the damn banana," Annabelle said after a while, nodding at my lap.

I wanted to say no, but then I brought the banana to my mouth and bit. Still tasteless.

I was a damn fool for asking them to tell me more. Now how was I going to keep walking with these shoulders?

"I'm leaving tonight," I told Annabelle, too numb to really feel anything for a while. "I'd really appreciate it if you can show me a map of the States, though. I need to get to Vermont, and I don't exactly know which way that is."

"I have a map," Annabelle said, so relieved to hear me say that I was leaving that it would have been painful if I was any less numb right now.

"Why Vermont?" Mikhaila asked, grabbing another apple from the bowl. It was cold out here.

The wind biting my skin was colder than I thought it would be. I had no jacket, but I didn't care. Maybe I could ask Annabelle for one of her shawls, just to cover my hair.

"I have a..." *Friend?* Lucien was not my friend. "I have someone there."

"It's a long way from here," Annabelle said.

"I have time." Until my father found me.

"I'm leaving, too," Mikhaila said.

"No, you're not," said Annabelle. It wasn't fair that I was *offended* that she looked concerned about her leaving.

We were strangers, she and I. *Strangers*. I needed to keep that in mind.

"I am. I have to. I feel fine today."

"Not fine enough to drive," Annabelle insisted.

"I am. Really—I'm fine. I can't stay here any longer."

Annabelle sighed. "Sure, kid. Knock yourself out. But I will warn you just this once—when you collapse again, I am letting you sleep out here, okay? I will not carry you back inside." And she stood up, throwing a look my way. "I'll get you that map."

Wow. She really couldn't wait for me to leave.

The worst part was that Mikhaila noticed because when Annabelle disappeared inside that house, I found her looking at me with pity in her pale green eyes.

So, I forced a smile to say that I was fine, and I ate the banana in silence.

SIX

"CAN YOU DRIVE?"

I looked up at Mikhaila, unsure whether she'd really spoken, or if that, too, had been a figment of my imagination. We'd been sitting in silence here for the past five minutes, waiting for Annabelle to bring me that map so I could leave. The night was so dark so suddenly. I'd just been studying the woods on the other side of the broken street. Even the moonlight that had been a friend to me last night seemed to have turned its back on me now.

"I said, do you have a driver's license?" Mikhaila repeated, her unblinking eyes on me.

"No." I wasn't allowed a driver's license. Mikhaila flinched. "I haven't driven in a few months."

Trevor had taught me to drive the fancy cars my father kept in his garage. I'd learned just because it was something to do, but I always preferred horses. They understood me.

"But you *can*," Mikhaila said, and the way she said it—so hopeful—scared me a little.

"I…I don't know. I think so." I'd only ever driven the roads around the manor in my father's estate. I'd never actually gone outside the walls.

Slowly, Mikhaila's thick lips stretched into one of those mischievous grins that I was learning was completely *her*.

"Here's the thing, Ella," she told me, putting the bowl of fruit to the side so she could come closer to me. I sat up straighter, suddenly perfectly aware of my surroundings again. "I need to get to Springfield. That's in Massachusetts. I am willing to take you with me if you help me drive."

My mouth opened and closed a couple of times.

"Busses are very slow. You'll be saving a lot of time. Springfield is a hell of a lot closer to Vermont than this place, so it's a win-win. You drive, I take you halfway there, and then you can take a bus or whatever." Her wide eyes sparkled as she looked at me.

I wanted to speak. I wanted to—I just didn't know how.

"Well? What do you say?" she said, and she grabbed my hands in hers, squeezed my fingers. I narrowed my brows, looking down at our connected hands. Hers were warm, like she was feverish. Or mine were ice-cold.

"It'll be fun. C'mon, we'll get there in a day, even if we drive slowly," she said, a bit desperate now.

Gods, I wanted to say *yes*. Of course, I wanted to go with her—was she kidding? But...

"You're not well, Mikhaila," I said because she wasn't. I hadn't forgotten last night. And this morning. And how was I going to help her if she needed it?

"Don't you worry about me," she told me, squeezing my fingers so hard I thought they were going to break, but I still didn't have it in me to pull away. "Trust me, I've gone through worse. I just need you to take me to Springfield, and then you'll be free, okay? I'll pay for gas." She smiled brightly, but it was fake. "I'm going to get there one way or the other. The thing is, there's a good chance I'll be knocked out cold with the wheel in my hands—and don't get me wrong, I don't mind at all. I just don't want to kill anyone accidentally, you know?"

I shook my head. No, I imagined she wouldn't want to kill anyone accidentally.

"So, you're not just helping me and yourself—you're helping potential victims, too." She tugged at my hands. "Let's just do it. Let's just go. You drive. I keep you company. We get to Springfield—and then you're on your own. No need to worry about me at all. Not even a little bit." She held her index finger and thumb together to show me how much she meant.

"Potential victims," I repeated, not sure why those words stuck with me.

"Yep. People who will most likely die when I crash that truck into their car—those people. You'll be saving them, technically speaking." She grinned like a little kid.

For some reason, I burst out laughing. That was the silliest reason I'd ever heard in my life.

"Is that a yes? Please say it's a yes," she said. "C'mon, Ella. Say yes. It'll be fun! A road trip. Just you and me—so much *fun!*"

It occurred to me that Greta would like her.

It occurred to me that about a million things could go wrong if I went with her.

"It's a yes," I said, anyway.

Mikhaila cheered. *Woohoo! It's a road trip!*

She seemed genuinely happy for about three minutes, and then she looked like she was about to pass out again.

By the time Annabelle came back outside with an old map, I'd already regretted the decision, but I didn't have the heart to take it back.

∽

POTENTIAL VICTIMS.

I looked at Mikhaila, doubt eating away at the little hope I had left.

If my father or his people found us, they'd kill her. I knew that.

She was a potential victim as well; she just didn't know it. How dare I not tell her?

Because if I told her, if I refused her offer, I'd have to steal. I wasn't good at stealing. If I got caught stealing, I'd could get locked up—worse, *killed* by someone else before my time. So much depended on my finding my way to Aither. Finding John. Summoning the Ether.

I'm not good at stealing. I will get caught.

I said those words to myself over and over again as I watched her dragging her feet to her beat-up red truck. I wasn't even sure I could drive it—the cars I'd driven with Trevor at the manor were...fancy. Very, very fancy.

Bile rose up my throat, but I pushed it back down. I'd slept for a few hours—Annabelle had insisted we leave with daylight. She had no problem with me leaving or driving, but she was worried about Mikhaila. Said daylight was safer.

I agreed. It had been better even—I had needed the sleep. I had needed the time to convince myself that this wasn't the worst idea I'd ever had in all my lives.

I don't know why I was so scared.

"Here. There's your plate and the glass, and some food in there."

I turned to Annabelle leaning against the door frame, handing me a small black bag.

"It's fine. We'll get something on the way," I said, glad for the plate and the glass to try the Water trick again, even though I wasn't sure how I was going to get food. I had no money. I had nothing but a spell to summon the Ether in my pocket. A spell that could potentially save the world...from my father.

I didn't even recognize what had become of my life anymore.

"Take it. It's been paid for, anyway," Annabelle insisted.

I took the bag. My body was weak, but I still couldn't imagine eating. I looked at her through the corner of my eye, the way hers remained on Mikhaila, who was sitting in the truck, eyes closed, breathing in the morning light. With the rising sun behind her, she looked more like a drawing than real.

"One day, I will be back," I said, despite my better judgment. Annabelle said nothing. "One day soon, I'll be back. You won't have to live like this forever." It was meant to be a promise, but...

"Don't you worry about me, Estella Azarius. I can take care of myself."

Her voice was bitter. There was no warmth in it. No warmth in the blue of her eye. No *feeling* other than irritation. We might have been of the same blood, but once more I was reminded, she and I *were not* family. Not in the way it mattered.

The thought of hugging her turned my stomach inside out. I wanted to and didn't want to. I wanted to look her in the eye and smile, and I wanted to run.

In the end, I only nodded at myself. In the end, I decided, no matter how bitter she was, and no matter what she said to me now, I *would* be back. I would make sure she lived a better life than this.

She was my blood. That meant something to me, it seemed, despite everything.

If I remained alive long enough to see the Ether back and my father dethroned.

Keeping my mouth shut, I made my way out of her yard

and to Mikhaila's truck. Annabelle followed me, and with every new step we took, I could almost *feel* the relief, the way her shoulders lightened, the way she walked a little straighter. It would have been easy to blame her, but one look at her face and I couldn't.

As she instructed Mikhaila on what to do and when to take her herbs—plus a little illegal potion she'd brewed for her last night—my mind did what it did best: it wondered. It filled up with questions before I could blink. Brand new questions.

Had my mother always been this way in my past lives?

Had she always almost killed her sister, had she ripped half her face off just so she could get to go to the tournament and win the right to marry my father? To be queen?

Had she really been so easy to fool once she succeeded?

Was she really as bad as she seemed to me right now?

"So long," Annabelle said, putting a small bottle full of brownish liquid in Mikhaila's hands before she closed the passenger door.

Plenty of space inside the truck. I was sitting on the driver's seat, too, with no idea what the hell I was looking at. Not nearly as many things and lights and buttons as in my father's cars. That had to be a good thing.

"Be careful, okay? And don't come back here again," Annabelle said, smiling as if she were joking. She wasn't.

"You'd be lucky to see us again, ya old hag," Mikhaila said, laughing. "Go back to bed. We'll be fine." Then she turned to me. "Right, Ella?"

"Right," I said automatically, then cleared my throat.

"The keys are in the ignition," she instructed, and she could see just how clueless I was, but she was trying not to panic.

It was okay. I had this.

Annabelle had already gone back to the fence gate and she was watching us with her arms crossed in front of her chest. I saw her face through the rearview mirror, the scars on the right, the smooth skin, the blue eye, the pink lips. She ripped my heart out by just standing there.

"Easy," Mikhaila whispered. "We'll take it slow. No rush."

And so we did.

I figured out how to turn the ignition on—there was no button here. The truck seemed *ancient* to me now, and Mikhaila was kind enough to remind me of the basics—*clutch, brake, gas. Keep the steering wheel straight. Don't forget to shift to second. Repeat.*

"You're doing great," she lied when we entered the wide, bumpy road that led down the hill and into the town.

"We haven't crashed yet," I said, which was pretty miraculous, considering I felt like I was riding a beast—and I don't mean the dragoness in my head.

"And we won't be crashing at all. Just keep your eyes on the road, and we go slow," she said. "We don't even have to play the radio. We'll just focus."

"Talk to me," I said instead because, despite what she thought, focus wasn't going to help me right now. Trevor once said that learning to drive was like learning to swim—the body would remember the motions forever. All it would take was to get back into the water.

My body knew the motions—I could tell it did. But the more I focused on what I was doing, the stiffer my muscles. So...

"Talk to you about what?" Mikhaila said from the passenger seat, her hand gripping the handle of the door tightly, even though she was trying to fool me into thinking she wasn't afraid.

"About...about where we're going. Why Springfield?" I blurted, going as slow as possible, which served me. The road in the middle of the small town was wide and open—no cars out at this hour. No people, either.

Thank the gods.

"Because I have a rendezvous with my ex," she said.

"Oh?" I checked the rearview mirror, side mirrors, and the road ahead—clear.

My muscles were beginning to relax with every new second.

"Yeah. The asshole dropped me off at Annabelle's door, paid her, left the keys to this old thing with her, and disappeared," Mikhaila said. "So, now I have to go find him, kick his ass, and return his truck."

"Why would he do that?" I wondered, slowing down at the corner of the street. "And which way do we go?"

"I'll be sure to ask him, but I doubt he'll be able to answer with broken teeth," she said, then put her phone on the dashboard. "Take a left, then the second right, and we'll be on the highway." The screen showed a map in various shades of green, and a blue arrow pointing me in the right direction.

Sweat dripped down to my brows. I exhaled loudly.

I had this.

"You okay?" I asked Mikhaila.

She settled on the seat, resting her head back, still gripping the door handle tightly.

"Don't you worry about me, girl. Just drive."

Nobody wanted me to worry about them today.

So, I drove.

SEVEN

ONCE I GOT THE HANG OF IT, DRIVING THE TRUCK wasn't all that bad. The strange noises it made every time I shifted gears did give me a scare, but the engine was working, the steering wheel was turning smoothly enough, and we were already on the highway.

Surreal. So much space, the road so wide. Nothing ahead, just the open sky, so blue it looked painted, and if I focused on it alone, I could pretend I was driving to it. I was driving into that blue, and to those white puffy clouds where my name didn't matter and my problems didn't exist.

Mikhaila fell in and out of sleep as I drove straight for a while. She scared me more than the car, but soon, we'd reach another town, maybe a city. Soon, there would be hospitals I could stop by if needed.

"Here's what's strange," she said after a long while, when the sun was higher up in the sky and my stomach was making pretty loud noises.

I turned to her for a second—I hadn't realized her eyes were open as she stared out the passenger side window.

"How did you find your way to Annabelle? Who brought you?"

My great, great, great, great-grandmother did some other kind of magic...or something like that. "I took the bus."

"And then?"

"And then, what?"

Silence for a moment. "How'd you make it from the bus station to that godsforsaken town? As far as I know, the closest bus station is in East Akron. That's far." I could feel her eyes on the side of my face.

I swallowed hard, trying to find words that would make any of this seem reasonable. There were none.

"Are you a serial killer or something?"

"What—no!" I turned to her so fast, the steering wheel in my hands turned, too, and I almost ran us off the road.

"Whoa, whoa, slow down!" said Mikhaila, holding onto the dashboard, gripping the plastic as if she was hoping to stop the truck from moving.

But I took control of the wheel again, and other than the car behind us honking a couple of times, everything else was fine. Other than my heart almost beating right out me, nothing was wrong. We were still alive.

"Okay, then, okay," Mikhaila said. "Not a serial killer. You don't have to kill us for real to prove it." And she laughed. It was a *relieved* kind of laugh, and I joined in, too.

"No, I just knew a good scare was going to take your mind off asking those questions," I joked, and she raised a brow, grinning.

"Not as innocent as you look, after all," she said, and my eyes moved to the rearview mirror on instinct. Why did everybody think I looked *innocent*? I didn't think I looked innocent. Sure—blue eyes and blonde hair and fair skin made you think that word, but there was a hardness in my eyes that had developed in the last couple of months that was *not* innocent at all.

"I'm really not," I said, shaking my head. Lucien thought I'd looked innocent, too. That's probably why he never even doubted I was Greta when I was in Aither.

"So, who are you then?" Mikhaila slipped in the question as if absentmindedly, but I could feel her watching me through the corner of her eye like a hawk.

The smile died on my lips. "I'm just a girl."

"No, you're not. I know what *just a girl* looks like. *I'm* just a girl."

I turned to her for a moment, but she was looking out the window.

"How old are you, if you don't mind me asking?" She didn't look like a girl, but not much older than me, either.

"Twenty-six soon," she said. Lucien's age. "You?"

"Twenty." For the seventh time.

"You look older," Mikhaila said, then settled back on the seat. "To be honest, I don't care where you come from or what you're doing, Ella, but as long as you don't try to kill me or steal from me, we'll be just fine."

She had her eyes closed and she sighed deeply, her skin already much paler than when we left Annabelle's. She worried me.

"I won't," I promised and kept my eyes on the road.

There was a feeling in my gut that insisted that something was *wrong*. Something was not right, and I needed to stop, see, think, *feel* whatever it was. Figure it out.

But I didn't have the time to stop. I didn't have the luxury to wonder. My father was searching for me right now. It was only a matter of time before he found me.

So, all I could do was keep on driving.

≈

IT WAS SILLY. The drop of water suspended on air, and I pulled the glass back, then offered it my hand. It floated over my palm just like it had done with Mikhaila the day before, but that's it. That was all. It didn't move in any direction. It didn't guide me the way it should. It just hovered there over my palm—*innocently.*

I could have laughed.

"Do something," I said to it again, focused on the buzzing that came off the water. It definitely had energy—I felt it clearly. Why it refused to just point me in the right direction, I had no clue.

Closing my eyes, I thought about the wyrm again—the large body, the blue scales, the four eyes. I saw it clearly, in as much detail as the artists had drawn it in that book. I almost touched it with my mind, yet when I opened my eyes again, the drop of water had only moved lower on my palm. Then, whatever energy held it up let go, and it spilled in the middle of my hand like it was exhausted. Just as exhausted as I was.

"Now what, John?" I mumbled to myself, spilling the water from the plate to the asphalt, and putting them back in the bag. More fruit in there, and a couple pieces of bread. I was going to save those for Mikhaila—she needed them more, even though I was really beginning to think I might starve before I reached Aither.

How ridiculous. I'd lived seven lives in pure luxury, never having to move a finger for anything—but look at me now. Wearing someone else's clothes, not a penny in my pocket to buy food.

Was it strange that I *liked* to feel this way? At least for a little while. It felt important to have the experience.

Or maybe I was just trying to make myself feel better.

When the door to the toilets of the gas station we'd stopped at opened, I looked up to see Mikhaila coming out. She looked fine, if not a bit pale. We'd driven for four hours, had passed towns and cities as fast as I could manage to drive, and now we had to stop for toilets and for gas before we continued.

If I could keep driving for much longer.

Mikhaila held up a finger as if to say, *hold on a minute,* and then she went to the other side of the building and into the convenience store. She had money with her—she'd paid for gas. Maybe she could buy something to eat for herself.

And if she did, maybe I could eat the banana and some bread, too.

When she came out of the convenience store, she had a plastic bag in her hand, and she barely took three steps before her legs let go of her. Her knees hit the asphalt almost as if by accident.

The fear gripped me by the throat, and I didn't even breathe until I reached her. I pulled her up and put her arm around my shoulders, saying, *you're okay, you're okay*—more to myself than to her. I had no clue how to handle someone sick. I had no clue what the hell to do, how to help her, and it freaked me the hell out.

"I'm fine," Mikhaila said with a hiss. "The cargo bed..."

I brought her close enough to the truck so she could hold herself upright, then pulled the panel of the cargo bed down. I helped her sit on it, and the look on her face—her eyes so angry they looked red—said that she *hated* having to be assisted to even sit down. But she was breathing heavily and there really was no room for complaints. She couldn't stand on her own, at least not right now.

"How are you feeling? Do you need me to get you anything? How about some water?"

"I'm fine," she muttered, closing her eyes and lowering her head for a minute. "I just need to eat, that's all. Hop on."

She brought the plastic bag to her lap and opened it. The smell of something delicious that I couldn't even place invaded my nostrils. My stomach sang so hard Mikhaila turned to look at me.

"I got us these shitty cold sandwiches. Best I can afford," she said and offered me something wrapped in brown paper.

"Oh, I'm fine," I told her. "I've got fruit."

"We'll eat that for dinner," she said. "Take it."

I stepped back. "I'm fine. I'm not hungry. You need to eat that. Just eat."

With a sigh, she lowered her hand to her lap, and she looked even more furious than before.

"I am six years your senior. Don't make me smack you. Sit the fuck down and eat!"

I flinched—she really did look like she meant it. I lowered my head, suddenly embarrassed. Was I really going to eat a sick woman's food?

"*Sit.*" And she pointed a hand to the cargo bed next to her thigh to tell me to sit.

So, I did.

She had a sandwich of her own, wrapped up in the brown paper, and she eagerly ripped it open before she bit into it. With her eyes closed, she moaned. I thought she enjoyed it, but...

"The most disgusting thing I've ever eaten," she mumbled, then bit into it again.

I tried it, too. The taste was strange—there was meat in it, maybe turkey or chicken. There was tomato and mustard, even a thin slice of cheese in there. It tasted like frozen food, but I kind of liked it. I don't know why—probably the hunger. I ate half of it like I was racing, barely breathing between bites.

Just like with magic, my stomach no longer screamed at me.

"Thank you," I thought to say when I remembered that Mikhaila was sitting right next to me.

"You're welcome, girl," she said, eating slowly now, just like me, to savor the last of the sandwich. "Where are your parents?"

"Mom's dead. Dad's...away." Hopefully *far* away from me. Hopefully so far away, he wouldn't find me at all until I reached Aither and became completely invisible to him.

"Life's a bitch like that," she muttered with a nod, like she understood. But she had no idea.

"Yours?"

"They're away," she said, looking down at the last of her sandwich.

"Are you...do you talk to them?"

"Not exactly." She smiled bitterly. "They kind of, sort of, think I'm dead."

I turned to her—definitely not what I expected. "That's...unfortunate."

Mikhaila burst out laughing, but it didn't last longer than a second. "Trust me, it's very fortunate. I was eleven when I faked my own death. You got any idea how hard that shit is?" She looked at me, brow raised.

I shook my head. Definitely no idea.

"It's hard. *Very* hard, but I was a clever little shit. I did what I had to do." She chewed on her sandwich for a while. "And then the likes of Torin Lopez drops me off at a stranger's door and disappears." Another one of those laughs.

"Why, though?" Why would anybody do something like that?

"Because he's a chickenshit," she said, almost sadly. "He's a coward—and I always knew it. I just...I like to ignore my own instincts often. I like to fool myself too much." She turned to me. "Like I'm doing with you."

Shivers ran down my back. "I'm not going to drop you off at a stranger's door and disappear." That, at least she could count on. I would rather die.

"I know there's something about you, Ella. That might not even be your real name," she said. "I know you're lying to me, but"—wiping her mouth with the back of her hand, she gave me a pointed look—"if you try something with me, I *will* kill you."

Her words rang true. "Okay."

"Okay?"

I nodded. "Okay."

She straightened on the bed again, feet dangling off the edge of the panel, then asked, "You ever killed someone?"

I looked at her just to make sure she wasn't kidding. She wasn't. "No." Such a strange question to ask. "Have you?"

"Oh, yeah," she said, nodding. "I've killed people." Again, her words rang true. I looked at her profile, the way she smiled and clenched her jaws at the same time. I *saw* so much more of her—the sheen of the layer of sweat covering her pale skin, the grease in her hair, the wrinkles in her clothes. It's like the sandwich was a magical potion and the strength it gave me made me realize just how much I'd always taken energy for granted.

"It's easy enough, actually. They tell you it's hard—it isn't," Mikhaila said after a minute. "What they *don't* tell you, though, is that you die, too." She flinched. "Parts of you, at least. Nobody ever mentions that."

In front of my eyes were the three men who had been about to beat me in that alley in Tearny—maybe do something worse. I remembered what they'd looked like while Lucien had taken the breath out of their lungs, had suffocated them slowly. I remembered the desperation in their eyes, the way they'd clung to life—had *tried* to. The way they'd collapsed.

Lucien hadn't looked like parts of him had died with those men, and I'd never asked him. Maybe I was a coward. Maybe I liked lying to myself, too.

Maybe...I didn't mind it as much as I thought I would that he would kill for me.

Because the truth, ugly or not, was that I would kill for him, too. Without hesitation.

"Did you have to?" I asked Mikhaila—and I wasn't judging her. Far from it. I was genuinely curious.

And she saw that. That's why she nodded. "I did."

"Then I'm glad you're here." Better them than her.

Surprised, her lips curled up as she watched me, a genuine smile this time.

"Glad to be here, too," she said. "I get the feeling you have even more secrets than me."

No way could I stop the laugh that burst out of me. "You have *no* idea."

"Then tell me something," she said, rolling the empty sandwich wrapper between her palms. I was done with mine, too. I felt incredible already, like I could drive for days at a time, like I could *run* all the way to Aither. "Tell me *one* thing that you've never told anyone before. It will be that secret that you told a stranger when you were young and naive. You'll remember it forever, and I will, too."

"A secret." I did have a lot of those, but which could I possibly share with her?

"Yes, one secret. How else can we mark this road trip and make sure we never forget?"

A secret...

I sighed. "Once, I read almost one thousand smut books within a year."

The way she shook while she laughed in silence had the entire truck vibrating. I bit my tongue to keep from doing the same—it was the one secret *nobody* knew about. Not even Greta. I'd been too ashamed to even bring it up with her, but I'd been a teenager, long before I got my memories back, and I'd been discovering my body. I was constantly curious about what I liked and didn't like, so sixteen-year-old Ella had taken it upon herself to figure it all out as fast as possible.

Gods, the things I'd read...they made me blush even now.

Eventually, Mikhaila stopped laughing. She looked at me. Smiled. Nodded. "Nice to meet you, Ella," she said, like she was just seeing me for the first time. And she jumped off the panel—right on her feet.

I smiled, too. "Nice to meet you, too."

Two minutes later, we were on the road again, and I felt as comfortable in that truck as if I were in Aither already.

EIGHT

QUESTIONS HAUNTED ME. SO MANY OF THEM—always too many. Mainly about my mother.

She'd always been pure to me—the synonym of peace and kindness and beauty. She was a goddess, divine and all-knowing. She felt like nothing else in the world. Her smile lifted me up the way nothing else ever did.

And now all those memories were threatening to tear me apart because of lies. Secrets. Truths hidden so well, I'd never even suspected them, not for a second. I wondered who Mom really was. I wondered if she really was someone who'd hurt her twin sister to get what she wanted. I wondered if she really was someone to have a purpose, a will so weak that attention and luxury and power would make her forget what was important. I wondered if she loved my father, too—*really* loved him.

I wondered if she was someone who would turn her niece away even though she didn't know her at all. If she would *hug* her for a moment, smile at her for once, tell her that she loved her.

I wondered.

And maybe that's why I saw her in my dreams.

I rarely dreamed about my mother. She was way too big for my imagination to be able to describe her properly. I always thought that. But tonight, she was there, though far away. She was smiling, though it didn't reach her eyes. She was speaking to me, though she could barely let out whispers—and I couldn't hear her. I couldn't understand.

Wherever I was, I couldn't move. I was too tired. Exhausted. Screaming my lungs out calling for her, but not being able to make a single sound.

But then the white dress she had on suddenly stopped floating around her legs. She appeared to be closer, though I still couldn't see her face clearly. And this time, when she spoke, I heard her loud and clear.

"*Where is your father?*"

My lips moved but no sound came out of me.

"*You have to find him, Estella. You have to kill him. You know that.*"

I broke to pieces and I cried, fell to my knees on the same *nothing* I stood on. I begged her—*stop, no, that can't be right, I won't do it*—but Mom just looked down at me, her blue eyes... strange. The color in them had always been clear. Pure.

Now, it was tainted. It was corrupted. It *wasn't her.*

It couldn't be her—that was not my mother. My mother would never say such a thing.

Not her, not her, not her...

And the light behind my closed lids disappeared.

I thought it was over. I thought the nightmare was done and I could wake up, breathe, remind myself that just because I knew *more* about my mother now, didn't meant that the lives I'd lived with her never happened. It didn't mean that all the good she was didn't exist simply because there might be some *bad* about her, too. *Might.*

She was still my mother.

But the nightmare wasn't over yet.

When my eyes opened, I saw the dark, heard the fire burning in the distance, saw the shape of the man bathed in an orange glow ahead of me.

"Time is running out," John told me, and his voice wasn't as light as it had been in my last nightmares. It was...irritated. "You have to find the wyrm, Estella." He didn't ask me this time—he *ordered* me.

I rose on my shaking legs. The anger gave me strength, like magic, like that awful sandwich I'd eaten with Mikhaila sitting on the bed of her truck.

"Tell me how and I will because your stupid Water trick doesn't work."

But John didn't care about that. He didn't care about his absurd demands, only made them again and again:

Find her, find her, find her...

MY EYES SNAPPED OPEN. Air rushed down my throat as if I hadn't breathed in years. I sat up, too, terrified to feel the cold of the air against my sweaty skin, to feel the thin blanket over my body, to feel my limbs shaking—from fear or the cold, I wasn't sure.

I had no clue where I was, but the nightmare was over.

I knew because the moon told me.

It was in the sky, right across from me, at the top of large pine trees on the other side of the lake. Their pointy tips seemed to be stretching out to touch it, but it was far out of their reach, surrounded by stars, unbothered.

I was okay.

John wasn't here. My mother wasn't here, either. It was just me, lying on the cargo bed, parked in front of a small lake, sleeping out in the open with a thin blanket over me, next to...

"Mikhaila."

She was lying to my right, clutching the thin blanket to

her chest, breathing worse than me. So much worse. Beads of sweat on her hairline. Her blue lips were parted, her eyes narrowed, and she looked like she was in pain.

"*Mikhaila!*" I said, rising on my knees, shaking her shoulders. She was shaking and she was panting, but she wouldn't open her eyes.

"Torin..." she breathed. "Please, don't. Don't..."

Oh, gods. I touched her forehead, and she was *burning*. "Hold on," I told her, as if I knew what I was doing. "Just hold on."

I grabbed the bag Annabelle had given us and took out the fruits we had left—three apples, two bananas. It was fabric, and the only thing I had right now, so I jumped off the cargo bed with my heart in my throat and ran to the lake, to the water, hoping it was as cold as the night. As cold as my heart right now.

It was.

I dipped the fabric in the water, then ran back to the truck as fast as my legs carried me. Small rocks bordered the lakeside and my tennis shoes slipped, but I managed to get back without losing my balance. Then, I put the wet fabric over Mikhaila's forehead, and tried to find her bag and the bottle Annabelle had made her. She had a change of clothes in there, some keys, and the bottle, filled to the brim with the brownish liquid.

"You'll be okay," I told her, pulling her up a bit so I could give her the concoction. "Drink, Mikhaila. Drink."

She did—slowly. She was delirious, eyes opening and closing slowly, but she couldn't see me. She kept calling for Torin, her ex who had left her, and it made me wonder if maybe he'd hurt her more than she let on. I was starting to think that Mikhaila was very good at hiding her feelings. I was starting to think that there was so much more to what she said than she let on.

I gave her almost half the small bottle before her body stopped shaking. The fabric of the bag I'd dipped in the lake had helped in lowering her body temperature. She stopped speaking, too, stopped opening her eyes. Stopped breathing so heavily.

Whatever mixture Annabelle had made worked.

Sitting back on the bed, I put the bottle aside and closed my eyes. I took in a deep breath and tried to calm my racing heart.

We were okay.

In fact, we were very close to Springfield, according to Mikhaila. We had stopped close to a small lake in Stockbridge when the sun began to set because we didn't have the money for a motel. It was a private place, lots of trees, and I parked her truck near one just off a low, narrow bridge. It was the perfect spot to sleep outdoors—something I'd *never* done before. It had been magic to sleep watching the sky turn from a deep blue to an all-consuming black, before the stars started twinkling and the moon shone silver. I hadn't seen it—it had been somewhere on the other side of the trees when I slept, but now it was right in front of me, which meant the night was almost over.

And now that I didn't feel like I was about to run out of breath soon, and Mikhaila was sleeping peacefully again, I could actually enjoy the view.

Gods, it was beautiful. The surface of the lake, moving only slightly, like liquid glass under the dark sky, the moon hiding half her reflection behind the sharp tips of the pine trees. It looked like a drawing, it *felt* like art, not a real moment.

I closed my eyes and breathed deeply, desperate to hold onto this moment forever. How I wished Lucien was here with me. How I wished I could feel the heat of his body against mine right now.

I had no plan. I had no idea how I was going to get to Vermont when Mikhaila and I went our separate ways. I had no clue how I was going to make sure my father didn't find me until I was safely under the magic of Aither—but I was smiling.

Even with the crazy turns my life kept on taking, even with the uncertainty that followed my every step, I wouldn't want to be anywhere else in the world but right here, with the moon keeping me company, the wind whispering in my ear, and the lake's magic in the air.

Eventually, I took the dishes Annabelle had given me and went to the lake, took some water, and tried to do the Water trick again. It didn't work. It *wouldn't* work. Everyone was right—it was just a silly story. It was definitely worth the try, though—especially since I got to run my hands in the water, watch the tiny ripples shining under the moonlight as they expanded, then settled into the water again.

It was the most peaceful night of my life. And when I lay down on the cargo bed near Mikhaila again, I knew deep in my bones that this was the calm before a storm I just might not survive.

"THIS IS IT?"

I looked at the crowded street, at the large brown brick building with huge windows on the other side.

"That's the bus station," Mikhaila said. "And this should pay for your ticket to Vermont." She put a hundred-dollar bill on my lap.

It was folded into a square, old and worn, like that piece of green paper had survived both war and peace.

I looked at her pale face. "No." I wasn't going to take money from her. Of course not.

Never had a piece of paper in my hand been so heavy, so I tried to give it back.

Mikhaila pushed my hand back. "*Yes.*"

"I can't," I told her. She was sick, she was alone, she wasn't going to give me money. I'd find another way.

"You can and you will," she insisted.

"But you need it—"

"And it's obvious to see that *you* need it more than me," she said. "Besides. You took care of me last night. I appreciate it. Now, get out."

I blinked. "You remember that?" She hadn't mentioned anything when we woke up at sunrise. She hadn't mentioned that she'd even known she was talking in her sleep or that she'd been burning up.

"A little bit," she said. "I remember you telling me I was gonna be okay. Dunno why I believed you, honestly." She leaned her head to the side. "But I like you, Estella. You're pretty nice for a liar." She gave me a cheeky grin. "Now, *get out.*"

I burst out laughing. "And where is Torin? Is he close? Because I think I should go with you, just in case." In case she collapsed like she usually did. I wasn't comfortable leaving her alone.

But Mikhaila reached right over me and pushed the driver's door open. "Get out, girl. Before I *make* you." And she pushed my shoulder playfully.

Tears in my eyes even though I was smiling. As soon as I was out of the truck, she jumped in the driver's side and closed the door, then rolled the window down.

"I don't mind," I said. "I can drive you there and back. Wherever you're going."

"See—that's the thing. I *don't* know where I'm going at all," she said.

I shook my head. "Then you can come with me. I know a

place—it's safe. It's...saf*er* than any other place out here." Aither and its Air magic and its happy people...would Lucien mind if I brought a friend along?

Was that what Mikhaila and I were—friends?

"Nah, kid. I'm good. I have a score to settle with a little bitch." She grinned. "Besides, tigers are lone animals. I'll be just fine," she said with a wink, like she was letting me in on a secret. And she was—she hadn't told Annabelle what she shifted into, but she'd told me.

"You sure? Because—"

"*Yes,* I'm sure! Go away!" And she rolled up the window in a rush.

I laughed, shaking my head. She was completely insane, and I most definitely liked her, too.

Waving my hand, I stayed there on the sidewalk as she drove away until she turned the street corner and I couldn't see her anymore. I tried not to worry—she could take care of herself. She was smart, she'd know when to stop and rest. She'd made it this far in life without me, hadn't she?

I looked down at my shaking fist where the hundred-dollar bill was. Something told me she didn't have many of those. No, this was most probably her last. And she gave it to *me.* A stranger. A nobody. Just a *nice liar.*

A couple tears slipped from my eyes, but I was also smiling. Because it wasn't just money she gave me. It wasn't even the solution to all my problems—it was more than that.

Mikhaila was the woman who faked her own death, ran from her parents, and even killed people—gods knew how many.

But she was also the woman who gave her last dime to a stranger in need. It reminded me that we can all be more than one thing. More than two, more than a hundred. That doesn't mean that we're all bad. It just means we're human, too.

Just like my mother was.

NINE

I WAS NEVER ON A BUS BEFORE. I NEVER KNEW IT would be so peaceful. I never knew how easy it would be to fall asleep if you sit close to the back wheels, and you rest your head on the window, and close your eyes and feel the vibrations of the machine go right through you.

So many firsts.

First bus station. First bus ticket. First two-hour wait for the bus to arrive. First bus ride.

I'd meant to stay awake and look out the window. I'd meant to enjoy this first thoroughly because I might never be on a bus again, but I must have been more tired than I thought. Much more hungry than I could have imagined.

I felt it when the bus slowed down, though. There were no dreams, no nightmares, just blissful nothingness while I slept —for over four hours. The sun was about to set when I realized we were in Manchester Center. Last stop.

I had to get off and somehow find my way to East Dorset, then beyond, to the Yuvelinne Castle. The little energy boost I'd gotten from sleeping in the bus helped in keeping my focus, but when I was in the middle of the sidewalk, watching the people pass me by, the panic wasted no time at all in settling in.

There were no busses to where I was going, and even if there were, I had no money to pay for it. Five bucks remained in my pocket, that's it. I was hungry, I was weak, I was a godsdamn mess—and worse of all, I had no clue how I was going to get to the castle. To the woods. To Aither.

My heart skipped a long beat as I tried to think up options. Where would I find anyone going to the Yuvelinne right now? How would I get them to take me with? I couldn't pay anyone. I could do nothing at all.

But I could still walk.

"Slow down," I whispered to myself and closed my eyes for a second. I had shoes on. I had five bucks to buy me a small bottle of water and something to eat—anything. Greta said that jalapeño sticks are delicious and cheap. All I had to do was find a grocery store, someone who could point me in the right direction, maybe show me a map on their phones, and I'd be good to go. It didn't matter how long it took, or how many highways I had to walk to get there—I would. As long as I was standing, I'd find my way.

My heart slowed down the beating a minute later. I let go of a long breath, knowing things weren't nearly as simple as I made them be, but I had to force myself to calm down. Freaking out wasn't going to do me any favors.

So, I started with the first part of the plan—grocery store. I spent four dollars, eighty-five cents on a bottle of water, and two small packs of turkey and diced cheese snacks. They tasted worse than the gas station sandwiches Mikhaila had gotten us, but they filled me up and they were cheap. My options were limited.

The sky was orange when I walked out, the sun almost completely disappeared behind the large two-story building across from me. I swallowed the last of the cheese and saved some of the water for later, and I looked around me, trying to find a person who wasn't walking, wasn't rushing, someone who would help me just because they wanted to be helpful. I literally had nothing to offer them other than a *thank you*.

I was so focused on trying to *read* people's expressions that I didn't even notice someone watching me. I didn't notice the two men across the street, and the third in the parking lot to the side of the building.

Instead, I just walked to a couple smoking near the trunk of their car, laughing at one another, who couldn't be much older than my father. They'd have phones. They'd let me take a look at the map app, just like Mikhaila had done.

The closer I got to them in the parking lot, the less *impossible* this whole thing seemed, and so when I called out to them, I was buzzing with energy.

"Excuse me, may I ask you a question?" I said in my most polite voice.

Both of them turned to me.

"Yes, sweetie?" the woman said, swiping her dark blonde hair behind her ear, an easy smile on her face, until...

Until her eyes landed somewhere behind me.

Her smile dropped. The man instantly threw the butt of his cigarette away and narrowed his brows, then slowly grabbed her hand, too. My instincts knew what was happening even before I did, so that when I turned around and saw what the couple was looking at, I was surprised.

I shouldn't have been.

Every inch of my skin rose in goose bumps when I saw his face, his dark eyes, the wicked grin stretching his lips.

Trevor and three other men behind him, *not* dressed as my father's guards, though they were.

"No," I whispered to myself, shaking my head, as if I could change reality if I decided to deny it.

Unfortunately for me, it didn't work.

"I knew I'd find you here, Princess," Trevor said, his voice thick, his shoulders incredibly wide—like he was about to shift into a wolf already. I stepped back, shaking, but I knew it was a done deal. He wouldn't be alone.

"Stay away from me!" I cried out anyway. The man and woman were already in their car, driving away.

"I've been waiting all day. I knew you'd want to go back to wherever you disappeared to last time, Estella," Trevor told me, shaking his head like a disappointed parent. "It's over. I'm taking you home."

Fuck.

That.

I turned around and ran.

Too close, way too close to Aither to accept that my fight was over. Too close to freedom, real freedom, to the Ether, to a life beyond the time loop, to a life with Lucien. How was I going to give up now? Even when I knew that Trevor wouldn't be the only one around me.

Even when I knew that I couldn't outrun his wolf if he shifted.

Even when I knew that I wouldn't make it away from my father's people even if I sprouted wings on my back—I still couldn't give up.

So, I ran.

Tears blurred my vision. The growing darkness didn't help, but I didn't need to see much. Just enough not to bump into something, just so I kept going until my legs failed me.

Or until my mind gave up.

My name was being called. Trevor's voice, like an animal's roar, ordered me to stop. If he was under my skin, he would have known not to waste his breath.

And I heard all their footsteps. So many—too many to count. They were all around me now, coming for me no matter how fast I ran. I couldn't tell where I'd gone, which direction I'd taken. Trees around me, but they wouldn't hide me. If I climbed them, Trevor would, too. If I dug a hole in the ground and hid, he'd be there to drag me back to the manor before I could blink.

Over.

It was over.

A scream wanted to rip from my throat when I felt the body right behind me, felt the fingers graze my shirt, but the soldier missed me by less than an inch.

The second time, he succeeded.

His hand wrapped around my arm and he pulled me back hard.

My legs failed me. I hit the ground on my back, unable to keep my balance. I rolled and rolled until I hit a tree trunk with my stomach hard. My lungs squeezed, desperate for air, but it hurt so much, I forgot how to draw it in. I forgot how to breathe, how to think, how to blink. Bells rang in my ears, and I heard the wolves howling, heard the tigers roaring, heard the footsteps and the shouts.

My eyes closed, tears coming out of me still.

And then I felt someone behind me.

Over.

Now, Trevor would put me in a car, on a plane, and I'd be standing in front of my father before the night was done.

I expected to be grabbed, put on my feet, forced to walk to wherever their cars were, maybe even be carried over Trevor's shoulder.

Instead, I heard a whoosh of air a split second before something hit the back of my head hard. The pain was so sudden, so all-consuming, it took away my vision instantly.

Everything went dark.

~

TIME MUST HAVE LOST track of itself because I was back.

Same darkness, same hard surface under me, all around me, same feeling—like I was being dragged over the bumpiest road, but...

Something was different, too. No wool on me, pressed to my skin, in my mouth and nostrils. No ropes around my wrists, either.

My body jerked, the memory of the night Izet kidnapped me and put me in his carriage fighting with reality. It was *almost* the same as that, almost, except for the missing sack of wool now and the missing rope around my wrists. My hands were free, but I was still in a box. I could have sworn it was that same box.

Panic gave me a boost of energy and I pushed my hands up against the wood over my head. I rose to my knees with all my strength, expecting to be trapped, expecting to be locked in.

Instead, the wooden lid fell back, setting me free.

Fresh, cold air filled my lungs, and I breathed as if I hadn't in ages. The night sky full of twinkling stars and the moon looked like they were chasing me. I was on a carriage, in a wooden chest—*exactly the same* as the last time I was kidnapped. A car was driving ahead, and the carriage was moving fast behind it, down a dirt road in a forest, with nothing but trees on either side. No lights other than the headlights of the car speeding down the bumpy road, making way for the carriage.

But the moonlight was more than enough to enable me to see.

The fox lay all around the wooden case I was in. She had raised her head and watched me curiously. Her fur, a deep black, shone indigo at the tips under the moonlight. Her eyes, two black orbs of darkness, glistened as she took me in—and I knew her name.

Izma. Izet's twin sister.

Tears rushed to my eyes. Nothing made sense to me yet, but I wasn't worried. The panic, the fear—*everything* let go of me and I rested my chin on the case's edge, eyes on Izma. Nobody was chasing us. I was in a woods, in the dark, and Trevor hadn't gotten to me. Somehow, Izet had kidnapped me again.

Why else would I be in his carriage with his twin?

Reaching out my shaking hand, I touched the black fox's head. I thought for a moment she wouldn't let me, but she leaned into my hand and purred, eyes half closed as I scratched between her pointy ears.

"Gods, you're beautiful," I thought I whispered. She purred louder, raising her head higher so I reached down her neck, too.

I was smiling and crying and feeling way too many things at once, but I was also calm. So, I closed my eyes with my chin still on the edge of the case and scratched the fox's head until unconsciousness took me again.

TEN

EYES ON ME.

I felt them even through unconsciousness. My instincts whispered in my ear and my heart was already beating faster.

My own snapped open.

A ceiling I'd seen before was over me. White, nothing special about it, but I knew it. I lay on something soft—a bed I'd lain in before, too. My body knew it, but my mind wasn't as quick to catch up because of the panic. Even the faint smell of roses in the air didn't make me realize where I was until I jolted up and saw the people standing around me.

Ezrail. Ron. Adeline. Janet. And...a man who looked almost exactly like Lucien, only younger.

I was breathing so heavily that the sound of it, and of my heartbeat, was all I could hear. Fear, excitement, *relief* that they were all okay made me feel like I was floating on air and sitting on burning coal at the same time.

The looks in their eyes...

Ezrail looked like he wanted to murder me just as much as always. Gods, the way that man hated me...

Ron hadn't decided yet just how pissed off to be that I was there.

Adeline...she was crying. Tears in her eyes, down her cheeks. Each one of them was like a stab in my gut.

And Janet had her arms crossed in front of her, a brow raised as she looked down at me, pretending she was pissed, but I knew her better.

"Good morning, *Princess,*" she told me, her voice as cold as the look in her eyes.

I couldn't speak if my life depended on it, so I just looked at the man I didn't know. Lucien's little brother, the one he'd told me about. It had to be—he was literally a younger version of Lucien.

"About time," he said, his voice light.

I swallowed hard, giving myself a moment to breathe. I was in the guest room, the old one where I slept after Lucien saved me from the aqarinnes. I was lying on the same bed where he unlocked a new part of me I didn't even know existed, where he showed me what it was like to truly be loved and wanted and *worshipped.*

This was more my room than the one I grew up in.

"You lied to us," Adeline said, her voice shaking, and it was like she'd slapped me.

"I...I-I-I..." I still couldn't speak. The words were in my throat, but they refused to come out, so the best I could do was to tell her with my eyes: *I'm sorry. I never meant to hurt any of you. I'm so sorry.*

But...

"Let's give her a moment, shall we? We have *a lot* to talk about," said Lucien's brother, and I was mortified that I didn't even know his name.

The others nodded and started to drag their feet toward the door slowly, their eyes never leaving mine.

It was too much. Too much guilt, too much panic, too

much fear. So, I squeezed mine shut until they all walked out and closed the door behind them.

The realization took a long time to finally reach me and make sense.

I was in Aither.

And Lucien wasn't here.

THE WARM SUNRAYS falling on my face wouldn't let me go. They warmed my tears and pulled up the corners of my lips, even if my heart was heavy. I was on the balcony of my old room, and I could see some of the town to my left, the buildings and the few people who were already going about their business. The fields, a brilliant green merging with the baby blue of the sky, surrounding it, and Yuvelinne standing proud in the far distance. I couldn't stop staring, taking in every little detail of the view, and I felt just as at home as I did the first time I stepped onto these gray tiles. The first time I held onto this railing.

The first time I felt *alive* in all of my lives.

I might have been a prisoner in this place then, but it was here where I experienced freedom for the first time. It was the best thing that had ever happened in all the lives I'd lived.

But I'd taken my time, and as much as I wanted to just stay here forever, I also didn't.

I didn't want to be here without Lucien, and somebody needed to tell me where he was.

My body should have been weak with hunger, but it wasn't. I still had Annabelle's clothes on, and her tennis shoes enabled me to walk down the hallway in perfect silence. I had no idea where everybody was, but I wanted to find Adeline first. Apologize to her. Tell her that I never meant to lie to her. It felt so important that I did.

The tears kept on coming with every new step I took in that house that had been both my prison and my home. So familiar, yet I felt like a stranger now that I wore my own skin and was known by my real name. My other lives had made a lot more sense to me than this one. And the day had only just begun.

When I opened the door to the kitchen, I froze in place. All the people who'd been in my room—plus Riad—were sitting around the long dining table where I used to eat meals with Ron and Adeline.

They all stopped talking and turned to me.

"Where is he?" My voice came out breathless, but they heard.

And the man sitting at the head of the table stood up, a small smile on his face. "You probably mean my brother," he said, and he looked so much like Lucien when he spoke, I suddenly felt like I was in a dream. His lips moved—those lips that were identical to Lucien's, and his hair just as dark, but it was the eyes that let me breathe easy. His were blue, an ordinary blue—like mine. They weren't like Lucien's.

"Yes," I said, unsure whether to walk in or get out or...

"Really? That's all you care about?" Janet was suddenly on her feet, crossing her arms in front of her chest again. "You haven't seen us in months, and you lied to our fucking faces, but you can't be bothered with a freaking *hello*? All you care about is where Lucien is?!" And she laughed an icy sound. "The same guy I warned you about—remember that? I *warned* you, Princess!" She said the last word like it was filthy, dirty, *wrong*.

"Janet..." Ron said—Ron with the kind eyes and easy smile and long limbs, but Janet didn't care.

And I could do nothing but stand there and listen, let her get it all out.

"I can't believe you!" she said, moving away from the table. "I can't fucking believe you—I trusted you!"

I shook my head. "I'm sorry." And I was. So sorry it hurt.

"Yeah, right. *Sorry* my ass," she spit. "You're not sorry. You're just the spoiled little princess we all knew you would be."

I saw red.

"You're alive, Janet," I snapped without really meaning to. "You're *alive*. If I were just a spoiled little princess, you wouldn't be."

And maybe that was too much, too mean, too unfair, but it was too much, too mean, too unfair to me, too.

Janet swallowed hard and spit fire my way with her eyes alone. She knew that I wasn't *bad*—she knew it. They all did; otherwise, Aither would be gone. My father would have burned it to the ground long ago if he knew it existed.

"Just tell me where he is," I said, shaking my head. "Is he... is he okay?"

They all looked at me like I was a three-headed alien with green skin.

"Just t—"

"He's fine," Lucien's bother said before I could ask again. "Sit down, Princess. Let's talk."

He's fine.

Lucien was okay.

I don't really know how I made my way to the table, but Ron offered me his seat to the side of Lucien's brother, and he and Adeline sat beside me, while Janet, Riad and Ezrail sat across from us. All those eyes on my face were slowly suffocating me. Gods, I just wanted to run and hide somewhere forever.

Preferably in Lucien's arms.

"I'm Rowan Di Laurier," the man said, offering me his hand. "We haven't had the pleasure yet, Princess."

I shook his hand reluctantly. "Ella is fine."

Janet snorted. "At least she's giving you her *real* name."

"Knock it off, Janet," said Rowan, but she got to me. She just got to me so badly—and it was probably because of all the guilt I was feeling, and I was ready to light up on fire, but I couldn't keep my mouth shut if I tried.

"May I remind you that I was *kidnapped* and held captive in this town?!" I hissed. "Of course, I couldn't tell you who I was—I didn't know any of you!"

"Oh, poor princess. You not only want me to feel *thankful* that I'm alive, but you want me to feel sorry for you, too? Do you want a hug or something? Would that make you feel better?"

My ears could have been steaming. "I don't want your gratitude or your pity. I just want you to understand."

"Oh, I understand plenty," she said. "I understand everything."

"You have no clue what you're talking about," I said, trying my best to keep my voice down. "You don't understand anything—"

"You *lied* to me! To all of us—you lied!"

"Because I had no other choice! Because I thought all of you wanted me dead!"

"If you'd have just told us the truth, if you'd been *real*—"

"I did! I was real—the only thing I lied about was *my name*!"

"I thought you were my friend!" she snapped, slamming a hand on the table.

It was like she drove a sword right through my heart.

"I *was*. I was your friend." I had been her friend for real.

"No, you weren't. You're just like your father."

I kept on bleeding. "And you make shitty beer."

Her eyes widened—I knew I was being petty. But she

stabbed me where it hurt most, and I knew *that* hurt her, too. I just wanted her to bleed the same way I was.

"Fuck you—my beer is the best in the world," she snapped, pointing her index finger at me.

"Whatever helps you sleep at night," I said, and I realized I was being childish, but I just couldn't help myself. "Asked for it in a shifter town. They told me they don't sell that crap to their customers."

Adeline actually gasped. I thought for sure Janet would know that it was a lie, but...

"*Crap?*" she whispered, slowly standing, looking at me like she was about to laser me with her eyes. "How dare you."

I swallowed hard. "You—"

"*Don't* speak to me again."

"Janet, c'mon," Adeline said, but she was already spinning around, rushing to the door.

And now I felt sick. "I was kidding!" I said, though it was in vain. "I'm sorry—I was just k—"

She slammed the kitchen door shut behind her so hard, the walls groaned.

The silence that followed kept squeezing my neck. I dug my fingernails into my palms hard enough to draw blood before I noticed that Rowan had his head lowered, and his shoulders were shaking like...like he was *laughing.*

Everybody else looked like they were stifling smiles, too.

And that made *me* want to smile as well—that had been silly. And unnecessary.

But, *Gods,* it was good to be back here.

"Sorry about that," I said, clearing my throat.

"No, please. That was the most entertainment I've had in ages," Rowan said, and when he raised his head, his cheeks were flushed, his eyes a light blue. Like that, he looked completely different from Lucien.

Lucien's smile was different. It was heavier and lighter at the same time. Much more intense.

Or maybe it was just me.

"Right," I said, reminding myself of where I was and what was important. Despite how I felt to be here—all the good and the bad—I still needed to focus. "Can you please just tell me where Lucien is?"

But it wasn't Rowan who answered—it was Ezrail.

"He's in Albany," he said, looking at me from under his lashes. I remembered how he'd hated me back then, how he'd threatened me, told me all about how he planned to chain me in his basement and torture me until I told him how to get to the princess.

"Yes—Albany. And he's waiting for you there," Rowan added, making my heart skip a beat.

"You've spoken to him?" I could hardly breathe.

"Yes, I have. He's called every hour to ask about you," he said, raising his brows at me. "I don't know what you've done to my brother, but he's not the same man I remember."

Tears in my eyes again. Lucien was really okay.

"I need to speak to him," I said, my voice already shaking.

"And you will—once he calls," Rowan said, looking down at his hands folded over the table. "But regardless of my brother, I'm going to need to know that I can trust you, Ella. Otherwise, none of this is going to work."

I nodded as if I understood, and I didn't even mind all the suspicion reflected in his eyes. All I cared about was that I spoke to Lucien.

"How did you find me?" I asked because I remembered Trevor. I remembered his soldiers—and they were fast. They were strong. How in the world had Izet managed to kidnap me again?

Had he?

Because I remembered the wooden case and the black fox.

The carriage. But it also felt like that could have been a dream, too.

"We were searching for you," Rowan said. "Lucien brought me back here when he came to Wisconsin with the St. Revents. A few days ago, he instructed me to keep an eye out for you until I found you. Well, last night we finally did."

I shook my head. "What about the guards? They were—"

"We took care of them," Ezrail said, his voice heavy with pride as he looked down at me.

I flinched. "Is he dead?" And he must have known I meant Trevor.

He grinned. "I don't know."

The sight of that awful smile made my stomach turn. The idea of Trevor dead made me want to throw up.

"I don't think anybody's dead," Rowan said, shooting Ezrail a pointed look. "Regardless, we found you and we brought you here, as my brother instructed. He said you would explain everything before we made a plan."

I shook my head. "A plan?"

"Yes. A plan to take you to him. He's waiting."

Just like that, all my troubles blew away.

"A plan," I repeated, my mind already working. How was I going to keep shielded from Trevor now when he knew for a fact that I was in Vermont?

"But first, the explanation," he told me. "I'm a sucker for a good story." But the way he analyzed my face said he wasn't so much interested in the story as he was in knowing he could trust me.

I didn't really blame him. I was the princess—what his father, his brother had been fighting to get to all their lives. Lucien trusted me, but Lucien wasn't here. And if Rowan was going to risk his life to help me, he wanted to know who I was.

I understood. It didn't mean I liked it, but I understood.

One look to the side, to Ron and Adeline, and I wanted to

tell them the truth. Gods, I wanted to get it all off my shoulders so badly, I could hardly breathe as it was. They deserved to know that I hadn't betrayed them—especially Adeline, whose eyes were still red with unshed tears.

There would be no regrets. My story was not a secret anymore. Lucien had believed me—maybe these people here would, too. And if they didn't, that was okay. What mattered was that I came clean to them once and for all.

So, I took in a deep breath, and I spoke.

ELEVEN

Surreal.

I was in Aither. I'd actually made it. Not by myself, but still. I was here, and I was sitting at a table with Lucien's little brother. I'd spoken so much for the past hour my jaw hurt.

And to my horror, when my stomach sang, demanding food, it felt like not only Aither—but the whole damn world heard it. My cheeks burned instantly—nobody looked at me, but they must have heard. They were all in their own heads, thinking about everything I'd just told them, and the silence was absolute.

They heard.

And a minute later, Adeline was on her feet, going for the fridge.

Gods, kill me now...

I had never been more embarrassed in my life.

"You were actually inside a Moving Forest," Lucien's brother said after a while. I looked at his profile as he scratched the tabletop with his fingernails, deep in thought.

"Yes—in Lyran," I said, and a second later, a big white mug full of steaming coffee was in front of me.

Adeline proceeded to put others in front of everyone else, too.

My stomach sang again, but this time they were all saying *thank you,* so I hoped nobody heard.

"And you actually are alive for the seventh time," Ron said from my side. "I mean...*seventh*?!"

"Yes, I—"

"What the hell did you do for *six lives*?" I looked up at Riad, sitting across from me, and he blushed instantly, looking down at the table. "With all due respect, of course," he mumbled.

"I died," I said, smiling. "Lucien killed me every time."

Rowan shook his head. "Fascinating."

"Not really." It hadn't been very fascinating to live those lives. I took a sip from the steaming hot coffee, and though it burned the tip of my tongue a little bit, I felt its taste. It was *everything*. "But I really have to get to Lucien. I have to—"

"Here's what I don't get..." Ezrail cut me off, and a plate suddenly appeared in front of me—a sandwich, two hard-boiled eggs, fresh tomatoes and dices of cheese to the side.

I almost moaned out loud—it smelled so good.

I looked up at Adeline, who smiled down at me—a strained smile so familiar, it hurt. I hadn't even realized how much I'd missed her.

"Thank you," I whispered, but she pretended not to hear me and went back to her seat.

"How did you get out?"

For a moment I forgot about the food and met Ezrail's eyes once more. To his credit, he didn't look like he wanted to murder me just now—he was simply curious.

"You said the king had you chained in the basement—how did you get out? How did you get separated?"

Oh, hell.

I looked down at the plate, and if I'd been any less starved,

I would have pushed it away. I hadn't told them about Alexandra—of course not. Magic *spells*? Yeah, they weren't going to believe that.

"I don't know," I said in a whisper. "The door exploded. I was knocked out. When I woke up, I was in Ohio."

What a pathetic lie.

They all knew it. That's why the weight of their looks was like a mountain over my shoulders. I refused to raise my head and meet their eyes—this was the only explanation I could give for now. Until I saw Lucien, until we summoned the Ether, that's the only explanation I could give to any of them.

"And Lucien somehow made it all the way to Albany," Rowan said, nodding, as if he wanted me to think that he believed me.

"Eat," Ron said, pushing the plate closer to me.

No, I'm fine, I wanted to say, but I swallowed my pride. My body was weak. I needed the food. I needed to stay awake —I needed to be able to make my way to Lucien.

So, I took some cheese and put it in my mouth, chewing slowly. Every instinct in my body wanted me to just eat the whole thing at once, stuff it all in my mouth, but I didn't. I still had some dignity left.

But gods, the taste of the cheese, the tomatoes, the hard-boiled eggs made it really hard.

That none of them said anything for a moment, only let me eat, made it even worse.

"Right, then," Rowan said, pushing his chair back to stand up so suddenly, I almost swallowed the food wrong.

He adjusted his leather jacket over his white shirt and smiled a plastic smile at me. "Eat. Rest. I'll let you know when we leave." And he started for the door.

"How?" I asked, standing up, too. "How are we going to get to Albany? How far is it?" Because Trevor knew that I was in Vermont. He would tell my father, and if my father was around here somewhere, he would find me.

"A transportation truck would be the best idea," he said with a sigh, as if he were suddenly tired.

"Covered in beer. Helps with the scent," said Riad.

"And lots of magic, of course." Rowan said. "I'll let you know when I find out for sure." And he walked out the door like his tail was on fire.

Or like he really didn't want me to ask him more questions.

I sat down on the chair again, feeling more awkward by the second. Out of all the people sitting around me, only Rowan had been a stranger, yet without him here, I felt like I was sitting on needles.

"I best get to work," Riad said, and Ron jumped to his feet, too.

"Yep, same," he said and kissed Adeline on her cheek. They didn't look at me, didn't even say *bye*. They just kept their heads down and walked out the door in silence.

It was just me and Adeline and Ezrail, and...

"I'll be right back," Adeline said, standing up, too.

My heart all but thundered out of my chest. I kept eating, though I didn't taste anything anymore. But my body needed all of this to function, so I didn't stop.

Ezrail. Out of all the people in Aither, he'd hated me even before he knew my real name. I knew he wouldn't dare to hurt me because of Lucien, but gods, I really didn't want to be in the same place alone with him right now.

I needed to leave.

Grabbing the second egg in my hand, I made an attempt to stand up—I could eat it outside in two bites. But...

"Sit."

I looked at his face, his eyes focused down on the table, his shoulders rigid.

"Is that an order?" I said sarcastically, and I expected him to start shouting in my face, to tell me about all the things he wanted to do to me as soon as he got his hands on me, just like last time.

But the day was only getting stranger, and it wasn't even noon yet.

"For fuck's sake, just sit. I'm trying to *thank* you," he said with an exhausted sigh, his large hand over his eyes.

"Oh." Thank me? Did he say *thank* me?

I put the egg back on the plate, feeling like I was in a dream again.

Ezrail cleared his throat, then raised his head, hands over the table fisted so hard his knuckles were completely white.

"Right. *Thank you*, then, Princess." His voice was so strained, I barely made out the words.

"You're welcome. And just Ella is fine," I forced myself to say. "But, um...just out of curiosity—for what?" *And why aren't you threatening me yet?*

Ezrail looked up at me, and I could have sworn he was about to lose his shit.

"For showing your face that day at the castle. If you hadn't, we'd all be dead right now," he said in a rush.

"Oh, that." I nodded. Yes, I'd showed my face that last day of the tournament because I'd seen Lucien and I'd known he'd attack, having no clue that my father was in the building. "Yeah, no problem." I grabbed the egg again—this was probably the part where he left.

But he surprised me yet again.

"And I'm sorry for...you know." He cleared his throat again. "All I was trying to do was to get you to tell me how to find"—he looked up at me again—"*you*."

"I'm sorry I didn't tell you the truth," I admitted, feeling like I was standing way too close to the sun just now. So hot in here so suddenly.

Out of everything that had happened to me the past few days, this definitely took the cake. It was *Ezrail*. The guy had dreamed about torturing me for as long as I stayed in Aither.

Look at us now.

And he laughed. A short laugh that sounded more like a scream, but he laughed.

"As well you should be. Everything would have been easier if you'd have just told us the truth," he said.

But how was I supposed to know what these people wanted from me, when all they'd say was that they were willing to *torture* me to get me to tell them how to find the princess? How was I supposed to imagine that Lucien, being the son of a man my father had killed, wouldn't want me for revenge?

I shook my head but said nothing. I appreciated his apology. I could leave it at that.

"So, you're really going to help us?" Ezrail said after a minute. "You're really going to help Luc summon the Ether?" I swallowed hard. "You're going to fight with us?"

My eyes closed for a second, and I took in a deep breath before I looked at him. "No." None of them were going to be in a fight, not if I could help it. "I'm going to fight for you. Not with swords or guns. This isn't that kind of a fight." It never had been.

"So how?" Ezrail asked, thick brows narrowed as he studied my face. I could hardly believe it, but none of all that hate he'd always had for me in his eyes was there anymore. It was just...*gone.* And it made me feel lighter.

I smiled. "The old Azarius way," I told him. "I will conquer in silence."

Ezrail shook his head—he didn't get it, and that was okay. He didn't have to understand. Lucien would. And when I met John, if he even was with Lucien, I'd explain it to him, too. And to Jack.

Together, we'd fight this fight without anyone ever hearing about it. We'd summon the Ether and set things right in the world before anybody knew it.

Just as long as my father didn't find me first.

MY IMAGINATION RAN AWAY with me more often than I could count. Here I was, fed and showered, dressed in *my* clothes, the ones Lucien had gotten for me last time. A pair of new jeans, white sneakers, a bra that actually fit me perfectly, a simple blue shirt—and I felt just like the girl I had been when I was living in this house. It had only been for a few days, but looking back now, it felt like I'd lived here years.

Like this house really was my home.

And these people were my family.

"I'm sorry I lied to you."

The words seemed to hang in the air, like Adeline refused to *hear* them.

I found her in the hallway, rearranging some crystal bowls inside a cabinet, and she finally turned and smiled at me—her smile just as forced as before. It made me take a step back.

"I'm...I'm really sorry. I didn't mean—" I said, and I must have had my hopes high because of the talk with Ezrail earlier, but they came crashing to the ground when Adeline nodded.

"Oh, I'm sure you are. I'm sure you're going to say that you didn't mean any of it, either," she said, and gone was the old Adeline, the sweet and kind Adeline who made me feel right at home in this place. Now, the look in her eyes was ice-cold, and her hands were shaking. She kept tugging at her fingers, like she was constantly stopping herself from slapping me or something.

The view tilted in front of me.

"I didn't," I said, lowering my head. "I really didn't."

And she laughed.

I'd never heard a stranger, colder laugh coming from her before.

"Adeline," I said, feeling like I might collapse all of a sudden. I'd been so sure that *she* out of all people would be easy to talk to. She would be reasonable. She would understand. She would take me back with arms wide open.

But now that I thought about it...*why* would she?

"Adeline, listen to me. I had no idea that Lucien didn't want to kill me, okay? I just heard his father's name, and I knew I had to lie. I knew he'd want my head if he found out, and...and I—"

"And you lied to everyone who offered you their friendship without a second thought." My mouth clamped shut. "You looked at my face and you lied to me—multiple times."

"I had to," I said, losing strength by the second. Gods, the way she was looking at me... "I had to, Adeline. I didn't know—"

"You knew enough!" she cut me off, her voice rising, shaking. "You knew there would be consequences—but wait, no. There are no consequences for *you*, the princess. You just get to come back here, and everyone is expected to take care of you again. They all just...*forgot*." She took a step closer to me. "But I haven't. I haven't forgotten who you are, Estella Azarius."

It was like a stab right through my gut—and she twisted the knife, too.

So godsdamn disappointing.

I took a step back and raised my chin. "You kidnapped me. You kept me here against my will—all of you—and you had the audacity to tell me that I wasn't *a prisoner*, when I couldn't leave. I didn't want to stay. I didn't want to lie—but my life depended on it!" And now she stood there and told me that she hadn't forgotten? "I haven't forgotten, either."

Adeline shook her head—she was just as disappointed as

me. And I realized we were never going to see eye to eye until the both of us calmed down. I realized it was too soon—I shouldn't have come to find her. I shouldn't have apologized yet.

Too late now.

"Your father took away the thing I loved the most in my life, and I brushed your hair. He ripped the heart right out of me, and I ironed your clothes. He's been killing me for decades, and I held your hand, smiled at you, fed you." Tears ran from my eyes so fast I couldn't keep count. "I felt sorry for you."

"Adeline," I breathed, but she was already stepping back.

"I know Lucien needs you. I know we all do, in a way. But I wish you'd have stayed in your palace. I wish you'd have rotted in hell before I ever had to see you again."

She turned on her heel and walked down the hallway with her head high.

I sat on the floor and tried to convince myself to stop crying for a good long while.

"Master Rowan wants to see you."

I looked up and blinked the tears away until I could make out Ron's face. He refused to look me in the eye—he just stared at the floor. "Follow me." And he turned to the other side of the hallway, to the painting of the sea beyond which was the entrance door to the house. That's where I'd met him the first time.

He'd been so friendly then, Ron. He was an ice shard through my heart now.

I stood up and followed him outside anyway.

TWELVE

I LOOKED AT THE LARGE WHITE TRUCK IN THE garage.

"This is it," Rowan said.

With us was Ezrail, Riad, and William, whom I hadn't seen at all until now. He barely acknowledged my existence with a nod before he opened the back doors of the truck and showed me the wooden cases and the barrels full of beer. Everything was branded with Blo's green logo.

"You'll be hiding in the back until we get there."

I looked at Rowan—he'd taken off his leather jacket and only wore black wash jeans and a white shirt. He was skinnier than Lucien and the more of him I saw, the more I realized that everything else about them was different. The hair color, square jaw, and general build was the same—but Rowan was much softer where Lucien was full of sharp edges.

"It won't be enough," I said, my voice weak, my eyes still red and swollen from crying. The sun shone in the sky, and I felt great physically. It was my heart and mind that were stuck in a sort of chaotic pain.

My pain had always made sense before, but right now it

didn't. Because Adeline's face stayed in front of me, her words in my ears.

"You're forgetting the most important thing," Rowan said, raising his hand and moving his fingers around. The air began to move, too, so fast I saw it, a tiny little tornado spinning around his fingers with incredible accuracy. He smiled, proud of that small display of his magic, then pulled his hand into a fist and the whooshing stopped.

It was incredible, yes, and Air magic could do so much—just as much as Water and Earth, but I doubted it was enough...

"On a scale from one to Lucien, how powerful is your magic?"

Someone snorted—I think it was William, but his head was down. And Rowan raised a skeptical brow at me—he didn't like that question.

"Eight and one quarter," he said, the sweetness gone from his voice.

I hadn't meant that as an insult or anything, but his face was hilarious. I had to pull my lips inside my mouth for a moment to keep from smiling.

"That's strong," I said with a nod. "Except my father will probably be on the lookout for me himself." Trevor had seen me. He knew I was here. "If he's shifted and he's searching—"

"He won't see you, and the beer and my magic will shield your scent," Rowan told me, then sniffed the air my way. "You smell like nothing in particular—merely a human."

"I know." Until I mated, I smelled like a human, and I could even be hurt by fire. My skin hadn't merged with the magic of my dragoness yet—that was my advantage right now. Because when I shifted, my Father would be able to feel my dragoness across worlds. There would be no escaping him then.

"Unless you've got any better ideas..." Rowan said after a moment—and he still looked bitter.

"None," I admitted. "May I?" I wanted to get into the truck, see what it was like in there, because with all the cases and with so little space, it seemed like there wouldn't be enough air to breathe properly.

"Sure," Rowan said, waving his hand forward, and Ezrail pulled something from the corner of the truck—a set of folded stairs made out of metal.

"Thank you." I got on the truck, feeling stranger by the second. It was colder in there, darker, and the smell of beer overpowered everything else. It felt like I was swimming in it by the time I made it to the middle of the truck. Cases, barrels, more cases—and a small square space at the right corner. That's where I would have to sit for...how long exactly?

I could already feel the pain in my limbs until we got there, but it didn't even matter. I would sit there for days if it meant my father couldn't smell me or feel me. There was always a chance—I was his blood. He'd been with me every day since I was born. Father knew my scent by memory, could feel my energy in his sleep, and if he shifted and went flying in the sky looking for me, no amount of beer was going to keep him from finding me for too long.

But the hope, that beautiful, deadly thing. The hope whispered in my ear that I would be okay, that I was going to Lucien, that everything would be over soon, and we'd somehow survive. All of us—we'd be okay.

"Ella."

I'd been so lost in my own head that when I heard the voice I jumped, barely holding back a scream.

Rowan was on the truck with me, and he was showing me something in his hand—a phone.

My heart stopped beating for a long moment.

"Would you care to speak to my brother? He's rather

impatient," he said, and I was already running before he'd finished talking. I grabbed the phone from his hand like a lunatic, and he muttered something under his breath, but I didn't hear it. I was too busy running down the tiny stairs and to the trees, on the other side of which I could see the surface of the lake glistening under the sun.

I'd never talked on the phone with anyone before. That it was Lucien on the other end had my knees shaking. I almost collapsed when I finally reached the cabins and the lakeside and stopped to breathe.

"Estella."

The voice was coming from the phone clutched to my chest. I was making a damn fool out of myself, I knew that perfectly, but I bit my tongue to keep the tears at bay before I had the courage to bring the phone to my ear.

"You're alive."

It was his voice—I knew it. Even through the phone, I knew his voice.

A long sigh from the other end. "You're okay," Lucien said, and he, too, was talking to himself more than me.

I sat on the grass, tears streaming from my eyes, phone clutched to my ear so hard it hurt. But it was okay.

The lake was in front of me, the surface of it like a mirror glistening under the sun, the trees and the mountains beyond more beautiful to my eyes than they had ever been before, though a bit blurry from the tears.

"What did you do, little fox?" Lucien finally asked when he heard enough of my breathing. "How did you...what did you do?"

He wasn't accusing me at all, but I still felt accused.

"What I had to," I said in half a voice. I'd done what I had to do to keep him alive.

"How bad?" he asked, and for some reason that made me smile.

"Very," I said, and I was laughing. "It's very, *very* bad." So bad I hadn't even realized it yet—I'd made a deal with Alexandra Azarius from beyond the grave. The consequences of that must be...so much worse than I had the capacity to imagine right now.

"It's okay," Lucien said. "You're okay. We're okay, too. We'll figure out the rest of it."

I nodded. "We will." That's the only thing I was counting on. "I'm coming to you, Lucien." Gods, I couldn't wait to see his face already.

"I know, little fox. I knew you'd go to Aither," he said.

I wiped my nose with the back of my hand. "You did?"

"It's home, isn't it?" he said. "You said so."

My eyes closed, and I laughed some more. I thought he hadn't noticed that—we'd been in my bed in my father's manor when I'd asked him about Aither. About *home.* And I was sure he hadn't thought much of it.

But I should have known that nothing ever escaped Lucien's attention. He always saw everything about me.

"Actually, I just wanted to find you," I told him. "*You're* my home."

He didn't hesitate. "And you're my world."

I closed my eyes and felt the tears slowly sliding down my cheeks. "I miss you."

"I wanted to come to you myself, little fox," he said, and he suddenly sounded like he was in pain.

I shook my head as if he could see me. "No."

"I wanted to, but Jack is alone. His brother is a mess. And if I leave them, they're completely unprotected," he said.

"Stay," I said in half a voice. "I'm coming to you, anyway."

"I know," Lucien said. "I know. I was terrified, little fox. If something happened to you—"

"Nothing happened to me," I lied. "I was fine. You did well to stay there."

"Not by choice," he muttered. "Believe me, not by choice."

"Keep them safe. Keep yourself safe, too. I'm coming, and then it will all be over," I promised him. "I have a plan and we'll see it through. This will all be over in no time."

Why did my words sound like *lies* to my own ears when I was sure I believed them?

"I will," Lucien said. "And you're with Rowan. You can trust him. He'll protect you with his life."

My eyes squeezed shut. "I think he hates me." *Everyone* here hated me...except Ezrail, which was comical.

"I'm sure he doesn't. He's a cynic at heart, but give him time," Lucien said, and I could have sworn he was smiling.

"Okay," I breathed, nodding, *hating* that we'd said everything already and that I had to hang up. I didn't want to—I wanted to keep talking to him until I saw him. Was that too much to ask?

"I thought I lost you, little fox," Lucien whispered. "I thought I lost you again, and I almost lost my mind."

"You didn't," I promised him. "I'm right here."

"I'm sorry I couldn't come find you myself," he said again, and I knew the guilt was eating him up.

"Don't be. I'm glad you stayed." If he'd been out here trying to find me, there was a good chance my father would have found him. If that happened, all of this—even my deal with Alexandra—would have been for nothing.

"I love you, my beautiful fox," he breathed. "I'll be counting the seconds until you get here."

"I love you, too. I'll be there soon, okay? I'll see you soon."

"Hurry up. There's only so much I can take," he said because he wanted to make me smile—he could tell I was crying—but he also meant it. There was only so much *I* could take, too.

"Bye now. I'll be on my way."

He chuckled and the sound of it warmed me to my bones even through the phone. My heart all but *exploded* in my chest, too. It still surprised me—I never even imagined that I could feel like this for a person. My capacity to love fascinated me all over again.

"Bye, little fox," Lucien said, then...

"May I have a word with my brother, please?"

I turned to find Rowan standing not five feet away from where I was sitting, a strange look on his face. One could say he looked constipated. "You know, if you're done with...whatever it is you're doing." And he looked disgusted as well.

"It's Rowan," I told Lucien, then stood up. "I gotta go. I'll see you soon."

"Stay safe," Lucien said, and I reluctantly handed the phone to Rowan, who was looking at it like it was a snake about to bite his head off if he wasn't careful. He took it between two fingers and brought it to his ear slowly.

Stifling a smile, I turned my back to him and went closer to the lake to give him some privacy. My sneakers sank into the mud a little bit, but I didn't mind. I looked at the sky, the sun, the water, the mountains, and I was lighter. I breathed easier. I thought clearer.

It wasn't over yet.

I'd been stuck in this limbo, refusing to *think* ever since I'd found myself in front of Annabelle. Refusing to try to figure out just how much damage I'd done, to accept that there was a chance I'd fucked things up beyond repair.

But now, it was okay. Because no matter what wrong I'd done, I'd also done plenty of *right*. Lucien was alive. Jack was alive. *I* was alive.

And the spell to summon the Ether was in my back pocket.

No, things were far from over.

"Just to be clear..."

I turned to the side to find Rowan coming toward me, brows narrowed and eyes on the ground as if he were in deep thought. The phone was no longer in his hands.

"When you said, *I love you, too,* does that imply that my older brother, Lucien Di Laurier, son of Michael Di Laurier, said *I love you* first? Did you hear that with your own ears?"

Oh, gods. "Were you *spying* on me?!" Was he serious?

He looked up at me as if he was *surprised* to find me there. "You don't understand—this is important," he told me. "Please, answer my question."

My mouth opened and closed a couple of times before I was able to speak. "That's none of your business!"

He laughed, but it was so strained it actually sounded like a scream. "Of course, it's my business, dearest Ella," he told me. "I have been studying my brother his whole life, and believe me when I tell you that I know who he is. And this is an issue of *safety* now—I have to make sure that someone else isn't trying to impersonate Lucien, that I haven't been talking to someone else on the phone this whole time."

Oh, gods, he was really serious.

"So, I'll ask you one more time—did you hear those words with your own ears?"

"*Yes!*" I said, still shocked with disbelief.

"And it was Lucien you were talking to?"

"Yes, it was Lucien!"

"Are you su—"

"Stop it!" I spit, shaking my head, not sure whether to laugh or cry. "Yes, I'm sure. It was Lucien. He's said it before —of course it's him."

His brows shot up. "My brother has said that he loves you before?"

Why was it so damn hot here? "Still not any of your business, but yes. He has." My eyes squeezed shut, and I felt like I might combust any second. "Look, can we just get going? Can we be on our way?"

I started walking back to the garages and the truck without waiting for a reply before my cheeks melted off my face. Rowan said nothing.

THIRTEEN

THEY SAID WE WOULD LEAVE AFTER MIDNIGHT because it would be safer. We'd be driving for five hours, give or take, and the dark of the night would shield us better, in case my father was really shifted and searching for me. The roads would be clearer, too. And even though I hated to have to wait, I agreed. They were right, but that didn't mean that I was going back to Lucien's house, to Adeline, to Ron. They both despised me right now, and even though it wasn't because of *my* doing, it was okay. I understood.

Maybe someday, we could talk again, Adeline and I. Maybe someday.

So, I spent the whole day in the town. Steven didn't hate me. Midnight, the gorgeous black mustang remembered me perfectly. And the animals of the woods were ecstatic that I was back. Plenty of new ones in the forest, too. They all looked so healthy I cried. Steven said they'd been taking their supplements regularly and everything was looking perfect, just as it should.

Not all of the townspeople hated me, though they all

knew who I was. How incredible—everyone knew my name now, and I wasn't wearing my artora. They could all see my face, and nothing happened. Nothing at all—nobody attacked me. Nobody came to even talk to me.

Lucien was my shield, even from thousands of miles away.

The day went by way too fast, and before I knew it, my eyes opened and it was dark. I was lying on the ground, resting against a tree trunk in the woods. Animals asleep all around me—rabbits and raccoons, even a couple of hedgehogs by my feet. I moved, and they all woke up. I must have fallen asleep without realizing it when I came here after dinner with Steven.

"Sorry, guys, but I have to go. I'll be back, though," I told the animals, who were all perfectly alert already. "I promise I'll be back."

The next second, they turned their heads east, then started moving west, hopping and running and walking like they did when someone was here, someone they weren't comfortable with yet.

I held my breath, thinking it was Rowan, but then I saw her face among the trees and I flinched.

"I honestly don't understand the appeal. They're *animals*. They can't even talk to you," Janet said, holding her hands in front of her as if she were afraid of bumping into a tree, even though the flashlight of her phone was on. It was pretty dark in the woods. The slivers of moonlight piercing thorough the canopy overhead weren't doing much to illuminate anything.

"Sure, they can. They just don't use words," I said, standing up, palms sweaty from nervousness already. It was just Janet—I didn't have to freak out. "What time is it?" Was it time to go yet? Because I couldn't wait to be on my way.

"Almost time to leave," Janet said, shining the flashlight of her phone on my face. "I was told to come get you."

"I'm ready," I said, desperate to start moving—and not

only because I was terrified of what she would say to me. Adeline had nearly broken me earlier. Janet would have no trouble finishing me off for good.

"Hold on a second," she said, then sighed. "Gods, I hate this already."

"Hate what?"

"This. *Us.* The *I'm sorry* I'm about to say. All of this bull-shit—you lying to my face, and then saving my people, and now you're *fighting* for us, too? It just doesn't sit well with me. I'd rather be far away from here right now," she said in a rush.

"I'm sorry," was all I could think to say. I was sorry that I'd lied. I was sorry about *everything.*

"You don't get it," she said, shaking her head, though I barely saw her eyes from the light she kept moving when she waved her hands around. "You're an Azarius. Do you realize what that means?"

"More than you do, actually." I knew what being an Azarius meant—so many things I'd read since I last saw her. So much I knew about my heritage now, about the people who had ruled over shifters for centuries. And it made me sick, but I couldn't change it. I couldn't change where I came from, only where I went.

"I *liked* you," Janet said, as if she were accusing me. "I genuinely liked you, and then you turn out to be my gods-damn enemy, and not only that, but you talk trash about my beer."

I shook my head, smiling. "That was a lie. I thought you'd know. Nobody said anything about Blo's—in fact, everyone at the bar was drinking it."

Janet paused. "Which bar?"

"Merkli's in Tearny. That's outside of my father's estate," I said, remembering that night that felt like years ago. "I snuck out one night and went to a bar and I said, *you wouldn't happen to have Blo's here*? And then the barmaid said, *I like your style,* and she filled up a glass for me. A large glass." Lucy had been the barmaid's fake name, and she'd ended up drinking my beer for me, too. "It was good. It was very good. Strong." Five sips had had me dizzy.

Janet thought about it for a second, then asked, "Why'd you sneak out?"

"Because my father doesn't let me go outside. Like ever," I said with a shrug. "I snuck out to search for information. I was chased and trapped in a dark alley, too, and almost got myself killed, but it was totally worth it."

Janet took a step closer, looking more curious than before. "How in the hell did you manage that?"

I laughed. "Gold. I paid for the beer with a golden ring, and for information with golden necklaces, because I don't have money. My father doesn't give me money. And then some people saw me, and they chased me, and they had me all alone, and they wanted gold, too, and...and..." Gods, why was I crying? I should have stopped crying, but I couldn't. "And then Lucien found me, and..."

I couldn't speak. The words got tied in my throat, and suddenly Janet had her arms around me, and she hugged me to her chest.

It was awkward and we were as stiff as the trees to our sides, but we hugged. The meaning of it had to count.

"I'm so sorry."

"I'm sorry, too, kid. I had this idea of who you were supposed to be in my head and it's hard to see past it. It's hard to accept that I'd gotten it all wrong."

"I didn't mean to lie."

"You had no choice," she said, pushing up my head so I looked at her, even though we could barely see one another. "Your life was on the line. I understand that."

"I thought you were out to kill me."

"Oh—*I* was. I wanted you dead regardless of what Master Lucien wanted to do with you. Couldn't care less—I just wanted both you and your father in the ground." And she laughed. "So, I guess it's a good thing you lied."

"Are you saying you'd have *killed* me if you knew who I was?" I said, only half joking, but she looked away.

"Just...just don't lie again." And she patted my shoulder. "C'mon, let's get you to Lucien now. It's about damn time all of y'all saved us from your lunatic father once and for all."

It hurt.

It hurt too much to be reasonable—I knew my father was much worse than a lunatic. She was being nice using that word —he was a murderous psycho.

But he was also the man who'd had to see his nanny being killed in front of him when he was eleven years old.

He was also that man breaking to pieces in the library, hating himself so much it made him sick.

He was also that man who'd hugged me in the hallway...

I hated that it hurt to hear people talking about him, and I hated myself for it, too. But try as I might, I couldn't stop myself. That would always remain my biggest flaw.

JANET HADN'T TRULY FORGIVEN me. I saw it in the way she looked at me when she dropped me off at the truck. There was plenty of light to see the dark look in her eyes, the way she smiled and wished me luck—it was painfully obvious that her heart wasn't in it. Deep down, I thought, she still wanted me dead, regardless. And I wondered what more my father had done to her that I never knew.

But I was in the truck, surrounded by cases of beer, cans and bottles and barrels, and I sat in my little corner, reminding myself not to cry. Not to panic. Not to fear. I was on my way to Lucien. Everything else could take a step back until I got there.

When someone hopped on the truck, then pulled the back doors closed, I was surprised—I was supposed to be in here all alone. Only a few blue lights were on behind the cases in the large space, but it was enough to enable me to see Rowan coming toward me slowly.

"Brother dearest insisted that I stay with you at all times," he said, and he didn't look particularly happy about that.

"Oh," I said, settling back under the cases. He reached the end of the truck in no time, and sat on the floor near me, back against the aluminum wall that separated us from the driver's cabin. He rested his elbows on his knees and pushed his head back, eyes closed. I could barely see his profile in the soft blue glow of the dim lights, and he looked exactly like Lucien to me again. My heart ached, so I looked away. Soon. Very soon.

The engine started. The truck purred. It reminded me of that bus ride a little, the most peaceful ride of my life. This was far more uncomfortable.

The truck moved. We were already on our way, and I prayed with all my being. I prayed to every god who heard that we made it. I prayed that we were safe.

The air was growing thicker by the second, too—Air magic coming off Rowan in waves. It was different from Lucien's, much less intense, but it would keep me invisible from the eyes of the world. It would do its job. It had to.

"Who were you hiding from?"

I opened my eyes and turned to Rowan—he was looking at me. Barely four feet between us, but I still saw his eyes, the reflection of the blue lights in them.

"Why were you in the woods all day? Who were you hiding from?"

Adeline. "Nobody. I just enjoy hanging out with animals."

"So I was told," he said with a nod. "I was told a lot of things, actually, and I'm a curious man—how in the world does one fall in love with her captor?"

Shivers ran down my back. I'd thought about this long and hard back home. And the only answer I was able to come up with was, "He actually saved my life. He gave me a safe place in Aither. Turned my prison into a home somehow." And I never knew how he did it. "He treated me like a human being." With wants and needs and fears of my own.

"I imagine that must have been very different from what you've experienced in the past," Rowan said, and he was right. Maybe what happened to me would have been different for people who'd always had their freedom to begin with, who were always treated *normally* by their family, by their friends.

But it really didn't matter now, anyway.

"Why did you walk away?" I asked Rowan, despite my better judgment. I hadn't really intended to talk to him at all on this trip, but since he started it, I was very curious, too. "Why did you leave Aither?" *Why did you leave Lucien,* was what I wanted to say, but I wasn't brave enough yet.

And Rowan raised his brows. "Because I could. Because I wanted to. Because I wanted to make my own life." And he turned me—his sparkling eyes *daring* me to judge him.

I did.

"You left him here all alone." He knew this already, and it was already done—I was merely pointing it out.

"*Alone* is such a difficult word—it never means what we think it means to other people," Rowan said. "My *alone* and my brother's *alone* are very different, for example."

"How so?"

"I was alone when I was here, surrounded by people who know me. He was alone when I left." He paused. "Make no mistake—it wasn't because he missed me. He just had one less person to order around."

I turned to him again. "That's not Lucien and you know it." He'd missed his brother, his sisters—I'd seen it in his eyes when he told me about them.

But Rowan burst out laughing. "There's another difficult word—*know*. What you know and what I know are very, very different things indeed."

I shook my head, incredulous. "He told me about you, about how you explained the old Light and Dark and Electricity shifters to him." Rowan sat up a bit straighter instantly. "It was just that small thing, but he looked very proud."

A second of silence.

"He...he remembered that?" Rowan asked in a whisper, and he looked confused for a moment.

"He did. So, don't judge—"

But that's as far as he let me go. "You think I'm *judging* my brother? I'm not. How silly of you to presume that, Princess," he said, leaning his head against the aluminum again. "You don't know what his life has been like, the way he was raised." Bringing the heels of his hands to his eyes, he paused for another moment. I almost asked him not to say anything else because it was Lucien's story, and he should be the one to tell it, but I was too curious. I couldn't help it. So, I stayed put and listened.

"My father, he..." Rowan stopped again, shook his head. "He was a difficult man. Never satisfied, always demanding more. A fair and just man, but he asked so much of us." He looked at me for a moment. "Of Lucien."

Pulling my knees close to my chest, I rested my chin on them. "I didn't know that."

"Yes, well, the rest of us, we learned eventually. We made choices," he said. "But he overworked my brother ever since I can remember. Lucien never got to choose. All his choices were made for him, and he just..." Rowan shrugged, looking ahead at nothing. "He accepted. There was never any fight in him for this. He just accepted."

Stabs at my poor heart. The more Rowan spoke, the more I understood everything Lucien had ever said to me better. When he'd been on his knees in front of me that first time, when he said that he wanted me, and that I had no idea how dangerous that was for him...

When we were in my father's manor, in my room, and he said he'd doom the whole world, but he wouldn't hurt me...I understood so much better. He wasn't used to allowing himself to have his own wants, make his own choices. He was going against everything he knew with me.

Just like I was with him.

The fates were so godsdamn cruel.

"He did fight it," I said after a while, wiping the tears from my cheeks. He fought it at the very end—with *me*.

"See, that I can't understand," Rowan said. "Because I meant it when I said that I've studied him my whole life—he is a very single-minded creature, my brother. He sees one thing, and one thing only. I don't understand that he would *beg* me to come back home—he is not the type. I don't understand that he would *beg* me to take care of you no matter the cost. It doesn't sound like him, and so I have to take into account that maybe someone is pretending to be him."

I laughed—he was a funny guy.

"You know something? *I* don't sound like *me*, either." I turned to him, legs crossed underneath me. "Do you have any idea what I was like in my other lives? *Passive*. Afraid. Terrified of my own damn shadow. Terrified of hurting people, of doing the wrong thing. All those godsdamn brains were wasted on me because I couldn't find courage to face my fears in any of those lives."

He raised his brows as if he didn't get my point.

"People change, Rowan."

"No, they don't," he said bitterly.

"They do—and that's a good thing. We're supposed to change. We're supposed to get better, aren't we? We're supposed to make mistakes, too. Gods know I have." Plenty of them. So many I lost count. "We're supposed to grow from them."

"Well, then we're doomed, I guess," he said, chuckling. "Because changing me and you and everyone—that's all well and good. But for Lucien to change? That's going to cost everyone their freedom."

I flinched. "It won't. We're fighting, remember?"

He turned to me. "And what about when the time comes to rise against your father? When you summon the Ether and when it's time to take over, what are you going to do—will you kill your own father, Ella?" His words were an invisible fist to my gut that took my breath away. "More importantly—what will Lucien do?"

My eyes closed. *I'll doom the world, but I won't hurt you...*

"My father will surrender. He'll give up. He'll—"

"He's a *dragon*. Dragons don't give up," Rowan spit. "If everyone stopped lying to themselves the whole damn time the world would be a better place already."

The truth was, he was right.

But I'd never stopped to think, had I? I had never even imagined that I could get here, so I'd never stopped to think things through to the very end.

I mate.

I summon the Ether.

And...then what happened to Father?

Because he would fight. He'd fight the Ether with all he had—and what if he won, and what if he *didn't*?

What happened to Lucien and to the nymphs' warning to stay away from him no matter what?

"We'll figure it out," I said, ignoring my tears and his words and my thoughts. "We'll be just fine."

"Sure, we will, Princess," Rowan said. "Sure, we will." And he didn't believe it for a second.

Fourteen

There he was again.

John, fused with the dark, allowing the orange light to only touch his shoulders, the shape of him, but never his face.

You have to find her, he said, over and over again.

I can't. I don't know how. I have to find Lucien first, I said, just as many times, but he didn't listen. I didn't think he could hear me. Because I explained that the Water trick didn't work, and I had no other way of trying to find a draca and I needed —*needed* to find Lucien first, make sure he was okay.

But John never listened.

Until someone called my name and my eyes popped open.

Rowan looked down at me, skin pale, thick brows narrowed.

"We're almost there."

I sat up so fast the entire truck spun around. I'd slept. I'd somehow lain down all the way on the hard surface of the truck's floor and I'd slept. Collapsed—possibly in an attempt to escape the questions in my head.

And nobody had attacked us.

I moved away from the tiny space I'd been in, and my

muscles screamed—everything hurt. Even my bones had felt the cold of the hard surface I'd been lying on, but I was alive. So was Rowan.

He was leaning against some beer cases with his hands in his pockets, and he looked tired. Exhausted. I realized what was left of his magic was still making the air heavy. All that magic for so long…it must have completely drained him.

"Thank you," I said with a nod. "For bringing me here. For coming with me."

He was silent for a moment, bringing a finger to his lips as he stared at the floor, then spoke.

"Oh, but this wasn't for you, pretty princess. After our little talk last night, I'm beginning to realize I haven't been quite honest with myself, either," he said, leaning his head to the side. He looked so much *older* today. The bags under his eyes were so much bluer, the look in his eyes so much colder.

"About what?" I dared to ask anyway.

"About my brother. About guilt. About *alone*," he said, waving his hand. "A bunch of things you have no use for." He straightened his shoulders. "But I brought you here. And you're safe. Now, we go find my brother." He turned his back to me and started walking toward the back doors of the truck, though we were still moving.

I smiled so big my cheeks hurt. I liked Rowan despite everything. And maybe it made me mean, but I was glad he'd felt guilty for leaving Lucien alone in Aither. I hoped that that same guilt would make him go back sometime. Maybe for a visit every once in a while. Maybe to help Lucien out with things he needed.

The truck stopped moving. I watched the doors, counting in my head, hoping that would make the seconds go by faster… until I heard movement outside.

I heard voices, something being dragged on the other side of the door—and then blinding sunlight slipped through the opening when they began to pull the doors from the outside, slowly revealing the world to us, and us to the world.

I hardly breathed until my eyes adjusted to the sunlight, and I began to see. William and Ezrail by the truck doors, and two men I didn't know, ten feet away, looking at us.

Near them was Jack, dressed in clothes, not his armor. No helmet on him, and he hadn't bothered to shave, either. He looked exactly the same, yet so different.

And a couple of feet to his side...

Lucien was there, looking right at me.

I ran.

No time to wait for Ezrail to pull out those stairs—the truck wasn't that high off the ground anyway. I jumped, my eyes never even blinking, afraid I'd lose sight of him. He was coming for me, too, looking like a broken man on the verge of becoming whole again, and when the world fell out of existence, I jumped and landed in his arms, locked my limbs all around him, and let go.

Home.

That's exactly what he felt like—*home.*

He was breathing and moving, whispering in my ear, one hand tangled in my hair, the other under my thigh, and he was alive.

"You're here," he kept saying, kissing my head, my cheek, my temple. "You're here. It's over. You're here..."

I was here. I'd made it.

Pulling myself back for a moment, I searched his eyes, touched his face, his skin flushed, his eyes exactly like I remembered them, the most beautiful colors in the world come together in a perfect moment in time. A strange gunmetal blue in four different shades, and silver flecks floating in it that mesmerized me just as much as the first time I noticed them.

I touched his cheeks, ran my fingers over his lips just to make sure they were real before I kissed him, starving for his taste, for his warmth. It all came back to me now with twice as much force, everything I'd repressed since I'd woken up with Annabelle. The fear, the exhaustion, the hunger, the uncertainty—it all fell on me at the same time because I could let go. Lucien was here. I could let go.

Except we weren't all alone in the universe the way I'd have liked to think. And when someone cleared their throat close to us, I couldn't ignore it.

"For a second there I thought you were running to me, Princess. Damn..."

Jack.

Closing my eyes, I smiled against Lucien's lips. He kissed them once, twice, then let go, and I unlocked my ankles from around his hips. I hit the ground, feeling stronger by the second, and Lucien's hand found mine, intertwining our fingers.

"Hey, Jack," I said, never looking way from Lucien. I couldn't—he held my eyes prisoner just like the first time we met.

"*Hey, Jack*? That's the best you got, Princess?" Jack sounded hurt.

Even Lucien fought back a smile as he pulled me to him and kissed my forehead. I looked away—at Jack, at the other men I didn't know...at Rowan.

Oh, shit, everyone was here.

Everyone was watching us, and Lucien needed to say hi to his brother. Blood rushed to my cheeks when I stepped to the side to give him some space, and Lucien reluctantly let go of my hand. I looked at Jack, his boyish grin, now transformed with a couple of days worth of stubble on his cheeks. He looked older, more mature. It suited him.

"Your Highness," he said, bowing to me, and I laughed.

"You're not dead, after all."

My father had taken him away that day, before he *gave me*

time to say goodbye to Lucien. He was probably going to torture the poor man, but Jack looked perfectly fine. Alexandra had really held her end of the bargain better than I'd hoped.

"Nope. Alive and well," he said, brushing imaginary dust off his shoulders.

I gave him a hug—not that he deserved it. He *had* been about to kidnap me that day, but I was still glad he was okay.

"That's more like it," he said, trying to hold onto me even when I moved back, when...

"You want me to free you of the burden of your arms, Jack?"

Jack froze, moving back instantly, his eyes on Lucien. "Take it easy, Frosty. I was just saying hi."

I turned around to find Rowan looking at Lucien like he'd just grown an extra head.

Then he turned to me and mouthed, *what have you done to him?*

I widened my eyes—now was not the time.

"It's good to see you, brother," Lucien said to him, then reached out his hand for me. I immediately moved to his side like he'd summoned me with magic.

"You look like shit," Rowan told him. "And I need a bed."

I rolled my eyes—he was impossible. But Lucien nodded. "That can be arranged." Then he looked at Ezrail and William —even Riad had stepped out of the cabin, and he looked relieved. Happy that they were all well, too.

"May I introduce you to my cousins," Jack said to me, waving at the two men standing to the side, watching me with strange smiles on their faces.

"Of course."

I had to let go of Lucien's hand again so he could go greet his men. And I finally had the thought to look around me.

We were in an open field with a wide road to my right, at

the side of which was the truck we'd traveled in. The sun had already risen on the other side of the trees to my left, and no cars were driving by. There were no other people that I could see around us. Just green—so much green, even more so than in Vermont.

"This is Raphael and Lenny, my first cousins," Jack said, and the men bowed their heads.

"It's an honor, Princess," the first said.

"Please, there's no need for that. It's a pleasure to meet you," I told them. It was easy to see Jack was related to them— they had the same jaws, the same golden-brown hair, almost the same lips. Their eyes were simply brown, though, and Jack's were full of green and gold.

I wondered what John's eyes were like, which reminded me...

"Where is he?" I asked Jack, and he knew I meant his brother.

That's why he sighed. "I can't believe you're actually here. I can't believe you're about to save my life, Ella," he said with a hand to his chest, then leaned closer to my ear to whisper, "I can't wait for this torture to be over."

I shook my head, smiling. "I'm sure it's not that bad."

"Oh, it's worse," he said, nodding at the trees on the right. "C'mon, let's get going."

"Go ahead, I'll catch up," I said, and he grinned.

"Don't worry. Your Frosty's not going anywhere," he said.

Mine. The word let butterflies loose in my stomach. Gods, I loved that so much it was kind of pathetic.

"Why *Frosty*?" I wondered, looking back at Lucien, who was talking to his brother and his men. The moment he felt my eyes on him, he turned to me.

The butterflies in my stomach multiplied at an alarming rate. It was incredible that he could still do that to me with a single look.

"Because he's *cold*, Princess. I honestly don't know what you see in him, but he's colder than a godsdamn snowman." And he laughed, putting his arm over his cousins' shoulders as they made their way toward the trees.

Cold. Lucien was everything but cold. He was fire, had been since the first time I met him.

But I was starting to think that that Lucien, *my* Lucien, wasn't someone anybody else knew. Not his brother, not Jack, not even his men. And the Ella that I was with him, *his* Ella, was not someone anybody else knew, either.

FIFTEEN

THE PLACE JACK REFERRED TO AS *THE TOWN* WAS nothing more than a small field near a famous country club. That's the only place any of the twenty families living here worked. They didn't pay well, said Jack, and so these people had to make do with hunting for food in the woods, and cutting trees on their own for warmth, and making repairs to their old houses by themselves, too. That's why they looked the way they did—pieces of wood, barely standing, definitely not fit for anyone to live in. So much worse than Annabelle's house.

And it sucked the soul right out of me to see the three small children half hiding behind a woman as we came through. I had my hand in Lucien's as we walked, and he seemed to be at ease among these people already, but I wasn't. Far from it. Men and women stared at me, some smiling, some not, as Jack took us to the second house on the left—the only one two stories high.

Shame filled me from head to toe, and the people moved to the side as they whispered to make way for us to go through, until we were on the porch. The wood underneath my feet creaked as if to warn me. Jack opened the door—it hadn't been locked—and we went through in silence.

"This is it," he said, leading us to the left of the small foyer and through a wooden door. A stairway was at the end of a simply furnished living room, smaller than my bathroom at the manor. "He's upstairs," Jack said and took us up the stairs and to the narrow hallway of the second floor.

He stopped by the first door on the right, and I held my breath when he looked at me. "Ready?"

I couldn't speak so I only nodded.

The door opened. Lucien guided me inside, squeezing my hand to remind me that he was there.

And I finally saw John.

My heart broke into a million pieces, and not because he looked bad. In fact, he was skinnier than I imagined, way skinnier than Jack, but his hair was short and clean, his skin pale and shaved, the cover over him crisp white. His eyes were closed, and his chest rose and fell evenly.

He looked like he was sleeping.

"Ella, meet John. John, meet your precious princess," said Jack, waving his hand from his brother to me and back with a grin.

Lucien stared at him dead in the eye, but Jack pretended not to notice. "Please, come in. Sit." And he waved at the four old armchairs around the bed. "This is a big day for me. It's the most important day of my life, okay? You want refreshments, anyone?"

I moved toward the bed, letting go of Lucien's hand, and I kneeled in front of John. He smelled of soap like he'd just gotten out of the shower. His black top was faded, old, but it was clean. Even the pillowcase seemed to have had some design in the past, but now it was almost completely washed out. Everything here was clean but old, about to fall apart.

My hand shook as I reached for John's cheek—same

eyebrows as Jack, same square jaw, though his lips were smaller. His hands were over the cover to his sides, and his fingernails were trimmed, his skin squeaky clean and soft.

"Right here," Lucien whispered, drawing my eyes at the end of the bed. I was crying and I hadn't even realized it. So strange that I still hadn't run out of tears. It felt like I should have a long time ago.

But I dragged myself on my knees closer to Lucien, where he'd pulled the cover to the side and was showing me John's left leg. He slowly pulled up his pajama bottoms to reveal a cut along his shin, a cut that looked deep. It was bleeding onto the red-stained pad they'd put under the leg, and green puss had gathered all around it. It smelled so bad it took all I had not to gag.

My shoulders shook from the sobs I kept from breaking out of me.

"Your father's poison, I think," Lucien told me, gently pulling John's leg to the side so I could see the wound better. It went all the way down to his ankle. My hand was over my mouth to keep from crying out.

"He was thirteen years old when he went hunting for food in the woods and didn't come back," Jack said. He was standing over me somewhere, but I was glad I couldn't see his face. It was enough that I heard the pain in his voice. "We found him unconscious, hiding under a broken tree, with this wound on his leg, and it refused to heal. As you can see, it still hasn't."

"It's infected several times over," Lucien said, his fingers hovering over the green puss hanging onto the open wound.

And I shook my head, looking up at him. "Why isn't he dead?" There was absolutely no reason why John wouldn't have died if this really was the poison extracted out of the chin barb of my father's dragon.

"I don't know," Lucien said. "I thought...I thought all

draca could handle it. I thought for sure it wouldn't hurt *me*, either." He shook his head. "That day when you found me in the woods with the arrow in my back, I thought I survived because my blood is immune to the poison. My father believed so."

I shook my head, unable to speak.

"But it's not true," Lucien said. "I realized it when I saw John. That day in the woods, you used your blood on me, didn't you." It wasn't a question. I nodded, more tears rushing out of me at the memory of seeing him like that, just hours away from death. "Yeah. Other draca are not immune to a dragon's poison."

"Maybe...maybe it works slower." It could be—John was still alive.

"For *six years*?" Jack asked from somewhere over my head.

I flinched—no, six years seemed a bit much.

"What if...what if it's something else?" I asked, my voice a shaky mess.

Lucien reached for something in his pocket—a small knife the size of my palm. "If it is, we'll know soon."

I offered him my hand eagerly—this man had already suffered so much. He'd wasted away *completely* on this bed, and if there was a chance my blood could help him, he could have all of it. He could have every drop.

Lucien grabbed my hand in his and pressed the sharp tip of his knife to the middle of my palm. Everyone in the room held their breaths.

"Do it," I told Lucien, and he didn't hesitate.

The sting barely lasted a second. We kept our eyes on each other as Lucien cut a clean line down my palm, then took my hand and put it right over John's wound.

I didn't dare look away from him, afraid I would fall apart. The tears kept on coming, and I could only breathe when I could see him, so I stayed there, kneeling on the floor, hand pressed to a six-year-old wound, praying with all my being that it worked.

Feeling so guilty I could contaminate an entire ocean with it.

And Lucien saw it. He saw it in my eyes, and it pissed him off to see me crying—I knew that, but I still couldn't stop. I just focused on his eyes, analyzed his pupils slowly turning to oval the way they did when his wyvern wanted to come out.

Gods, he was so beautiful, even as exhausted as he looked. The bags under his eyes looked like bruises—I doubted he'd slept for more than a couple of hours every night. His cheeks were hollowed out a bit, too, but it suited him. Every inch of him drawn to perfection for my eyes only.

"That's enough," he said after a while. He took my hand away from John's leg and turned it over to see that my wound had closed. Just a thin red scar remained, and my skin smeared with blood.

I risked a glance at John's leg to find that the green was gone. The puss that had been coming out in bubbles around the broken skin wasn't there anymore—or maybe it was just smeared with blood?

I looked at John's face, breath held, heart hammering, so much hope inside me I barely contained it...

His eyes were closed. He hadn't moved a single inch.

"Come on, now, Johnny," said Jack, running his hand through his brother's hair. "You've got your royal blood. Now's time to wake up, you little shit..."

His voice was strained and there were unshed tears in his eyes.

John didn't wake up.

SIXTEEN

I SAT AT THE TOP OF THE STAIRS, WATCHING JACK and Lucien talking to Rowan and the others, before Jack took them out of the living room, and Lucien turned to me.

When he looked at me, I breathed a bit easier. I felt less of a monster, like I must have done *something* right to deserve to be looked at like that. He climbed the stairs two at a time until he squatted in front of me and took my hands. He didn't say anything when he pulled me to my feet, then guided me back into the hallway of the second floor, this time taking me to the other side, into the last room on the left.

It was a small room, an old queen-sized bed to the left, a wooden dresser, two windows across from the door.

"I'm staying here," Lucien said, guiding me to the bed.

I sat at the edge of it, but he grabbed me and put me on my back, then lay down next to me. The sheets smelled like him. The room smelled like him. The *air* smelled like him. Or maybe it was just me.

He wrapped me in his arms and held me to his chest like he knew exactly what I needed. I put my head right over his heart, hungry for the sound of it, for the reassurance that we were both okay. For now.

I thought I wouldn't be able to stop crying at all once I let go, but I did. My tears dried somewhere between Lucien's kisses on my head, his hands running down my body, touching me, the warmth of him pressed to me the way I dreamed possibly over a million times. It took a while, but they dried.

And I was calm. I breathed evenly.

So did he.

We stayed like that for a long time, holding onto each other, breathing each other in, until the world didn't seem so dark anymore.

I thought Lucien had fallen asleep at some point because his heartbeat had slowed and I barely felt him breathing, but one look at his beautiful face, and I found his eyes half open. A small smile curled his lips—my favorite kind.

"Are you thinking what I'm thinking?" he whispered.

"Um…" Was *he* thinking that he was my favorite thing in the world, too?

"There's way too many clothes between us," he said lazily. Impossible not to smile.

"True," I mumbled, raising my head to reach his lips.

He kissed me gently, his hands under my shirt, warm palms pressing to my back, so I did the same. To feel his naked skin against mine was everything. He was absolutely right— way too many clothes between us, which was why I pulled up his shirt all the way to his armpits, and he pulled mine.

Gods, it was so easy to get lost in the feel of him, the sight of him, the sound of him. His moans fueled me while we kissed and touched slowly, like we had all the time in the world. Every inch of me had missed every inch of him, and even if I had another two lifetimes of this—*only* this—it still wouldn't be enough.

"How did you get us out of there, little fox? Where did you go?" His voice was barely a whisper, but it cut right through me.

Lucien kept kissing my cheeks, my closed lids, the tip of my nose, but the question remained.

The question I *had* to answer.

No more secrets between us. I'd sworn to myself that I wouldn't keep anything from him again. All our secrets had done was make everything more difficult than it already was.

Never ever.

"I made a deal with the devil," I said, not really trying to joke, but I found myself smiling anyway. Because it did feel exactly like that—and I *still* didn't regret it.

How could I when we were here right now, alive and breathing?

"You did?" Lucien said, moving back so he could look into my eyes as he smoothed my hair away from my face.

"Mhmm," I whispered, my eyes begging to close, to just focus on the feel of his hand on my cheek, caressing me, his thumb running over my lips.

"You're my undoing, little fox," he whispered, his breath blowing on my face. "The gods were cruel to make you so perfect. I could spend a lifetime just looking at you, and I'd die a happy man."

My toes curled and my heart picked up the beating instantly—the idea that he saw me the way I saw him, like the best thing the gods had ever made in the history of the world, made me want to burst into flames.

"And I could spend a lifetime just listening to you talk," I said. I'd always loved the way he spoke—with such ease and determination, commanding the air around him even with his words. But I'd never loved it as much as I did when we were alone and he spoke to me in whispers, when he told me how completely hopeless he was—just as hopeless as me.

"You're my favorite thing in the world, Mr. Di Laurier."

He pulled me closer, digging his fingers onto my back. "Maybe not so cruel, after all," he said and kissed me.

But it didn't last long, not nearly as long as I wanted. My leg was draped over his, and I was dying to pull his shirt off completely, but he stopped me again.

"Who's the devil?" he asked, and my body cooled down a bit instantly.

The talk. The truth that I'd promised myself to tell him.

That came first. That was more important.

"Alexandra Azarius."

I felt it the moment he stopped breathing and every muscle in his body locked down. I closed my eyes and let that sink in for a moment...

"Little fox," he whispered, still unsure whether I was joking or not.

Unfortunately for the both of us, I wasn't.

So, I told him. I started from the beginning—how I'd found the library, the diary entries, the mirror, how I'd given it blood. I told him about my father and about Alexandra. I told him *everything*—up until I made the deal with Alexandra in that basement.

It took me a while to get to the end—I left nothing out. Gods, it felt so good to get it all off my chest. So freeing. Like I'd always had a lump in my throat that I hadn't even noticed, and I finally swallowed it down.

"My father did it—in small amounts. Very small," Lucien said when the initial shock passed and he was no longer speechless. "One needs incredible power. *Incredible* power, little fox..."

"For what?" I wondered, confused about what he meant for a moment.

He looked down at me—I'd only ever seen him that pale at

the castle, when I first pulled my artora off and showed him my face.

"Magic. Spells. Incantations. Stretching the limits beyond the element," he whispered, playing with the strands of my hair. "He could only do it a handful of times. Said it drained him, depleted him of his energy completely for a few hours." He shook his head, eyes squeezed tightly. "I don't understand..."

"Alexandra was powerful. Very powerful." I'd known that even before I'd *met* her. My father had always told me stories about the incredible way she was connected to Fire.

"Even so, how would she be able to do what she did from the grave?"

"Time," I said—it was just a guess, but the best I had. "I think she just pulled me into her timelines. She was always doing whatever she was doing back in the days I sort of *went* to see her. She always said it was important that she continued." The dead bodies in the library. The man chained to the wall in the basement...she'd always kept going, doing whatever she had been about to do that day.

"Time traveling," Lucien whispered, then shook his head again.

"Or maybe just...projecting. I didn't technically travel through time—I wasn't there. The mirror never showed my reflection. My father never saw me—Alexandra never saw me. She just *heard* my voice."

Which...now that I thought about it, was very strange. Very curious.

"The mirror," I whispered. "She said she could hear my blood."

"Blood is powerful," Lucien said. "The most powerful bond of all. But even so...*how*? How powerful was she?"

I shook my head—I had no answer for him. I just ran my hands down his back and his stomach, tracing the lines of the tattoos on his chest. They were like ink spilled over his skin by accident in the most beautiful shapes, like the wind blowing color all over him. I wanted to kiss each and every one of them slowly, but...

"Where did she take you? Did she bring you here?" I asked instead.

"No," Lucien said. "We were still in the manor, except...it was just us. Me—and Jack in a different room. Nobody else was there."

I looked up at him, confused. "What do you mean? Where was my father?"

But he shook his head. "I don't know. The entire manor was empty—just us two. I didn't wait around to see for how long. I shifted, grabbed Jack, and flew out of there. Everything else outside the walls of the manor was just the same."

His words made no sense to me. "Are they...is everyone..." But the words died on my lips. Trevor had been at the manor that day—and I'd seen him in Vermont just yesterday. He'd looked perfectly fine.

"They're all okay. I managed to talk to Arthur on the phone two days ago. They're all fine—your father included." Shivers ran down my back and my cheeks heated in embarrassment to be caught *caring*. "What about you? Where were you? I searched everywhere, but you weren't in the manor."

"I was in Ohio, believe it or not. Except I didn't get there myself—I woke up there, right in the middle of the street."

Lucien propped himself on his elbow, looking down at me, his fingers tracing every line of my face. "How?"

"No idea. But I was...I..." I shook my head, smiling because of how ridiculous it was that this *hurt*. "Remember my mother's twin Alexandra told me about?" Lucien nodded. "Yeah—I woke up in her town in Ohio."

His eyes widened for a second, then he kissed my forehead. But I'd already started, and I wasn't going to stop until I told him everything. "She knocked me out, put me in her van, then took me to her place. My grandparents' house, just atop a hill with the town below it. Turns out, she's a healer. My grandparents had been healers, too, before their death. And turns out, my mother really did almost kill her to take her place at the tournament. Ripped half her face off. She only has one eye."

Tears falling out of me again. Just when I thought I got rid of them.

"She...uh, she didn't really like that I was there. Said, um... said that I had no family with her, that we were basically strangers. She did feed me, though. And let me sleep in her house, gave me clothes." And then she'd practically told me to never go looking for her again.

Lucien held me to his chest tightly, and again, his proximity, his warmth, kept me grounded, stopped the tears much sooner than they'd have stopped by themselves.

"I have the spell," I said, reaching behind me for my back pocket, for the page I'd ripped out of that book with Alexandra's spells in it. "To summon the Ether—I have it right here."

Lucien took the folded piece of paper and opened it carefully, like he was afraid he'd ruin it if he moved too fast. Then, he started at the small letters scribbled in black ink—the words in old Gaelic that Alexandra had infused with her own magic.

"I saw her do it," I said to Lucien. "I saw the Ether, too. She spoke to him. I heard his voice."

He folded the piece of paper again and put it back in my pocket. "Then we'll do it, too. We'll summon him just like she did."

I nodded. "I think that's it. Once the Ether is back, the balance will be restored, and the reign of dragons will end." Once and for all.

I would never be queen. And my father...he'd hate me for

it, I was sure of that. But I'd take it. I'd take his hate any day of the week.

Lucien grabbed my chin and turned my head until I met his eyes. "As soon as John wakes up, we'll do it," he said, using his thumb to wipe away the single tear slipping out of the corner of my eye.

I nodded, trying not to think about the *other* thing. Trying not to think about the nymphs.

"What is this place? Why are these people living like this?"

"They're all Earth," Lucien said. "Most of them don't have any magic at all."

I swallowed hard. "Annabelle had a lot of trouble with her magic, too. I never...I had no idea..." I never even knew there were people out there who couldn't do magic. Gods, just when I thought that I couldn't feel any worse...

"The elements are weak," Lucien said. "They're very unstable, especially in these parts. I mean, some of the people can't even shift."

"I don't get it," I said, trying not to cry again. "My whole life, the people at the manor, they all had access to their magic. And the people in Aither. They were so powerful."

"In the manor, they're close to your father and you. In Aither, the people are close to *me*," Lucien said, smiling sadly. "Why do you think so many of them agree to live there in isolation like that?"

"I don't...I don't understand."

"The draca were always sources of power, directly linked to the Ether. They kept the elements fueled, so to speak. But since the Ether disappeared, the magic of people who live away from these sources of power is almost nonexistent," Lucien explained. "These people here, before Jack and John were born, had nothing. Then, they figured it was just an anomaly that they could suddenly do magic and shift without trouble —it has happened before. But then three years ago, when Jack left, their magic slowed down almost all the way again. I assume it's because John is unconscious the whole time."

Sources of power.

That's why the people at the manor never had trouble with their magic.

That's why everyone else in the world was *never* going to have trouble with their magic again as soon as we summoned the Ether.

"My father's family has been trying to put a stop to this for the past two centuries. Dethrone the dragons and bring back the Ether so that the draca may live again. So that magic will be distributed across all shifters equally. So that the people won't have to suffer anymore."

I was crying so hard the bed shook. *Dethrone,* he said, but he meant *kill* instead.

"It's okay, little fox," Lucien said, pulling me until I was lying completely on his chest.

"Why didn't you tell me?" Why would everybody keep this from me? Why hadn't I seen it?

Why hadn't I realized it in my other lives, too?

"At first, I though you knew. And then...I don't know. I don't like to see you cry, little fox." He kissed the top of my head again and again, rocking me gently to the sides. "Please, don't cry..."

And it broke me even more. Because he really would doom the world just to keep me from crying. This silly, beautiful man.

I leaned back and looked at his face, kissed the tip of his nose, smiling and crying, a bigger mess than I ever had been in my life.

"It's fine," I promised him. "Just because I'm crying doesn't mean I'm giving up. I'm just making way for the pain to settle, that's all."

He grabbed my face and kissed my lips hungrily. "I don't want you to hurt, either."

"But if I don't hurt, how am I going to grow?" How was I going to know what it was like? Where was I going to get the strength to keep going until I saw the end of it? No, I needed the pain. I needed the fuel. I needed the truth. I'd went six lives without any of it and look where that got me.

Not anymore.

"I'll carry your pain," he told me. "If you smile for me, I'll carry all of it for you."

I smiled against his lips. "I'll always smile for you, Lucien. And I'll carry all the pain in the world doing it."

He kissed the breath out of me, put me back on the bed and hugged me to his chest until he was all I knew. Like that, I felt safe. Like that, I felt like I belonged even in a house I'd never seen before, miles away from any place I knew.

We were only just beginning, Lucien and I, and this beginning was my fuel, too.

I'd be damned if I didn't see the end of it.

SEVENTEEN

SLEEP TRIED TO TUG ME UNDER, BUT THE HEAT OF his body didn't let me go, and I was glad for it. Sleeping was something I could do any time. Being with Lucien? That was like a treat, and I never knew when we'd be separated again.

So, while he ran his hands down my back, under my shirt, caressing my skin, I stayed awake, completely motionless, taking every little thing he could give me.

I'd always been selfish when it came to this man—since the day I found out who he was, and the day I decided to let him touch me. But I could have never anticipated that my need for him would just keep growing and growing the way it did.

"How are you so soft?" he mumbled lazily against my forehead, then kissed it a million times as his fingers grazed my skin. His hand closed on the side of my waist—he always did that, like he was measuring me up. "Every line, every curve..." His voice trailed off as he nudged my head up so he could kiss my closed eyes.

A lazy smile spread on my lips, and I slowly lay down on my back. He lay on top of me instantly.

"Every little inch of you is perfect," he said against my

parted lips. I locked my legs around his hips tightly and he moaned into my mouth. To feel his cock hard and ready against my center lit a different kind of fire in me that only he could control. "I'm addicted to you, little fox." He took my bottom lip between his teeth and bit, moaning like it was the most delicious thing he'd ever tasted.

"And I need a hit right now," he said, leaning back for a moment, grinning like the devil.

The past and the future no longer existed, just this perfect moment in the present. There was no need to think when we were like this. We only moved and felt—that was enough.

"Take as many as you want," I said breathlessly, pulling the shirt off him. *Finally.*

His lips were on my neck, biting and licking and sucking until he reached the collar of my shirt. I could feel the light layer of magic in the air—Lucien would make sure nobody heard us. I was free to be as loud as I wanted—and I always wanted to be loud with him. I was already panting, so wet I was a waterfall, but I knew Lucien would want to take his time, and I was looking forward to the way he touched me, savored me, *looked* at me. He rose on his knees between mine, slowly pulling my shirt up again. I sat up and raised my arms until it slid off me.

"Look at you," he whispered so low I barely caught it. I stayed like that, resting my hands back on the bed while he looked down at my chest, at my breasts, ran his hands up and down my stomach, his eyes bloodshot. He squeezed my breasts hard, and I threw my head back with a moan. The next second, his mouth was on my neck again, kissing and biting violently, and the pleasure climbed so fast I was already shaking with it. He unclasped my bra, too, groaning as he kissed me.

"Lay down," he instructed, and I fell back on the bed with a sigh. He pulled the bra off me, throwing it to the side, his eyes taking in my naked breasts like he was seeing them for the first time. He was completely mesmerized as he ran his fingertips on my skin, nudging my hardened nipples as he went.

"Lucien," I begged, back arched, body desperate for his touch.

"Yes, baby?" he said, smiling sneakily though he knew exactly what I was saying. The way he touched me, lowering his fingers all the way to the waistband of my jeans, slipping them under just to tease me before he pulled them out again, left no room for doubt.

"Come here," I said, reaching for his hands, trying to pull him down, but he resisted.

"Tell me what you want, little fox. Tell me, and I'll give it to you," he said, his hand on the bed near my head propping him up. I locked my arms around his neck and tried again, but he didn't budge.

"Everything," I whispered.

"Everything? Do you want the whole world?" he teased with that boyish grin I adored. So easy to imagine him as a wyvern, a beautiful beast sizing me up before he came to devour me completely. Gods, I could hardly breathe... "Do you want the moon, baby? Say so, and you can have it."

"I want *you*," I panted, running my hands down his stomach, sticking them under his jeans. And when my hand wrapped around his hard cock, we both moaned. *This,* I thought, then said it out loud. "I want *your* everything..." I leaned up and kissed his chin, his jaw... "I want your mouth on me. I want your cock inside me. I want all of you." The entire solar system couldn't compare.

Lucien was no longer smiling. He just watched my parted lips as I breathed heavily, undoing the button of his jeans with one hand while I stroked him with the other, until the zipper was down and I could wrap both hands around his cock. Gods, I'd missed him more than I could have imagined, and at the same time, it felt like we'd never been apart a single second.

He finally lowered over me and the heat of his skin against mine set me on fire.

"You could get my heart to stop beating if you just ask it," Lucien whispered. Then he kissed the breath out of me, his tongue in my throat, his hunger matching mine, and his lips never moved away from my skin for a while.

He trailed kisses down my neck as if he was in a hurry now, before he took my nipple in his mouth and sucked hard. I could no longer reach his cock, so I tangled my fingers in his hair. My back arched as he played with my nipple, tortured it until the skin was raw red, then moved to the other. My hips were moving, but he grabbed them and pushed me down, holding me in place as he trailed fire with his lips down my stomach. His teeth and his tongue were on every inch of me, sometimes slowly, sometimes rushing, until he reached the waistband of my jeans and began to undo the button.

I could come just by watching him worship me with his mouth.

When he finally pulled my jeans and panties down, his every movement became more urgent. He raised to his knees again, pulling the denim off my legs, watching me writhe underneath him, desperate for his touch. I gripped the sheets tightly, drinking in the sight of him, his naked chest so perfectly built, those jeans hanging so low on his hips, the button and zipper undone, and I could see the tip of his cock just a little.

Pushing my legs to the sides, he leaned down again, whispering things I was too gone to understand as he pressed kisses on the insides of my thighs. He moved higher and higher, his lips searing my skin, then settled between my legs with one arm curled around my thigh to keep me in place. I called out his name, unable to breathe properly until I felt his lips where

I needed them most. When his mouth closed on my pussy, every inch of me felt it, down to my very bones.

He pulled and pushed me over the edge all at once—his tongue pressing against my throbbing clit urgently, the tips of his fingers teasing my entrance gently. My hips moved against his face and my hands tangled in his hair again. I was a savage —all I knew how to do was cry out, lost in ecstasy, and take, take, take everything he was giving me.

When he sucked in my clit between his teeth, held it there and continued to tease it with his tongue, I was a goner. There was no point trying to make it last—I couldn't. So, I cried out his name and I dove deep into the sky where nothing and nobody could reach me but him.

"YOU TASTE BETTER EVERY TIME," he said, trailing kisses up my stomach and chest while I lay there, completely surrendered to him. "Here..." He stuck his tongue in my mouth, and I moaned, the feel of him and the taste—a mixture of Lucien and my juices—igniting me again.

"So juicy," he said, running his tongue over my lips. "So fucking sweet."

My shaking legs wrapped around his hips, and I pulled him to me, but he still didn't let go.

"I need more," I told him, and he knew that already, but he wanted to make me say it. He loved to watch me beg for it, and I loved to please him.

"How much more?" he teased, licking my cheek, biting the tip of my nose gently...

"All of it," I said, raising my hips to meet his cock, still covered by fabrics. "Everything."

With a growl, he bit the side of neck hard until I cried out. I already couldn't wait to see all the bruises he'd leave on me.

"Greedy princess," he said, nudging my head to the side so he could stick his tongue in my ear, then bite my earlobe until he almost tore it off. He was a savage, too, right now, and I had no complaints.

I throbbed with need for him already. My hands were on the waistband of his jeans, pushing them down as much as he let me, until his cock was in my hands again. I moaned, throwing my head back, twisting my hands up and down until his hips started to move in rhythm.

And when I pressed the tip of him to my throbbing clit, his arms let go of him and he finally fell on top of me. *Thank the gods.*

He propped himself on his elbows, looking down at my face as I played with him, nudged his tip to my clit, moved it down to my entrance the way he liked to do, then up again. He looked like his soul was in my hands, not his cock. My hips moved, my pussy desperate to be filled by him, and as much as I wanted to keep playing just to see that wondrous look on his face, I needed him too much.

So, I held him in place, then raised my hips up, taking him in.

The way he slid between my slick folds and all the way inside me was otherworldly. We were made for this, to exist like this, connected together. One.

Lucien took over and thrust his hips forward, filling me so completely, until he was inside me to the very hilt. Gods, the way he felt. He filled every inch of space inside me, lit up every cell of my body with his fire. I wrapped my arms around his neck and took in his face, half hooded eyes glazed over, lips parted, brows slightly narrowed...

"Don't move," I whispered, and every muscle of his body tensed as it locked in place.

Then I moved.

I pushed my hips up as far as they'd go, then let his cock

slide back out of me slowly. I held onto his strong body and found my perfect rhythm, fucking him from underneath for a while, focusing on his pleasure alone. The way he moaned my name was the best thing I'd heard in my lives. I kissed his face, bit his lips and his jaw, dug my fingers into his shoulders as I picked up the rhythm, clenching tightly around his cock until he couldn't take it anymore.

He took over.

Gripping my hip with one hand and a fistful of my hair with the other, he sucked hard on my bottom lip and grinned.

"My turn," he whispered, and he thrust inside me before I could breathe.

Hard. Fast. Violent.

I forgot my own name in three seconds when he pounded into me like that, like he wanted to break me open and see my insides. I cried out so hard my throat was sore, but his cock was pulsating inside me, reaching new depths with every thrust. My skin was covered in sweat, my heart about to beat right out of my chest, and I tried my best not to come right away.

I failed.

"*Fuck!*" he cried out, pushing himself as deep as he could go inside me, face buried on my neck, my skin between his teeth as he let go, too.

I continued to hold onto his shoulders for dear life as the orgasm filled my mind with fireworks and chased away every bit of darkness that had ever existed inside of me.

EIGHTEEN

I MUST HAVE FALLEN ASLEEP AT SOME POINT because, when I woke up, Lucien wasn't in the bed with me. My first instinct was to panic—where was he? Had something happened? Had my father found us?

I sat up only to realize that I was completely naked under the covers, and despite everything, a rush of warmth went right through me. My body was sizzling with energy, completely satisfied, and though my thighs hurt a little bit, it was the best feeling in the world.

Before I could put my clothes on and go search for Lucien, he was already coming through the door, a wooden tray full of food in his hands. My stomach twisted and turned, not because I was hungry, but because of the look on his face.

When I first saw him, he'd been pale, blue bags under his eyes, hair all over the place, shoulders hunched. Even his eyes hadn't sparkled the way they used to—until now. Lucien looked like a different man, a small smile playing on his lips, his eyes wide and full of color, his hair combed back. Even the air about him hummed the way it always did.

And I couldn't keep a stupid smile off my face, either.

"Hey," he said, putting the tray on the floor when he came to sit on the bed with me. He opened his arms, and I practically jumped at him, holding the covers to my chest as if I were embarrassed. As if he hadn't already seen and tasted every inch of me numerous times.

Lucien chuckled, pulling me on his lap. I missed that easy sound. I missed waking up and finding him there. I missed everything I never thought I could have with him again.

"Sleep well?" he said, and I nodded.

"How long?" It felt like I'd slept all night, but the sun still shone outside the window.

"Just a couple hours. I figured you'd be hungry," he said and put me back on the bed before he grabbed my face in his hands and kissed me. He was smiling just as big as I was.

We were hopeless.

"I don't want to eat these people's food." By the looks of it, they barely had enough for themselves—and there were kids here, too.

But Lucien shook his head. "There's enough for everyone. We've been working on pulling out water from a nearby reservoir. I've already created Air pipes like we have in Aither, so there's plenty of clean water coming in. And the people have been able to access their magic again now that Jack and I are here. Things are moving," he said with a nod, like he wanted to confirm it to himself, too. "We've also been working on the houses to prepare them better for winter, though I suspect the people will be able to do that themselves if Jack doesn't leave. And, of course, if John wakes up."

Things were moving. He'd been here a few days, and things were already moving.

It occurred to me how much it would take to manage an entire town, let alone one as big as Aither—and Lucien did all of it alone. Rowan was gone. His sisters, too—it was just him and his people.

I grabbed his face and pulled him to me. "I love you," I told him because it just felt like I hadn't said it enough times. Then I kissed him until my toes curled under the covers.

He almost looked surprised, like he'd never heard those words from me before. I could have sworn his cheeks turned a light pink.

"I love you, too, baby. Which is why I have to insist that you eat," he said with a grin, then brought the tray to my lap. "Breakfast in bed, as is fitting for a princess."

I laughed. "I thought you hated the fact that I'm a princess." And the fact that I was a dragoness. And that my father was the dragon king.

But Lucien shook his head, coming to sit closer to me. "I merely hated the fact that I thought I couldn't have you," he said, kissing my shoulder. "I've always known you're too good for me. I don't deserve you, little fox."

My poor heart. "But you do." It was *me* who didn't deserve him. After everything my family had done to his, to this world for centuries...Gods, all the Azarius dragons were good for was *ruin,* while Lucien fixed. He just made everything better.

He put his arm around my shoulders and pulled me to him for a moment. I breathed in his scent, woody with a hint of mint, and instantly felt calmer.

"I also hate the fact that you were here another six times, and I wasn't with you," Lucien said.

I held onto his shirt tightly. "You were. You alway came at the end."

"To kill you," he said, and his voice was strained.

"But we didn't know each other then."

"I don't know, little fox," he said with a sigh. "I have trouble believing that I'd look at you and wouldn't fall completely and helplessly in love with you within the second, in any timeline or life or world."

"It doesn't matter," I told him because I could hear the guilt in his voice, and it really didn't. We were here now. The past didn't matter—for all anyone was concerned, those lives didn't even happen.

"What about the nymphs?" Lucien said, and it was like I swallowed a sack of rocks. He leaned back to look into my eyes, and I tried to smile for his sake.

"The nymphs didn't know you, either. Everything was different then. Everything is different *now*."

"I don't want to risk your life in any—"

"Don't." I couldn't let him say more. "Don't even think about it. I am not leaving your side."

He clenched his jaws so much I saw them popping. Slowly, he wrapped his fingers around my chin and brought his lips against mine. "What if being close to me hurts you?" he asked, his whisper so low, like he was terrified of uttering those words.

"Maybe, but I know for a fact that being away from you *kills* me."

It had. Slowly, soundlessly—but it had sucked the life right out me to be away from him.

He sighed, shaking his head, and I hated that he still looked uncertain, that he didn't take my word for it.

And I knew I needed to take his mind off that completely. That's why I asked, "Who's Ingrid, really?"

Lucien was surprised. The question had burned me ever since that night he'd snuck me back into my father's manor, and Ingrid had spotted us in the hallway. I'd hidden behind Lucien's back so she hadn't seen me, but I'd heard. I'd her heard ice-cold voice, and I'd been able to imagine her face just fine—her long black hair, lips painted a dark brown that looked black.

And I was curious.

"She's my sister's best friend," Lucien said, shaking his

head. "Terrible human being."

I nodded, the jealousy spiking my blood. Gods, I'd hated that woman so much it had made me blind. "That's how she knew your real name."

He nodded. "I had no other choice but to turn to her. She was the only one whom the boy's father listens to. Has him wrapped around her little finger. That's why he agreed to send me to the king without complaint," he explained.

Boy, he said. He always called Gabriel that.

"Just surprised that she agreed to it," I said, and gave him a pointed look.

He knew there was a question in that statement because I'd heard what she'd said to Lucien in the hallway. She'd wanted him in her bed—*ugh.*

"I *paid* her," he said. "With money.*"

I don't know why I was so relieved.

"I don't think I've ever hated anybody more in my life," I mumbled—and I knew it wasn't fair. I just didn't care.

Lucien chuckled. "Eat, little fox," he said. "You need your strength."

"I do," I said, letting go of that conversation with a sigh. We both needed to be in a brighter mood, anyway, so... "You exhausted me pretty quickly there," I teased.

His eyes gleamed with mischief instantly. "You think I'm done with you? The day isn't even over yet," he said, biting my cheek.

I laughed. "You better not be." Because I wasn't done with him, either—not even close.

"Eat. All of it," he ordered, closing his eyes for a moment as if he were struggling to control himself.

And I did. The scrambled eggs were heaven.

"Oh, wow. Who made these? They're delicious," I said, taking another bite.

"I did," he said, and I looked at him, the fork halfway to my mouth. "What? I can cook."

"That is certainly news to me." I'd never seen him cook before in my life.

"I do. I used to pester my mom in the kitchen when I was a boy. She couldn't cook anything without my dragging a stool around to climb on it and watch her," he said. I never thought one could be so incredibly happy and suffocating in sadness at the same time, but that's how I felt. "Adeline won't let me near the kitchen anymore, but I used to cook every day. I love food."

I reached out a hand and touched his cheek. He didn't look sad—on the contrary, he was beaming. And I wanted to keep it that way forever.

"I have a confession to make," I said, and he was already chuckling because he knew. "I can't cook for shit. Literally—I didn't even know how to boil an egg." He full on laughed now. "I tried it once—it *melted*. I swear, I broke the shell and the yolk melted onto my hands. How was I supposed to know it takes *minutes* to boil an egg completely?"

I wasn't joking—I'd been a teenager, sneaking into the kitchen with Greta, who'd been busy stealing us dessert. And I don't know why I had this crazy idea that the egg would be hardboiled if I simply put it in boiling water for like a minute. Needless to say, I was disappointed—and the object of Greta's (rightfully) ruthless teasing for years.

Lucien's shoulders shook as he laughed, pulling me to him again. "Little fox," he said, kissing my cheek. "You're a princess through and through." And by some miracle, he now seemed to *love* that fact. "Don't you worry about a thing. I'll take care of you. I'll cook for you every day."

My cheeks flushed. "You will?" Something told me I'd eat a lot more if he was the one doing the cooking. I could already picture myself in the kitchen, sitting there watching him cook until I had enough and ripped his clothes off. All the fun we could have on dining tables and chairs and kitchen islands...

"Of course," he said without hesitation. "It's a privilege to cook for the people I love."

I kissed his cheek. "Then you'll teach me how to cook, too, so I can make delicious things for you."

"You don't need to cook for that. You just have to lie there and let me eat you," he said, and my toes curled again. "Nothing in the world is more delicious."

My eyes closed and I sighed. To be like this with him was even better than in my daydreams.

"Now eat, before I get carried away and serve you to myself right now," Lucien whispered.

Oh, gods. "It's my turn," I reminded him. Just as soon as I was full—and showered, I was going to take my time with him, too. Slowly.

But...then I remembered.

"How is John?" I asked, afraid of the answer already.

"He's the same, but the wound is looking much better," Lucien said, bringing the glass of milk to my lips. I didn't comment, just drank. "The infection seems to be gone, and the bleeding has slowed down, too."

"He needs more blood," I guessed, and Lucien nodded.

"If it's your father's poison, he's had it in his body for over six years. It will take a while to *clean* it, so to speak."

"He knows," I whispered, shaking my head. "John knows about everything. I've been seeing him in my dreams."

"You have?" Lucien looked up at me, hopeful again.

"He told me to find the wyrm—that it was a *she.* He told me to do the Water trick, and I did, but it didn't work."

He flinched. "Not surprising. They say the tricks used to work before, but now there's not enough magic in most places around the world."

"Except Izet did it," I said in wonder. "Remember, when he first kidnapped me? He said he did the Fire trick."

"It was just dumb luck, I think. He was there, and you were in the woods. He'd have kidnapped any other woman he saw around that castle because he just wanted the money."

That's what I'd figured, too. Izet just got lucky.

Gods, was I glad that he did...

"I still remember that day, though," Lucien said. "When I first saw you."

"Oh, I remember, too." I couldn't help the smile stretching my lips. "You held a sword under my chin, and you were half naked." The most perfect thing I'd ever seen, though I wouldn't have admitted it then.

"I never had a harder time looking away from something in my life. You were dirty and tied up, your cheeks flushed—a beautiful mess that somehow demanded all my attention," he said, shaking his head as he smiled. "I thought it would pass. I thought I'd get used to you."

I closed my eyes, resting my head on his shoulder, food forgotten again. "I thought I'd get used to you, too." I'd even fooled myself into thinking I could handle him.

"But then I saw you in town with Janet, and it was all I could do not to grab you and hide you in my room forever," he said, chuckling. I just about melted.

"And then you saved my life, and when I kissed you to say thanks..." I looked up at him. "That was a very shitty move, by the way." The way he'd locked down, had looked at me like I'd killed his puppy, then had told me to *never* do it again.

I'd been mortified then, but it was funny as hell now, especially when Lucien's cheeks turned a light pink again.

"You had no idea what you were doing to me, and at that point, I was still fighting with myself. I still refused to accept that I wanted you more than I wanted to breathe," he said, kissing my temple, my cheek. "And then you were close, and your lips were on me, and I was hanging on by a thread, little fox."

"Not for long, though," I said, fire lighting up my skin at the reminder. "The way you touched me that night in your office..." My voice trailed off. We were breathing heavily now, the memories perfectly vivid to the both of us.

"You were impossible," he whispered against my hair. "Too beautiful. Too pure. You felt too good to be real." He coaxed my lips open with his. "You still are."

Food forgotten, I gave in to the kiss like it was my lifeline. In a way, it was. I only ever felt alive when Lucien was there, when he was kissing me, holding me to him. We'd gone through a lot together, even if we hadn't met too long ago, not in this life, but it was all worth it. The confusion, the pain, the guilt—everything had been worth it. I had no regrets.

"Eat, little fox, before I forget John and everyone else again. Eat," he said with a groan against my lips, and John's name was a wakeup call to me, too.

We had things to do first, and I needed the energy. I needed to see John for myself, then I'd be calmer.

So, I moved away from him reluctantly and ate the last of the eggs he'd cooked for me without daring to even touch him again.

NINETEEN

THE WATER FROM THE OLD SHOWER WAS COLD, which served me. By the time I was out and dressed in my old clothes, I was wide awake, and the sun hadn't even begun to set yet. It felt like I'd slept for ten hours, but Lucien was right —it had been just a couple.

And John's wound was definitely looking better, too.

I didn't cry this time when Lucien cut my hand and held it to it. No puss, no green, just an ordinary-looking wound— large and open but not infected. I gave him all the blood that would come out of me, squeezed my fist right over his open flesh, and I prayed again with all my heart that it worked. That he woke up and helped us summon the Ether, helped us put an end to the reign of dragons—*before* my father found us.

I waited, heart in my throat, for him to open his eyes, but he didn't.

John looked the same.

"Come on, Johnny," Jack kept whispering for a while. The look in his eyes was so hopeful it broke my heart. Maybe he had come to find me because he wanted to be free of his brother taking his energy all the time, but he also cared about him, it was easy to see. Of course, he did—they were *twins*.

Which made my mother's actions seem even stranger.

Gods, what had she been thinking? How had she figured that almost killing her own sister would somehow make sense?

What were you thinking, Mom?

"Ella, this is my grandfather, Austin," Jack said when an old man came into the room, slightly limping and holding his weight on a light wooden cane. It reminded me so much of Farin Azarius and the statue of him in the library, that I almost couldn't hold back a flinch.

"It's a pleasure," I said, shaking the man's hand.

His eyes were almost completely glazed over like he could barely see me, but his handshake was firm. He was old, possibly the oldest man I'd ever seen before, with no hair on his head, square teeth, and short white stubble on his wrinkled cheeks.

"My dearest—you've finally come," the man said. "Please, please—sit." And he waved at the chairs around John's bed.

"This guy right here raised us himself," Jack said proudly, helping his grandfather take a seat. Lucien stayed at the corner of the room, arms folded in front of him as he watched me and *almost* smiled. I loved what being with me did to him—it had happened at my father's manor, too. The way his mood changed when we were together spoke volumes to me.

"You did a great job, sir. Jack here turned out pretty...*okay*," I said, just to tease Jack, who looked at me, then put a hand to his chest like my words had been an arrow to his heart. I bit my tongue to keep from laughing.

"Please, Austin is just fine, deary," the man said, folding his hands over the cane between his legs. "Tell me, how long will it take for my boy to wake up? I haven't been able to die, you know. I'm old, but I can't go yet, not without seeing that he's okay first. And I'm tired. Very tired. I have to die eventually."

"He's just joking," said Jack while the man laughed and shook his head.

"Oh, no. No, I'm not," he said.

"What about...what about your parents?" I asked Jack, and I don't know why I thought that would be a good idea.

I realized it wasn't the second his face dropped.

"They, erm...they left. When we were two. They left town and didn't come back," Jack said, and it would have hurt less if he'd have stabbed me.

"I'm so sorry," I said, mortified, but he smiled.

"Don't worry about it. They made their choices—it's fine. Besides, Pops here was everything we ever needed." And he patted the man's shoulder lightly.

Gods, I didn't know this man at all. I thought I knew Jack, but I had no clue what he'd been through. And for his parents to just walk out on him and his brother? I couldn't even imagine.

"I don't know how long it will take, Mr. Austin," I said. "But I'll be back here to give him blood every hour until he wakes up. He'll have to wake up eventually." I looked at John's peaceful face as he slept, then at Lucien. With his eyes alone he comforted me.

"Good, good," the man said. "It's a messy world out there, deary. But it's bearable when we're with our loved ones. Jack here needs his brother, you understand? They need each other."

Jack blushed bright scarlet. "What I *need* is for him to stop sucking the energy out of me, Pops."

"Sure, sure," the man said, laughing. "That's all you need, my boy."

"Would you mind me asking you a question, Austin?" said Lucien, coming closer to sit on the floor near my chair.

"Not at all. You're very welcome to ask me anything you please. You saved my boy—" He turned to me. "Did they tell you? He saved my boy," the man told me, smiling as much as he could, but it was like the weight of his years, of his life, tried to pull the corners of his lips down. He fought against them anyway, as he looked at Lucien. I could swear my heart was about to burst inside of my chest.

"They did, yes," I said, feeling like I might sprout wings and fly any second. I was so proud of him it was ridiculous.

And Lucien asked his question. "What do you know about magic spells? What do you know about magic *beyond* the elements?"

My smile faltered instantly, and even Jack looked curious.

"Oh," the man said, nodding his head before he lowered his eyes to his hands folded over his cane.

"My father knew a little bit about it, but not much. I was just wondering if maybe you heard..." Lucien said, and the man nodded again.

"Oh, I heard, my boy. I heard, alright." My heart all but fell to my heels. "There's a reason why we were only given control of the elements. Most do not understand that power comes with responsibility twice as great, and nature knows us best." He spoke slowly, stopping to breathe every few words. His watery eyes looked at Lucien for a moment. "There are those who've meddled with powers they do not understand. Things *I* don't care to understand, either, but they paid the price."

"What price?" I asked in half a voice.

"The ultimate price, deary. The elements give and take, but anything beyond that is one-sided—only *take*. We were not made for it. It consumes us. We're left with nothing—no life, no soul, no body."

I shook my head, unsure of what to believe. I'd seen

Alexandra—she'd seemed perfectly fine, even though she'd done those spells of hers constantly, I suspected.

"Thank you, Austin," Lucien said with a nod.

"Have you known someone who's crossed that line, my boy?" he asked, blinking his eyes too fast, like he suddenly couldn't see much. "Because they must be warned—now, before it's too late."

Lucien and I looked at each other.

"No, I was just curious," he said, and Jack must have figured something was off because he patted his grandfather's shoulder again.

"Time to go lie down, Pops. Enough wandering for today."

But even after they left, and Lucien and I were alone with John again, his words stayed in my ear. *They must be warned before it's too late.*

I swallowed hard, the fear only increasing inside of me. Because I was warned—and I was still going to go through with it and summon the Ether.

"How much farther?" I asked, looking up at the small mountain Lucien had me climb. The sun was already setting, the sky a deep orange beautifully merged with purple. I'd wanted to just stay out there and look at it, but Lucien had insisted he knew a better place, so I'd followed him—behind the houses and across a small meadow to a small green mountain barely four miles away.

And then...

"We're here."

He reached for my hand and I took it without thinking. Then, he pulled me up, behind a tree trunk and around a large grey rock.

"Oh, wow," I breathed when I saw the view—the sun was setting right across from us, and the colors of the sky were otherworldly. No way could they be real—and the way the clouds gathered around them, like they wanted to dip and dive into those colors, too, made it all the more magnificent.

"Come here," Lucien said, tugging at my hand, and he took us up a couple of square rocks, and close to a bunch of trees that stood apart from the rest surrounding them. I could see why—on the biggest branch of the one in the middle hung two chains as thick as my wrists, and a thick piece of wood connected them.

"You're joking," I said, smiling and shaking my head.

Behind the swing, there were two seesaws, one of them broken, and a metal slide painted blue. They all looked like they were put there by mistake, like someone had misplaced them, then forgot all about it—except the swing.

"A playground—for the *kids*. Like the edge of the mountain isn't right there." He chuckled, showing me the rocky edges just ten feet away. Then he bowed to me, waving his hands toward the swing. "Your Highness."

"Thank you, kind sir," I said, smiling so big my cheeks hurt. I went and sat on the swing—by some miracle, it fit me just right, and Lucien was behind me, kissing the top of my head.

"It's the best view I found around here. Look at that," he whispered, nodding ahead at the setting sun, at the colors, at the green earth underneath...

"It's perfect," I breathed. Even a painting couldn't do it justice.

"Hold on tight, little fox," Lucien said, and began to push me forward.

My laughter echoed down the mountain, but nobody else was there with us. I was so happy I could burst into a thousand ribbons. I realized it wasn't a big deal, just a swing. But to me, it was *huge*. To be able to share something so simple with Lucien in the middle of my chaotic life, it meant *everything* to me.

He swung me slowly until the colors dipped in darkness, and the sun was barely there anymore. Then, he wrapped his arms around me from behind and kissed my cheek.

"You're even more beautiful than that," he whispered in my ear. "Imagine that."

I laughed again. "I think you just love me, Mr. Di Laurier."

He squeezed me to his chest. "More than the moon loves the dark."

I turned my head and kissed his lips, holding onto his forearms with all my strength.

"As much as I'd have liked to take you out on a proper date, little fox, this is the best I can do right now," he said, and I melted all over again.

"This is perfect." It was more than perfect—the best date anyone could hope for.

"For now, maybe," he said, slowly moving around the swing to get in front of me. It was dark now, the moon hiding somewhere, but its light still let me see his face. I stood up, too, wrapped my arms around his neck and raised on my tiptoes to kiss him again.

"I have a question," I said against his lips, feeling every inch of me come to life as he ran his hands up and down the shape of me.

"Hmm," he mumbled, sucking on my lower lip until I moaned.

"It's important," I said, already breathless. I was both terrified and excited to ask him. My heart was beating so fast it shook me.

"I'm waiting..." Lucien said a minute later when I refused to speak.

I had to do it. It was a simple question, and I already knew the answer...didn't I?

I swallowed hard. "Will you...will you mate with me?" I blurted.

Lucien stopped moving. He leaned his head back, looking at me with his brows narrowed. For a moment, I thought maybe he'd say *no*, that that was a ridiculous question, that I'd lost my damn mind because despite what we felt, our history couldn't be changed. Our families couldn't be changed. *The world* couldn't be changed.

But...

"Of course, I'll mate with you, little fox." He shook his head like he was confused. "You're already mine."

My eyes closed. Tears pricked the back of my eyes, but they were happy tears for once.

"And you're mine," I whispered, more to remind myself. We'd made promises, Lucien and I, even before we knew things could get so complicated, but they still meant something. They meant *everything* because they were made from the heart.

"For as long as I live," he said against my lips. "We'll mate any day, any time you want. Just say the word and we'll do it."

I smiled, feeling like I was standing on clouds and could touch the sky if I reached out my hands.

"Let's wait for John to wake up first." It felt important that we did.

Lucien nodded. "Deal." And he kissed the breath out of me.

The relief was incredible. Everything I knew, at least about us two, was right. Nothing had changed the way *everything* changed by the week in my life. I could always count on what we had here.

It took him less than a minute to fire me up—he just knew how to kiss me, how to touch me, how to moan the way I liked. It was dark and we were outside, and if the air was cold, I didn't feel it. All I felt was Lucien, arms wrapped around me, body flush against mine, his hard cock pressing against my lower stomach.

And I was dying for a taste.

He moved us to the rocks, pressed me against a cold surface and pulled me up until my legs locked around his hips tightly. We kissed like it was the first time, and we couldn't get enough.

I let him have his way with me, kissing and biting every inch of my skin he could reach—until I was about to explode and let go of him. I landed on my feet, then grabbed his shirt and spun him around so that his back was against the rocks. My hands were on the button of his jeans, shaking, until I grabbed his cock in my hands.

We both froze for a second, him groaning like he was in pain, me holding my breath.

"I need you to open your eyes and look at the sky," I told him, then fell to my knees in front of him.

I licked his smooth pink tip just a little at first. He moaned that sexy sound that vibrated throughout me. His head fell back, and I knew he'd keep his eyes open. He'd stare at the darkness, the stars just firing up, and maybe he could even see the moon, too. And I knew he'd love it just as much as I did.

I ran my hands up and down him, then took him in my mouth—as deep as it would go all at once, just like he liked. I went slow at first, tasting every hard inch of him, running my tongue over every swollen vein, every smooth surface, until I was satisfied. Then, I began to lick and suck his tip, taking my time, letting the sound of him guide me. I used my teeth— only slightly, just like he taught me, and I picked up the pace slowly. My knees were numb from the small rocks on the ground, but I wouldn't have had it any other way.

The night was filled with his moans and whispers, and the

wet sounds of his cock sliding in and out of my mouth. He grabbed fistfuls of my hair and pumped into me faster, like he'd die if he didn't get his release soon. I choked on him so many times, and my face was wet with tears and saliva, and my throat was raw already, but every second was worth it. I'd get on my knees for him every single day for the rest of my life, not just for the taste of him against my tongue, but for the way it made him feel. I could live to please him, and I would be a happy woman.

With my name on his lips, he came, pulling my hair and thrusting his hips desperately. I swallowed his cum like I'd already done it a million times, and I'd missed the salty taste of it so much it was ridiculous.

Even before he stopped moving completely, I wanted more.

"I wish I had a violin," I said when he pulled me up to my feet and kissed me, searching my mouth for his taste. "I wish I could play it for you while you played with me."

"I'll make you one," he said breathlessly. The way he devoured my mouth said he wanted more, too. So much more. And his hand closed around my breast as he bit my neck, and his other one moved lower, to my jeans and under them before I could blink.

His fingers pressed onto my clit and I cried out, already delirious.

"You were right," he said, slowly spinning me around again until my back hit the rock. "Look up at the sky, little fox. The stars have never been closer."

And he fell to his knees, too.

My jeans and panties were around my ankles before the second was over, and his hungry mouth sucked on my clit hard. I raised my head and looked at the open sky, and I was freer than I'd ever been before.

The more Lucien licked me, the closer the stars came,

until they were all I could see. My hips picked up the rhythm of his mouth, and when he realized that I couldn't move properly with the clothes around my ankles, he took off one sneaker, and one side of the jeans and panties. Then he pulled my leg over his shoulder, and like that, he had full access to my pussy. He pumped his fingers in and out of me as his tongue flicked over my clit. I could hardly breathe as I moved with him, ground against his face until the stars were within my reach.

But Lucien pulled his fingers out of me too soon and stood up. With his hands around my thighs, he pulled me up until I locked my ankles around him. The anticipation had me shaking. He was hard for me again, and he was going to fuck me under the open sky tonight.

When I felt the tip of him against my entrance, my eyes rolled in my skull.

"Keep looking," Lucien whispered against my jaw, and with his hands on my hips, he pushed me down hard on his cock.

I cried out his name as I floated with the clouds, touching the stars with my fingertips, completely full of everything—light and love and life and pleasure.

Lucien didn't take it slow—he pumped in and out of me fast and desperate, face hiding under my chin as he breathed in the scent of me, telling me how much he loved me, how good I felt to him with every new thrust.

Then...

"Do you want my magic, little fox?" The question alone almost tipped me over the edge.

"Yes!" I cried out, and he grinned.

"Good girl," he whispered, and his magic fell over every inch of my skin as if it were snowflakes covering me up completely. It slipped into my pores and spread inside me, searching my lungs and my throat, closing around them so naturally, you'd think Lucien had *made* my body himself.

"Let me hear you choking, baby."

His magic closed all around me at once, just as he thrust deep inside me, rising on his tiptoes.

As much as it terrified me, the pleasure blinded me completely. I couldn't breathe, couldn't see, couldn't *think* at all, but the pleasure consuming every inch of me took me to another dimension where thinking wasn't required. I locked around him, squeezing tightly to try to hold onto this moment for as long as I could. I tried to draw in air on instinct, and when I couldn't, it somehow made the pleasure twice as powerful. I knew Lucien knew what he was doing, and it was so relieving to give up control like that, that I became light as air.

And it lasted a long time.

When I began to breathe again, Lucien continued to fuck me, slow at first.

"You okay?" he whispered, fingers digging into my ass as he pulled out of me, then thrust himself in again. I was so wet, the sound of it was intoxicating.

"I've never been better," I promised him, my voice hoarse, my throat dry, but my body was alive.

"I love that you trust me enough to do that to you," he said, pumping into me harder, faster, deeper.

"I trust you more than anyone in the world." More than I trusted my own self.

And I continued to hold onto him, to take in the blinking stars, to feel him sliding in and out of me, giving me strength with each new thrust, until he let go, too.

We held onto each other on the side of that mountain, covered by the dark—and Lucien's magic—the stars our only audience. Every time I was with him like this, every new time was like a first, a better first—the best first anyone had ever had.

"I think we should take this back inside now," he said, resting his forehead to mine, breathing as heavily as me.

Fire in my stomach. We weren't done yet. *Thank the gods.*

I grinned. "Yes, sir."

TWENTY

WE STAYED UP LATE THAT NIGHT.

We woke up early that morning—John needed my blood.

His wound was healing, it was easy to see. No more pus, no more bleeding, and his flesh was coming together, his skin knitting more with every hour. He was still not awake, but we had faith. We had to—the wound was closing.

To give him my blood every couple of hours was the least I could do. Lucien cut me in different parts of my hands because my wounds didn't heal in two hours, and he didn't want to reopen old ones before the skin healed completely, so both my hands were crisscrossed with thin red scars. And everyone was always rushing to bring me freshly squeezed juice, tomatoes and carrots to eat, and by the time the second day was about to end, I felt like I belonged in this small town.

Lucien was always busy, talking to the townspeople, his brother, his men, always making plans. Right now, as I sat on the porch of Jack's house and watched him and Ezrail talking to a couple, whose house apparently needed a new roof, I couldn't help but be in awe of him. The things we'd done to one another last night were still imprinted all over my body, and every time I remembered, my cheeks flushed.

Gods, I wanted to live like that every single night of my life. I wanted him to fuck me under the stars and under a roof, and under a damn mountain, too. I wanted it so much I almost wished that John wouldn't wake up until tomorrow, just so I could have one more night like that.

One more day in this place, to get Lucien to take me to the small woods behind the houses. There would surely be small animals there, but Lucien's shielding magic didn't extend all the way to it, so I hadn't had the chance to visit yet. But if we stayed a bit longer...

"You do know there are other things around here, right? Not just your counselor."

I turned to see Jack standing by the door of his house, grinning mischievously at me. Then my eyes went back to Lucien again, as if by a magnet.

"He's not my counselor," I said when he came to sit on the porch with me.

"What is he then—your *boyfriend*?"

Shivers ran down the length of me, and for some reason, I smiled. I'd never had a boyfriend before, but I hadn't really talked about it with Lucien. We did say that we were going to mate, though....

"He's a friend," I told Jack.

"A friend. Right," he said, rolling his eyes. "His brother looks positively pissed, though."

"What?"

But my eyes found Rowan instantly—he and William were sitting in front of one of the houses, on two chairs with a small table in between them, and he was looking right at me. He'd probably been looking at me the whole time while I was staring at Lucien, and I hadn't even noticed.

My cheeks burned from embarrassment, especially when

the corner of his lips turned up. I knew he was mocking me, the asshole. I almost flipped him off.

"He's just curious, that's all," I told Jack, though I wasn't entirely sure. In fact, I thought Rowan and the others would leave as soon as they dropped me off, but so far they were still here.

"I can't believe it actually worked out," Jack said, rubbing his face and his overgrown beard that he refused to shave off. Maybe he was tired of having to shave every day for the past three years as a guard of my father's. "I can't believe he actually turned out to be a *good* guy. Ugh." He nodded at Lucien.

I laughed. "That bothers you, doesn't it." It wasn't a question.

"Yeah, it bothers me—he almost got me and John and this whole town killed with his stupid heroics. *Come with me, little fox,*" he said, doing a terrible imitation of Lucien's voice when he'd been chasing us in the basement of my father's manor. Back then, I'd had no idea he was trying to *help* me, save me from Jack.

"What is up with that, anyway? Why *fox*?"

I smiled, eyes on Lucien, and he turned his head to me whenever he could. Those small smiles he gave me made my heart skip beats on the regular and my toes curl inside my sneakers. "When he was keeping me captive in his town, he thought I was Air. A little fox."

Jack blinked at me hard.

"Now, that's just fucked up," he said, scratching his head. "I can't believe he held you captive and you still chose him over me." I smacked him on the shoulder, and he laughed. "Kidding! I'm just kidding, okay?"

"You're worse. You were trying to kidnap me. All that talk about *you can trust me,* and *I want to be your friend*—it was just to make your own life easier when you asked me to follow you. And I did—ugh. Low move, Jack. Low move, even for you." I'd been stupid enough to trust him when he told me to follow him that day.

"It *worked out,* didn't it?" He rubbed his arm as if I'd really hurt him. "I mean, John's not up yet but it worked out. We're here. We're safe."

Safe. I didn't like that word. It gave me hope. Too much hope. We weren't really safe from my father, not yet anyway. Not until we summoned the Ether.

"Almost," I whispered, grinning at Lucien when he winked at me. Gods, I loved that face. I loved those arms—and his ass, too. I blushed at the thought, but I did love it. He was a fine specimen, indeed.

And Rowan was *still* staring at me, shaking his head. I could almost hear the thoughts in his mind: *are you seriously just going to stare at my brother the whole damn time*?

I raised my chin. *Why, yes. Yes, I am.* And I went back to staring at Lucien. What better thing was there in the world to look at, anyway? The way he walked, and the way his biceps flexed when he moved his arms...damn.

"You're not even listening to me," Jack complained—and for a moment, I thought about Greta. I wished I had a number to call her. I wish it were safe to just hear her voice—but it wasn't. Even if Lucien could somehow get me in contact with her, I wouldn't risk her life like that.

"I am," I said absentmindedly. "You're asking what happens when John wakes up, and I don't really know. We'll have to talk, I guess. Figure things out."

"About the Ether?" Jack asked, and I nodded.

"Yep. About the Ether." And about my father, too, because I'd want to know. I *had* to know what would happen to my father before we did anything.

A pause.

"And *then*?" Jack insisted, making me laugh.

"I don't know, Jack. But you'll get your life back, I guess." Nobody would be sucking power out of him anymore.

"What if it's true, though? What if we're really what Lucien says we are? He drew the thing for me—it was scary, not to mention *ugly*. I'd rather just be a bear, thank you very much," he said with a flinch.

I grabbed his fingers and squeezed for a moment. He was so surprised, he almost jumped back. Despite everything, I still thought of Jack as a friend. Even if all I'd known about him were lies, I still liked him. Cared about him.

"I think you're going to love it, Jack. You just wait," I said, the image of the drake I'd seen drawn in that book coming before my eyes. It had been magnificent—brown scales, two heads, large paws, and no wings. Just as beautiful as the rest of the draca.

"Yeah, yeah, I—" His voice cut off abruptly.

His eyes were wide open, pupils completely dilated, and he was staring ahead at nothing, his jaws locked tightly. He wasn't even breathing.

"Jack?" I said, unsure whether it was just a joke, but...

He sucked in a deep breath and met my eyes. "John," he said and jumped to his feet and ran into the house before I could blink.

"Lucien!" I called, and the second he saw my face, he knew something was up. I rushed to the door, and he ran after me.

My heart beat a mile a minute, and I barely made it up the stairs to the second floor. Jack had opened the door to John's room and had stopped just inside the threshold, still as a statue.

"Wha..."

The word died on my lips when I saw the room, the bed, John lying in it.

He was awake.

TWENTY-ONE

JACK'S EYES WERE FULL OF TEARS, BUT HE REFUSED to let them shed. Instead, he smiled so big he looked completely transformed.

John was really awake.

Did I dare to believe that something actually went right?

His eyes were open, and he was smiling, too, holding his brother's hand as Jack said something, kneeling in front of his bed. I couldn't tell what they were saying—my ears still rang, but I could hardly breathe.

He was awake. The man who was there, in my house, the nights I died six other times, and the one who knew just as much as me...the man who remembered.

I needed some air, and Jack needed some time with his brother, so I grabbed Lucien's hand and I turned to leave, but...

"Estella."

His voice.

It was *his* voice, the same one I'd heard in my dreams.

I faced him again, and he smiled bigger, looking at me like

I was an old friend. "It's good to see you," he said, and my tears slipped out sneakily.

"It's good to see you, too," I said in half a voice, and Lucien squeezed my fingers as if to reassure me. I looked at him, and he smiled, nodded toward the room. It was okay. I could go back in.

It was just John. I knew John.

I *knew* John.

"I could really use some more of your blood, if you don't mind," John said, pulling the cover over him himself.

Jack burst out laughing, those tears still in his eyes. John looked at him, and he was *proud*—so proud we could see it from across the room. I had never been in a more *intense* situation, and I had no idea how to act, what to say. Luckily, Lucien was with me.

He pulled me under his arm and guided me closer to the brothers, both of them laughing, both of them crying silent tears. *Happy* tears, same as mine.

The sight of John's wound made my breath catch for a moment—it was barely there. Earlier, when I gave him my blood, it had been open still, the flesh torn at least an inch deep. Now, the skin was knitted together, and the scar remained—red and raw, three inches long, but a scar like that would heal within a day on a shifter.

I could hardly believe it. It had *worked*.

"Give me your hand," Lucien said, and I don't know why I was so overwhelmed, why I felt like my insides were made out of air and I was going to deflate soon. Maybe because I'd been searching for answers for so long, across so many lives, and I'd been secretly convinced that I would *never* find them, but my hand was shaking, and I didn't feel the sting of the cut at all. "Squeeze." Lucien held my hand over Jack's leg and pulled my fingers together.

I squeezed my fist as hard as I could.

Dark red blood dripped onto his skin like paint. I couldn't stop looking at it, *drip, drip, drip* onto the scar, erasing it like it was pure magic, spilling all over the white sheets—and then John moved his toes.

It startled me so much I almost screamed.

"Thank you, Princess," John said, and there was color in his cheeks, a sparkle in his eyes.

He was so much like Jack—and so different, too. His face had sharper edges, and his eyes were more brown than green, and there was a depth to them that Jack didn't have. Like he'd seen things. Like he knew things, things I was both terrified and desperate to find out.

"It's good to have you back, John," Lucien said, pulling me to stand, taking me closer to the bed. Jack was sitting on one of the chairs, elbows resting on his knees as he looked at me—*admired* me with his eyes. My cheeks flushed. I hadn't really done anything—it was just my blood.

"Thank you, Lucien. For everything," John said, as if Lucien was his old friend, too. "Have you mated yet?"

I stopped breathing for a second, as John looked from Lucien to me, then back again. I couldn't speak if I tried, but Lucien didn't seem to have a problem with it.

"Not yet," he said. "We wanted to wait for you to wake up first."

John brought a shaking hand to his chest and smiled. "I am honored."

This was officially the strangest conversation I'd ever had in my life.

～

IT WAS LIKE HE KNEW. Like he'd been here all along, pretending to be asleep, but wide awake and listening. He'd heard everything—he knew about Lucien and me, about Jack being away, about how many times I'd had to give him blood since last morning, and it freaked me out a little bit.

We'd given them a moment because his grandfather had wanted to see John for himself, and now the three of them were in the room talking and laughing, while we waited in the guest room down the hall.

"Don't you think it's strange how he...*knows?*" I asked in a whisper, for some reason feeling like I was committing a crime to doubt John.

Lucien brought me closer to his chest and kissed my forehead. Just to be lying with him on this bed took half the bad of things away, but the questions still remained.

"It is," he said. "It's very strange, but also...exactly what I expected."

"I can't believe that guy in my dreams was actually really him," I said, shaking my head, hiding my face under his chin. I felt better when my lips were pressed to his skin.

"You know, I think I've heard that voice, too," Lucien said in wonder. "Maybe in a dream, or maybe...I don't know. It's a familiar voice, like it has been in my head before."

Shivers ran down the length of me. He felt them, so he ran his hands down my arms to chase them away.

"You're worried," he whispered, then pushed me to lay on my back. He propped himself on his elbow and was right over me, his lips inches away from mine.

"A little bit."

"Don't be. We're together," he said, and it was the most sense I'd seen in the world today.

We were together. Little else mattered.

"That's more like it," he said, before I even realized I was smiling. His kisses all over my face were soft, gentle —*reminders.* And I lay there with my eyes closed and charged on them.

"I just can't shake the feeling that something is...something is..." *Off,* but not exactly. *Strange,* but we'd already established that. "...different from what I thought it would be. Just...just a feeling." Like the sky was barely holding on, and it was about to fall on me any second. But I didn't say that out loud.

Lucien leaned back to look into my eyes, and I got lost in his instantly. Such an unusual blue. Such a perfect shape. He must have really been made for me.

"Instincts should never be ignored, my father told me," he said, and for a moment the conversation that I'd had with Rowan in the truck came back to me. About Lucien. About their father. Rowan had avoided me the past two days, but I understood that I made no sense to him, not with the way Lucien seemed to be *different* from what he thought he knew. I still hoped I could talk to him again, though.

"Rowan said that he was hard on you. That he was... demanding," I said, even though there was a good chance that Lucien wouldn't want to talk to me about it at all. I expected him to flinch or shake his head or just change the subject, but to my surprise, he smiled.

"He was. Very demanding," Lucien said. "But I loved it. I loved the challenges he gave me."

I blinked—Rowan had had a different opinion of their father's demands. "Really?"

"More like..." He closed his eyes for a moment, as if he was searching his head for the right words. "More like the way he was proud of me for completing them, I think. They were easy tasks—magic always came naturally to me. It was no bother, but he could be a bit too much at times."

I kissed him with my whole heart simply because he was so open, because he didn't hesitate. We'd always kept secrets from one another, Lucien and I, ever since we met. And I always expected him to hesitate to talk to me like he did back at the manor, but...he didn't. He seemed so perfectly comfortable talking to me about this, I felt *honored,* just like John said.

"And your mother?" I asked, my voice shaking, but it was just the excitement. The thought that Lucien trusted *me* the way I trusted him that made a mess of my chest.

"Oh, Mom was different. I never understood how they worked so well together, but she was very kind. Always knew the right thing to say," he said, and sadness touched his eyes. He was so open that I saw it clearly, and it fascinated me all over again. "She had this thing where, no matter what went on during the day, we always gathered for tea before bed to watch the moon in my father's garden. He built it for her for that purpose."

My heart melted. "That's beautiful."

"It was. It didn't matter if we fought, or if we were pissed at one another—mainly at my father—we were all obligated to meet in the garden before bed. She believed that deep down, we're creatures of the moon, and that our souls and our animals belong to it, and that we should show our respect by giving it a little of our time. We didn't even have to talk at all— we just had to sit there and think for a little while, and then we could go to bed."

"I want to do that," I whispered. "I want to do that every night." I wanted to talk to the moon, too—I'd tried it while I was away. After our talk in the basement of my father's manor, I'd talked to it on my way to Aither, and I'd always felt so much better afterward. Like talking to a friend.

"Then we'll do it," Lucien said, kissing me slowly.

"Every night."

"Every night," he whispered, his kisses becoming harder, more desperate. He fell on top of me, chasing the air from my lungs but giving me so much more in return. The world fell away bit by bit just like always, and I was already floating with the clouds. The more I tasted him, the more his tongue slid against my own, and his hands gripped my waist and squeezed me, and the tighter my limbs locked around his body, the more the need for him grew to a throbbing ache all over me, especially between my legs.

But...

Lucien broke the kiss with a groan, eyes squeezed shut, his hair all over the place. He looked like a god laying over me like that, breathing heavily, lips red and eyes bloodshot...

"He's coming." Cursing under his breath, he rolled off me and jumped to his feet in a second, running his fingers through his hair.

I barely had the time to check my shirt and sit on the bed before someone knocked on the door.

"You guys decent?" Jack said, but he didn't wait for a reply. "I'm coming in!"

He came in with a hand over his eyes, his fingers open as he looked at us.

"You're an idiot," I said, unable to hold back a laugh.

"Just making sure I don't see anything I'm not supposed to," he said with a grin.

"How about *don't come in* then?" I said and stood from the bed.

"Why wouldn't I?" Jack said, as if he really didn't get it. I looked at Lucien standing by the window—his jaws were locked, and he was still trying to get control of himself, his back turned to Jack because of the delicious—*so* damn delicious—bulge in his pants.

I pulled my lips inside my mouth. "Just get out."

"Right," Jack said, and he knew—I could tell that he knew exactly what was happening by the way he looked at Lucien's back, then wiggled his brows at me. My cheeks all but melted off me. "Right, well, Pops is downstairs, and John wants to see you. Just thought I'd tell you that." And he still didn't move.

"*Get out!*" I shouted, and he finally stepped back.

"Okay, okay, damn!" he said, closing the door behind him, mumbling something about being kicked out in his own house.

"He really...tests me," Lucien said with a sigh when the door closed. I went and hugged his side, kissed his shoulder.

"He's a good guy."

"He's annoying," he said, kissing the top of my head. "And you're impossible to resist."

Oh, I liked that very much. I stepped back, grinning like I was trying to impersonate Jack. "You got something in your pants, Mr. Di Laurier."

His face broke into a smile instantly. "I do."

Fire under my skin even though I was stepping away from him, toward the door.

"It's big," I said with a nod, looking at his hard cock pressing against his jeans. Oh, yes, it was.

"But you take it so well," he whispered, and it was painful between my legs.

My jaw hit the floor. Why was that so damn sexy?

"John," I reminded the both of us. "We need to talk to John."

Closing his eyes, he sighed and ran his hands through his hair once more, but the strands that always fell in front of his left eye refused to be pulled back. They were just as stubborn as him. I pulled the door open, unable to get enough of the sight of him.

I just couldn't believe it. I couldn't believe that *that* was mine.

"Keep looking at me like that and John will have to wait a while," he said in that low voice of his that had chills running down my spine the same time it ignited fire inside of me. It was a damn warning.

"Don't," I said, turning to the hallway. "Later. Just...later." He could do with me whatever he pleased later.

But we had to talk to John first.

"Later," Lucien said, stepping out of the room, no longer hard.

And *that* was a damn promise.

TWENTY-TWO

JOHN LOOKED EVEN BETTER THAN HE DID A COUPLE hours ago. He'd eaten some soup all by himself, without anybody feeding him, Jack announced proudly. It had served him—he looked fuller somehow, his eyes livelier, even under the strong yellow light overhead. Night had fallen, and the moon sat right outside the window, watching us.

"Please, sit," John said, and he was sitting, too. They'd put pillows against the headboard of his bed, and he was resting against them. He'd even changed his pajama top for a blue short-sleeved shirt. He suddenly looked very...ordinary. Just a guy sitting on his bed, relaxing, not someone who'd been asleep for six years.

"How are you feeling?" Lucien asked when we sat on the chairs Jack had put in front of the bed, and he joined us.

"Better by the minute," John said. "I still can't stand—my muscles will need some work, but other than that, I feel great. The poison is almost completely out of my system." His eyes fell on me. "So, thank you for that, Princess."

"Ella is fine," I said. "And you're very welcome." It was the least I could do to heal him, but... "I don't understand how you're still alive, to be honest."

John smiled, looking at Jack who was sitting to my right. "Because of him," he said. "We're a strange pair of twins, Jack and I. We're connected on a deeper level. He literally kept me alive by loaning me his life force and his magic. That's why he looks older than he should. Much older than me."

I looked at Jack, about to say *no, he doesn't,* but...he did. Compared to John, he had fine lines on his forehead, and around his eyes, and his laugh lines were more pronounced. If I focused hard enough, I could see the few grey hairs around his ears as well.

"He's only twenty-one years old," John said, and I gasped.

Twenty-one? He looked at least thirty.

I shook my head, at a loss for words.

"Thanks, dipshit," Jack said to his brother. "You literally stole my life from me. I didn't consent to that shit."

But John laughed. "You'll get it all back, brother. Don't you worry about it."

"It's fascinating," Lucien said. "That you were able to tap into his life energy at all..." He shook his head, holding John's eyes. "You *are* a drake. You have to be—normal twins are not connected in this way."

"There you go again," Jack whispered, rubbing his face, but John wasn't laughing or shaking his head or asking what the hell a *drake* was. Lucien was right—it was the only explanation. Normal twins didn't work that way—my mother was dead, and her twin was still alive.

"We are," John said in a whisper, and it was like the whole world held its breath for a moment.

Then...

"What?" Jack had raised his head again, and he looked at his brother like he'd lost his mind.

"We are a drake," John said. "And that's the only reason why I'm still alive."

Jack was on his feet, shaking his head. "Nah, nah," he said to his brother. "That's not...I'm a bear—we're *bears*, not *drakes*. Fuck that—I ain't some two-headed, ugly ass creature that's not even supposed to exist."

"Draca," John said, and my heart skipped a beat.

I was right. He knew.

"We're draca," John said. "The first to be born after almost two centuries."

Every inch of me raised in goose bumps. Lucien felt the same—I could see him shivering visibly, so I took his hand in mine. Things didn't seem like such a big deal when our fingers intertwined like that.

Jack fell down on his chair with a deep sigh.

"You were there," I whispered, still in disbelief that I was actually sitting here, talking about this. "In my past lives, you were there. I remember you."

John didn't hesitate. "Yes, I was. I was always there. I had to watch you die twice, Ella." The way he smiled, you could tell that it made him sad.

"You died in my fourth life," I said because it was the only death I didn't remember.

"Yes, I did," John said, but before he could say anything else, Jack was on his feet again.

"Hold up, hold up, wait a sec," he said, raising his hands. "What do you mean, *you did*? When—I was with you the whole damn time?!"

"It was a different life, one that...technically never happened," John said, and he was already feeling uncomfortable.

"What the hell are you talking about?!" Jack shouted, his voice pitched high. He really was taking this worse than I imagined. I thought for sure he was prepared to hear some strange things after what Lucien and I told him, but I had the suspicion that he thought we were full of shit or just wrong about him and his brother.

Now that he saw we weren't....

"Sit down, Jack. I'll explain everything. Just sit down," said John.

But Jack didn't. "You didn't think to tell me about any of this *before?* Huh, Johnny? You didn't think it was important to let me in on this *before* you almost got yourself killed?"

"I didn't know," John said, his own voice rising. I squeezed Lucien's hand tightly—loud voices were always a trigger for me. They sent me right back in front of my father, and nothing scared me as much as his wrath.

But Lucien pulled me closer, and he kissed my temple, as if he knew that was exactly what I needed. My heartbeat calmed down instantly, and my eyes opened to his. He looked at me like he could read my mind, and he was concerned.

I really wasn't on my own anymore—and that realization kept catching me by surprise somehow.

"I didn't know before I got shot," John said with a deep sigh. Jack sat down again, head down and hands fisted tightly. "There's always something that triggers the memories, and I was too young to have remembered when I got chased and shot with that arrow. This time, it was the wound that triggered it, but I had no energy to wake up, stay conscious. If I did that, I'd have taken even more out of you, brother, and I refused to do that. I refused to endanger you in that way. So, I took just enough to get by. To stay alive. I was awake inside my head—perfectly aware. I saw through your eyes." He looked at me and Lucien, too. "Through all of your eyes. I saw the world. Heard and felt. Even if I wasn't awake in this body, I was here."

Jack raised his head, and I saw the tears slipping down his cheeks in silence.

"I never saw you before," I whispered. "I understand what you mean, and I think my mother's death always triggers my memories. I never remember while she's alive, but I've never seen you before. Just this time, in this life. Just after I met Jack and we talked in that basement."

So overwhelming. I didn't know which way to think yet, and John nodded.

"We can't be expected to remember *everything*, of course. There are some things in our past lives that we'll never get back. I think we only remembered what most affected us, things that really left a mark on our souls," he said, and the more he spoke, the heavier my shoulders.

What more had happened in those lives that I didn't know? What had I missed? Who had I been, and why did I feel like I should *mourn* all those Ellas? There were parts of me that didn't make it. They were gone forever.

"Tell me what you remember," John said, trying to make himself comfortable on the bed. Jack no longer said anything or cried. He just rested his elbows on his knees, kept his eyes on his folded hands. And Lucien rubbed my knuckles with his thumb in silence.

It almost felt like I was all alone with John.

My voice shook when I spoke. "I remember the fire. The fire *you* made..." The same one Jack had summoned the morning of my wedding to serve as a distraction. In my other lives, it had been John. He'd been standing at the bottom of the stairway, perfectly comfortable among the flames—flames that could burn me.

"Yes," John said with a nod, but he didn't offer any further explanation, just looked at me like he expected me to say more. So, I did.

"I remember I can't shift. Nobody can shift that morning. It's always the same morning—right after my twenty-second birthday." John closed his eyes and took in a deep breath, as if he could *see* what I was saying behind his lids, but he didn't comment. "And I remember...I remember Lucien. I remember him killing me. He always kills me." Lucien squeezed my hand tightly but didn't look up at me at all.

John's eyes popped open, and he didn't blink for a while, analyzing my face like he was just seeing me for the first time.

And then he said the words that changed my entire existence forever.

"Lucien never killed you, Ella."

My heart refused to beat.

"What?"

John shook his head. "Lucien never killed you."

A second lasted an eternity.

"He did," I said when I found my voice. "I remember it. He always kills me. I always die that morning. He kills me."

But John looked at me like he was about to break me wide open.

And he did.

"You die that morning, but Lucien doesn't kill you, Ella. Your father does."

TWENTY-THREE

SOMETHING ABOUT THE AIR AND THE WAY IT BECAME thicker. It refused to go down my throat—and it wasn't like Lucien's magic. It wasn't comforting.

It was *death*. A brand-new kind of death I'd never crossed paths with before.

I looked at John, blinked, and looked at him again, but his face didn't change. Reality didn't change.

Lucien brought my hand to his lips and kissed my knuckles.

I pulled it away.

"No." It wasn't possible. I knew this—I'd *seen* it. I had been there. I'd alway been there.

Lucien was the one who killed me.

"Estella," he whispered, wanting me to look at him, but how could I?

"*No.*" It was *him* who killed me—him. Not my father. "I remember it clearly. I've lived it five times. *Five* times!" My voice rose, but I was shaking so badly I didn't care.

And John had the audacity to shake his head. "I'm sorry, Ella."

I stood up just to stretch my legs, just to get my body moving, just to remind myself to breathe and to think and to *know* what I knew.

The morning. The fire. The masked man coming up the stairs to end me—Lucien.

Lucien, Lucien, Lucien...

John was saying something from somewhere behind me—when had I come to the window? Why couldn't I see anything outside it?

"No," I said again. "He comes up the stairs through the flames. He wears that mask—I've seen that mask on him. And he kills me, the way he's always killed me, and my death resets everything. It's never over—it just starts from the beginning."

Someone was close to me, then the window pulled up. Fresh air in my nostrils.

"You okay?" Jack whispered from my side, but I couldn't really answer.

"Not *your* death specifically," John said. "*Our* deaths. I died three lives ago, and that reset time, too. I came back, and I remembered. I only remember those lives, Ella, since I died. Three lives, and in two of them, he kills you."

He. My father, Archibald Azarius, the king.

Not Lucien.

"Little fox." He was behind me, hands on my shoulders, forehead pressed to the back of my head.

And I wanted him *gone.* I wanted him to stop touching me—why was he touching me?

Why did I want him to stop?

This was Lucien. It was my Lucien—kind and sweet and full of passion. He would doom the world before he saw me hurting. I trusted him more than I trusted myself.

So why did his hands on me feel like they were burning me —in an awful, *awful* kind way?

"Please, talk to me," he whispered, and I almost sobbed out loud.

It wasn't fair. He killed me. I knew that, I remembered it, I'd *accepted* it. I'd made my peace with it despite everything. I'd accepted it.

And now this man was sitting there and telling me that it was all a lie?

That once again, everything I knew, everything I thought was certain, wasn't?

When, when, *when* was I ever going to see the truth for what it was? When was the world and my senses and my mind going to just stop lying to me?

"I don't get it. I don't get any of it," Jack was saying, and I barely heard his voice over the screams in my head. "How does the time reset? Does this mean I've lived all those lives, too?"

"Look at me," Lucien whispered, and my eyes closed. I didn't want to. "I know it hurts, but we'll get through it, I promise."

But he didn't know how it hurt. He had no clue.

"The Ether..."

John's voice got stuck in my ear, those two words filling up my mind. *The Ether.*

I turned, careful not to look Lucien in the eyes. Careful not to remind myself of what I felt, what I thought, what I feared. "Let's get to the bottom of this first."

And then I could break. Then I could cry. Then I could die, if need be, before I could get myself together again.

"Of course," Lucien said, and he didn't try to take my hand. He didn't try to get me to look at him. He just stayed by the window when I went to sit in front of John again.

"The Ether," I said, and I hated that he looked at me now like he *pitied* me.

"Yes, the Ether," John said.

"He's a man. I've seen him...technically." Only the shape of him and had heard his voice in Alexandra's.

"And I believe that the only power he has left is over time," John said.

My mind was blank now, blank of thoughts of my father, and of Lucien and of *me*. All of it could wait.

"But how? And why now? Why wait so long, why not—"

"The draca," John cut me off. "He was waiting for all of the draca to be alive in the same timeline, and once we were, he must have tied the time to us, so that it resets whenever one of us dies."

I shook my head, my thoughts buzzing. "Two hundred years." It had been almost two hundred years since one of my ancestors had killed the last of the drakes, wiping out the other kind of draca from the world. And the Ether had waited that long...

"We give him power," Lucien said from behind me, and the sound of his voice made me shiver.

"We do. He's stronger when we're alive," John said.

I reached for the back pocket of my jeans and the page I'd torn from that book. "I have the spell to summon him." I put the folded piece of paper on John's lap.

He took it, his hands shaking slightly, his eyes sparkling.

"It's all come together," he whispered, reading the words Alexandra had scribbled on the edges of the page.

"Once we summon him, he'll be able to...come back," I said. "Won't he?"

"I think so," John said. "We're alive. And he'll be here. And..." He looked up at me, like he was suddenly surprised.

"Where did you see him, exactly? What did he look like?"

"In a memory," I whispered. "A memory of my ancestor, Alexandra."

John narrowed his brows, but before he could speak, Jack beat him to it.

"I don't get how that worked," he said, and he no longer sounded as pissed off. "How do you just *see* into a memory?"

My mouth opened to speak, but...

"The same way we do." I looked at John. He wasn't joking. "The same way I've been able to see you guys."

I shook my head, unable to say anything.

"We're all connected," Lucien said. "My father told me once that the draca used to be connected differently. We all lose power apart and are stronger together."

John looked at him. "Except dragons," he said. "They're the strongest existing creatures in the universe. Even when they're at their weakest, they're stronger than anything else out here." His eyes fell on me.

"How does it work?" I asked in half a voice, my thoughts coming back to me. "How would I *connect* to you?"

And it was like he already knew exactly what I wanted to say. "I'd give you access to my memories, and you'd search for me. The same way I've done it with you."

"I never gave anyone access to anything." If anything, I'd wanted to keep everyone away from my mind.

"You did," John said. "In your dreams, you always did."

"But I never saw you before. I never saw you—"

"You could never make me out, yes. You needed to be reminded about my existence on your own before you could see me there," he said, and I remembered the first time I'd seen him in my dreams, days ago. The way he'd said, *you finally see me.* That's what he'd meant. "But I was there. And..." John swallowed hard. "If you want, you could be, too."

White noise went on in my head.

"No." Lucien was standing next to me, looking at John. "Absolutely not."

But I was already hyperventilating. "I can *see* into your memories?" I asked John, and he nodded reluctantly. "I can see the last time I died...from your eyes."

"Ye—"

"Estella, no," Lucien said, and he kneeled before me, grabbed my hands on my lap. I had no choice but to meet his wide dark eyes. He looked pale. He looked terrified.

And I loved him so much it knocked the breath out of me.

Because I also wanted to *resent* him for not being the one to kill me.

It wasn't his fault, I knew that. Maybe it was just me. Maybe I was just a bad person—an Azarius. Maybe I was no better than the rest of them.

"You don't have to see that. There's no need. Things are different this time—everything is different," Lucien said. It was like he knew things even I didn't know yet, but my mind was already made up.

I touched his cheek, tried to will myself into remembering what it felt like when we were together, but I couldn't. Right now, I couldn't. The need to know was too great.

I had to see.

"I have to," I whispered and watched him turn his head and kiss my palm. Just now, it felt good, that kiss. It calmed me a bit. "I have to know. I have to understand."

I'd spent six lives believing he killed me. I saw it all in my head—everything was perfectly clear to me. I *saw* it, and if I was going to choose to not believe my own eyes, I would need proof.

"I think you do," John said from the bed. "I think you really do."

And Lucien stood up, looking like he was about to sprout wings any seconds. "It doesn't matter," he said through gritted teeth. "What does it matter—those lives didn't even happen. We're all here now, aren't we?"

But John looked at me, and I shook my head. He understood. Even though those lives didn't happen to the rest of them, they happened to us. They happened to *me*. And I had to know how my father killed me.

I had to see it with my own eyes; otherwise, there would be nothing left of me by the end of this day.

John understood it. That's why he nodded. "Hold my hand," he said calmly.

Every inch of my skin raised in goose bumps, but before I could move, Lucien grabbed my face in his hands and forced me to look up at him.

"Please, don't," he told me. "Listen to me, Estella, nothing good will come out of it. You don't need to see what never happened."

It's because he knew. He knew me better than anyone else, and he knew what it would do to me if I saw.

But what he didn't understand was that *not knowing* would be worse. So much worse.

I was tired of secrets. I was tired of lies. I just wanted to see. So, I forced a smile on my lips for his sake. "I'll be okay."

When I stood up from the chair, he had no choice but to let go of my face and step to the side. I sat at the edge of John's bed, holding his eyes.

"Whoa, whoa, whoa..." Jack was saying. "This is getting out of hand. Is anybody going to pass out? Just tell me if somebody's going to pass out because I need to be prepared..."

John offered me his hands and I took them. "I'm ready."

TWENTY-FOUR

NOTHING HAPPENED AT FIRST.

My eyes were closed, my hands in John's, and I could hear Lucien and Jack breathing somewhere close by, but I was still there. Still in that house, sitting on John's bed.

And then there was this sound, like a bell that I was pretty sure I'd heard in movies, and it kind of lured my thoughts, pulled them to follow it. So, I did.

It was dark behind my lids, just as dark as in my dreams. I felt the heat of the air around me, felt my heart beating steadily, and then I was sucked in gently until there was light out there in the world again.

My eyes opened. It was as easy to do as when I'd woken up in Alexandra's memories. In my father's memories.

We're all connected, John said. And he was right.

Because right now, there was fire all around me, a blazing inferno burning every inch of space around me, clinging to black and white marble floors, white walls, shattering windows...and I saw it as clearly as I'd seen it on the days I died.

Except this time, I was at the bottom of the stairs. This time, I saw a lot of different things.

I also *felt* very different. The thoughts in my head were those of a stranger's, too.

It took me a little while to realize where I was, what was happening, and understand why the fear that felt like it should have paralyzed my body completely was doing nothing to slow me down.

That's because it wasn't *my* body—it was John's, and my emotions didn't affect it.

"Hurry up!"

My head turned to the side, toward the stairway and the man walking up slowly, looking around him, a mask on his face.

Lucien.

So many thoughts that didn't belong to me...

I can't believe we actually made it inside the manor...

I can't believe I have to wear this stupid mask, but Lucien was right. If the king survives and knows our faces, there's nowhere we can hide. It's important to keep our anonymity...

I tried to breathe, tried to scream, tried to get myself away from whoever was implanting those foreign words into my brain, but I couldn't. I could do nothing but watch Lucien climb up the stairs, think things I had never thought before, and feel the nervousness, the excitement, the fear of the body I was a guest in, for as long as this lasted.

The princess...

My eyes landed on a dark figure at the top of the stairs, in the hallway, coming closer. Lucien froze for a moment when he saw her—*he did this last time, too...just stood there and watched her, wasting precious seconds...*

The princess...

It was me. I was there, at the top of the stairs, and I was

wearing a white nightgown made of silk that reached all the way down to my ankles, and my hair was tied behind my head in a loose tail, and I was saying something, hands to my chest, shaking...

Lucien wasn't moving again.

Godsdamn it, man!

I looked around——*John* looked around, at the hallway of the second floor, at the burning walls and the orange flames that danced like they were made out of liquid. *Safe,* he thought. Still safe.

Then he turned around and took off running up the stairs, taking me with him.

"What are you doing?!" John said, and I heard his voice as if it were mine.

And I saw through his eyes—saw Lucien with his arms raised toward me while I was frozen perfectly still, eyes closed, flames on the hem of my nightgown—but only for a second.

"She's *burning!*"

Lucien.

I heard his voice, saw him moving, pulling the mask over his head and revealing his face. That same face. Same eyes and same lips and same brows...

And he was running toward me while I fell back, slowly, about to be devoured by the flames—until Lucien caught me in his arms.

He caught me in his arms, and he fell to one knee, looking up at John, screaming— "Turn it down a notch!"

"I can't—it's out of my control! I'm not a godsdamn dragon!" John cried out, then looked at the stairs again, his thoughts popping into my mind: *where the hell are you, Jack? Better not be dying...*

"Keep moving—what are you doing?!" he shouted at Lucien, as Lucien put his hand over my chest and looked at my face like he was scared. *Terrified,* though I simply looked like I was sleeping.

I wasn't dead yet. I was...breathing. I could see my own chest rising and falling steadily.

"This was a mistake—she's burning," Lucien said, his voice transformed. "Her skin is burning. I need to cool it down." And I noticed how the flames couldn't reach him at all. He'd created a shield with his Air all around himself.

All around *me*. My limp body, still in his arms.

"Are you kidding me? We need to go—*now,* before she can't keep the king back any longer and he finds us! Screw the burns—let's go!"

Lucien finally rose to his feet with me in his arms. "This was a mistake. It's not her fault," he said to John, and when he looked at him, I could see the regret flashing in his darkened eyes. "*Look* at her!" And he raised his arms a bit as if to show me to John.

My gods, I couldn't breathe. Wherever I was, I felt my lungs expanding, but I couldn't breathe at all.

John put his hand on Lucien's shoulder. "Yes, Lucien, I can see that you're smitten by the princess—but now is not the time, my brother. We *need* her. We *have* to go!"

Lucien looked like he might explode any second. "It's not her fault," he insisted.

But John said, "It's not the world's fault, either."

Lucien looked down at my face—so peaceful, eyes closed, hair stuck to my cheeks...breathing steadily.

Breathing. Alive.

The men ran.

They ran down the stairs, and I began to notice the bodies. *Dead* bodies of soldiers on the ground, burning. Where was the staff? Had they made it out in time?

Gods, it felt like I should have been throwing up...

I was divided—my mind with John, my body in Lucien's arms still. Down and down the stairs we went, the three of us, past the burning flames and the bodies, down the second floor, and to the main hallway, behind the stairway and to the doors of the kitchen. In my last life, the manor had been much the same as it was in this one, but the dragons on the doors and on the walls were different, and now that they were ignited by the fire, the gold paint melting off them made them look like they were coming to life.

We went through the back doors and walked outside into the morning light, and through John's eyes I saw more soldiers, dead on the ground. I saw Jack, too. My heart all but stopped beating—he was standing and he was waving, smiling as big as always, which only meant one thing, and John thought it loud and clear: *the king is still contained.*

"Let's g—" John started to shout, so excited he was *flying.*

...and then everything changed.

I saw my father through his eyes rising over the flames, his clothes torn and burned, his skin bloody, but his eyes...

"*You dare to touch* my *daughter?!*"

His voice was like lightning and thunder, and he rose from the flames like he couldn't feel them burning him when I knew they did. I'd felt them myself—and Lucien said it, I'd been burning. This wasn't normal fire—this was fire straight from the Earth's core that Jack and John had pulled out just for us. For my father.

And he looked pissed.

He laughed and his laughter echoed, and he moved so fast he was a blur. He slammed onto Jack just like he had done in the basement of the manor days ago and threw him to the side with incredible ease. Jack flew in the air so far we lost sight of him within seconds.

And John felt it all. He felt the *failure*, and I felt it with him.

He stepped back as my father laughed, coming closer, stepping onto the flames burning the grass and his feet, but he didn't care.

He was mad. He was completely mad. And he was coming.

"Lucien," John said, looking down at Lucien, who'd kneeled on the ground, and had put me on the grass—a patch of land that wasn't burning. And he was whispering to me, *you'll be okay, you'll be okay,* pushing my hair away from my face, folding my hands over my stomach...

Then he looked up at John.

Both of them knew. Both of them knew for a fact that it was over, but...

"We fight," said John, and in his mind, the words—*we lose* —echoed right after.

"We fight," Lucien repeated, pushing the mask off his head, and John did the same. They threw them to the sides and looked at my father, coming closer by the second, raising his hands...talons. He had talons instead of fingers, and the shock that went through John shocked *me* as well.

The thoughts in his head turned chaotic.

He's shifting...

How is he shifting? He said he wouldn't be able to shift!

We can't shift—how can he shift?!

Did he shift last time—oh, great fucking job, John, for not remembering THE MOST IMPORTANT THING!

He said we'd be safe from the dragon, damn it! He said—

"Too powerful," were the words that fell out of his lips "Way too powerful. We're fucking doomed..."

"Not yet," Lucien said, raising his hands toward my father. He didn't sound half as afraid as John, and that gave John confidence, too. A false sense of courage he clung to...

"Ready?" Lucien asked.

"Let's do it," John said, though he wasn't.

And the fighting began.

It was all so chaotic in front of me that I missed most of it, maybe on purpose, maybe not.

Fire and Air and Earth collided with one another, and talons pierced through skin, ripped clothes and flesh off bones. John was bleeding, Lucien was bleeding, my father was burning and bleeding and never slowing down.

Please, I said, but nothing came out of John's lips except the screams whenever my father sank his talons in his body. John attacked him with large pieces of the ground, and Lucien slammed blow after blow of Air magic onto him, but my father refused to fall. He refused to back up.

When he gripped John by the neck and threw him to the side, I barely felt the pain—John's body had turned numb. He fell to the ground full of holes that he'd made in an attempt to trap my father. He then dragged himself for a couple of more feet before he stopped, eyes half open, his consciousness hanging on by a thread.

In my head I screamed because I saw Lucien standing up to my father, and I felt John trying to shift but he couldn't, and I knew Lucien was trying, too.

He slammed his fists onto my father's face fast, and Air magic attacked him from all sides at once, but it still wasn't enough. My father could barely stand, but he still managed to sink those large claws right into Lucien's shoulder.

Lucien moved, twisted around like he didn't even feel the pain, and he slammed the tip of his foot onto my father's knee, making him tumble and fall to the ground.

Hope bloomed in John's chest for a moment, then...

Lucien went for me—my body still lying on the ground ten feet away from them. Sleeping.

"No," John whispered. "F-f-finish him first. F-f-f..."

But Lucien was too far away and couldn't hear him. And while my father was still on one knee, half the hair on his head and the beard on his face burned to a crisp, Lucien grabbed me in his arms and tried to make a run for it.

My father raged. I saw it all happen in slow motion, and my heart stood perfectly still until it stopped beating for good.

He pushed himself up and large wings erupted from his back, and he launched lightning fast at Lucien with both arms open. He slammed onto him with all his strength within two seconds. Lucien was still holding my body in his arms, and the three rolled and rolled on the ground until they reached the side of the manor and John lost sight of them completely. I couldn't see, either, because I was still stuck inside of him.

"Not again," he breathed, and he tried to prop up on his elbow to see better, but he could only hold himself up for a minute—the left side of his gut was torn completely open and bleeding still.

But that minute was more than enough for me to see.

Lucien, on his stomach, being consumed by the flames on the grass.

My father on his knees, with my body in his arms, his large hand around my neck...

My *bleeding* neck.

His head fell back and his wings spread wide and he roared at the sky until the entire earth shook, trying to stop me from bleeding, though he knew it was too late.

John's heart skipped a beat.

He thought, *she's dead.*

It's over.

She's dead...

THE WORLD FELL out of existence.

TWENTY-FIVE

THE THINGS ONE FEELS ABSOLUTELY CERTAIN ABOUT are never true.

I SWAM in the dark like it was water. I breathed it in like it was air. I touched it like I could feel it caressing my skin, and it helped. It helped in piecing things together—like a blank canvas I could use to draw the picture I'd been missing my whole lives.

But it still wasn't complete.

"Estella," said the voice that was trying to wake me up, and I recognized it. My heart recognized it even if my mind was still too numb to make sense of the real world.

Lucien's hands were on my face—my body felt the weight of them perfectly, and it came alive at his touch. He was here, in this world, and he was alive, and I wanted to be alive with him.

My eyes opened to his. I was lying in his arms, just like I had seen through John's eyes in a time that didn't exist. He was caressing my cheek and pushing my hair out of my face, calling my name gently, coaxing me awake.

Gods, he was beautiful—the kind of beautiful that had character, that went deep, that told stories so rich they could go on forever. He was the same Lucien, looked at me the same way—*it's not her fault,* he'd said to John. *Look at her,* he'd said to John. *She's burning!* he'd shouted.

Beware of the man who takes your life.

It wasn't Lucien.

It was my father.

I must have broken down at some point because I felt the tears, warm and big, sliding down my cheeks. I felt his thumb and his lips catching them as they fell, and he told me that it was going to be okay, just like he had then, though I'd been unconscious and hadn't heard it.

Unconscious—that's it.

I'd always thought he killed me when he knocked me out to spare me the pain of the burns, to *cool* my burning feet. I always thought *that* was my end because I was never conscious again. I always thought he took my life because I wasn't awake to see my true death.

And so much had gone wrong because of it.

But I knew now. I'd seen, and when the time was right, I'd see more. I'd see my fifth life as well, just to understand better. Just to say that I knew how things that happened, though they never really did.

Right now, I just needed to keep burning, keep dying until I shed all of my old skin. And when I woke up among the living again, I prayed to all the gods that I'd be ready to fight once more.

～

THE NEXT DAY went by and I still failed at understanding the thoughts in my head. I could tell time, I could tell where I was, I just couldn't tell how to react to the truths revealing themselves around me.

"Not yet," I said to Lucien when he asked if I wanted to talk.

I didn't want to talk—why would I talk when I knew I wouldn't understand anything yet?

I understood the touch of his hands, though. I understood his kisses. I understood the worry in his eyes.

"Just talk to me," he whispered, framing my face with his hands, coming so close his nose touched mine. "Talk to me, baby. Tell me what you saw. We'll figure it out—just talk to me."

"Not yet," I repeated, then wrapped my arms around his neck and pulled him on the bed, right over me.

His kisses were my lifeline. He kept me grounded in this reality when my mind wanted to wander off to others. My limbs locked around him, and he groaned as if he were in pain—because he wouldn't stop me, and he thought he should. Because he couldn't stop kissing me, even when he thought we should *talk* instead. He'd been trying all day—he couldn't. He wanted me too much.

And for now I preyed on that.

His hands were under my loose shirt—one he'd had on that I liked to wear because it smelled like him. It felt like him.

"I'm going to learn how to say *no* to you some day," he told me between kisses, his hand closing around my breast, the other gripping my ass as he thrust his hips against mine. Too many clothes between us still, but his hard cock against my pelvis made me feel light as air. I needed that more than I knew how to say.

"Until then, I'll just keep taking advantage of you," I said breathlessly, sucking his lip inside my mouth hard until he moaned my favorite sound.

I rubbed against him, moving my hips faster by the second until I wanted to rip his clothes off completely.

"So, you admit that you're using me," he said, rising just a bit so I could reach the button of his jeans and push them down.

"Absolutely," I said with a moan when I took his cock in my hands and began to jerk him off.

He laughed, then hissed like my touch burned him, thrusting his hips against my hands desperately.

"As long as you don't misuse me," he finally said because we both knew that he was *never* going to learn how to say no to me, not for this. And he'd already accepted his fate.

"Not too much," I teased, and he rose on his knees to take my clothes off. He pulled my shirt up and my bottoms down so fast, I almost didn't feel them at all.

Then he stayed there, kneeling between my legs and touching my thighs, watching me, growling and moaning like it *pained* him to see me like that, spread wide open for him to do with as he pleased.

"Do you think you would have looked at me like this in my other lives, too, if we'd met before?" I wondered, drinking in the sight of him—the curves of his muscles, of his tattoos, the rough touch of his hand, the color of his eyes...

"How do I look at you?" he whispered, leaning closer to my chest to take my nipple in his mouth.

I moaned, my back arching, my fingers in his hair pulling him to me. "Like...like...you want to eat me," I breathed, watching him playing with my breast, eyes closed, completely intoxicated. "Like...you love me."

He let go of my nipple and looked up at me for a second, and it struck me, that face. The way he *adored* me. The way he looked with my hands in his messy hair and his eyes burning with desire and his lips parted, desperate for the taste of me...

"I do love you, my beautiful fox. And if I've lived a thousand lives, I've loved you in each one of them." He was so sure of that, it was impossible not to believe him.

His tongue flicked over my hard nipple, and he played with it for a bit, all the while looking at me, never breaking eye contact. Then, he ran his tongue down my stomach, to my thighs, biting and kissing them—and just the sound of it brought me close to the edge.

When he thrust his tongue inside me all the way, I fell back on the bed, breathless.

"*Gods,*" I choked, grinding against his face as he licked me and sucked on my clit and fucked me with his tongue.

"You taste like my dreams, baby," he whispered, sliding two fingers inside me, then curling them up. "I think you're made of them."

"Lucien, please," I breathed, moving my hips faster against his hand, feeling his tongue pressing against my clit.

"Use me," he said, and he sounded completely mesmerized. "Keep moving. Use me whichever way you like."

I cried out so hard my throat hurt, and I grabbed his hair again, pushing his face down as I rode it and his fingers until I jumped over the edge.

Impossible how well he played my body. Impossible how freeing it was to be like this with him—and I'd always thought sex was something purely physical, that it could be separated from emotions.

Not this, though. Not with Lucien. It was everything, all of it rolled into every little movement and whisper and moan that went on between us.

He raised on his knees again, and I opened my eyes to see him, a lazy smile on my lips. He looked down at me, completely spent for the moment, still high with the aftermath of the orgasm.

"*Look at you,*" he whispered, grabbing his hard cock in his hand, stroking it as he slowly pulled my thigh to the side.

Look at her, he'd said to John.

I raised my hips, a mess of emotions suddenly taking over me. He ran his free hand up my stomach, then down again, and slipped his fingers inside me as he continued to stroke himself. I'd never seen anything sexier in my lives. And one day soon, when I had some self-control to spare, I would ask him to sit there for me and make himself come as he watched me. I wanted to see that so badly my entire body shook at the thought.

I called out his name, and he took his time, touching me, teasing me with the top of his cock, slipping it down my folds, before...

"Hold on tight," he told me, wrapping his hands around my hips when he positioned himself at my entrance.

Then he pulled me to him and thrust forward with all his strength.

The way he filled me was out of this world.

We fell on the bed, our skins covered in sweat, our bodies moving as one, and he fucked me hard and fast until my eyes rolled in my skull. He had no mercy the way he pounded into me.

My legs were numb by the time he rose again, grabbed me and spun me around. But when I wanted to kneel on all fours, he put his hand on the small of my back and stopped me.

"Don't move," he whispered, breathing just as heavily as me. Then he brought my legs together, put his knees on either side of them. I felt the weight of him on the back of my thighs, and his hands on my ass, massaging, spreading my butt cheeks apart, bringing his cock between them. I closed my eyes, hands tucked underneath me, and I just felt what he was doing to me with my breath held.

"Raise your ass a little bit," Lucien ordered, and I did.

The way he moaned when he brought his cock to my entrance again, then slid all the way inside me, filled my head completely.

There was no gentle with him tonight—he just gripped my ass in his fists and pumped into me until I could no longer even scream. My face was buried in the pillow, and he lowered himself down on my back until he was on top of me. He wrapped his arms all around me, then kissed my ear, my cheek, until I turned my head and gave him my lips, too.

He held me to his chest like that and continued to thrust, his hips bouncing on my ass as he sucked on my tongue.

When he came, he almost squashed me to his chest completely.

His cum was dripping out of me, but he wasn't done. Still breathing heavily, he lowered one hand under me until he reached my throbbing clit.

He made me come again so fast it almost surprised me. But the pressure of his fingers was just right, and he was lying on my back, his skin was flush with mine, and his cock was still inside me, and his cum was dripping out of me...I couldn't hold back if I tried.

I was completely, utterly spent, way too tired to think about anything else but the pleasure that consumed me even now.

Lucien pulled himself off me, running his hands down my back, then gripped my hips and pulled my ass up in the air. I smiled against the pillow—he still couldn't get enough of just looking at me.

"My gods..." He slowly slipped his finger inside of me, and I could feel his cum coming out as he did. "You're going to be the death of me," he whispered—and his face was right there in front of my pussy, and he slowly pumped his finger in and out, unable to look away.

"I literally was," I said—the way my father had slammed onto him, and those flames that had been burning him. He'd have died if I hadn't first. If the world hadn't fallen out of existence.

John, too.

"And it was absolutely worth it," Lucien said, his teeth sinking in my ass suddenly.

I jolted up, laughing, but he pushed me back down on the bed again, and continued to bite every inch of my back until he was satisfied.

By the time he lay down next to me, I was halfway asleep already, knowing he'd still be right there when I woke up.

Twenty-Six

LUCIEN WASN'T THERE WHEN I WOKE UP.

After a quick stop in the bathroom, I went to John's room, knocked and walked in—it was empty. John wasn't in his bed.

It scared me.

The sun had already set. I'd lost the entire day. I was hungry but full of energy from all those naps and from being with Lucien.

I headed for the stairs to go search for him in the kitchen, when I heard the voices coming through the open door of the living room that was at the bottom of the stairway.

Lucien, Rowan and Jack were in the foyer right outside, talking. About *me*. I stopped on the stairs and listened:

"She needs time," Lucien was saying.

"We don't have time," said Jack. "We really don't—you heard John."

"I'll have to agree," said Rowan. His voice, compared to Jack's, was ice-cold. "I'd rather get back home, and I can't do that without a definite plan."

I flinched, closing my eyes for a second.

"I understand that. But none of you are talking to her," Lucien said, his voice growing heavier.

"Lucien, we—" Jack started, but Lucien wouldn't hear it.

"No," he cut him off. "She needs her time and she's going to have it. What you make of it is your business."

A snort—probably Rowan. "Congratulations—you sound just like him."

I flinched again—he meant his father.

They said something else, but my mind was busy, my shoulders heavy with guilt. I loved Lucien more than I did anything in the world, but...

I remembered the feelings that had come over me when John told me it was my father who killed me, not Lucien. I remembered how I'd resented him, how I'd wanted to *hate* him, how I didn't want to even touch him. And it made me sick to my stomach because it felt like it wasn't *me* at all.

It made me feel guilty, too—so guilty I could claw my own heart out and offer it to him and beg him to forgive me.

"I don't care how much time we have," Lucien was saying. "She's not—"

"I'm fine."

Only when I heard my voice did I realize I'd spoken. The men heard.

Footsteps—the door of the living room opened all the way and Lucien walked in, his eyes on me. He wore a grey shirt and faded jeans, string of his dark hair covering his left eye completely. He looked good enough to eat. Or maybe it was just me.

He came up the stairs to me, never breaking eye contact. Rowan and Jack came into the living room, too, but they didn't come closer.

"Hey," Lucien said, grabbing my face in his hands. "You okay?"

"I'm fine," I told him, and the guilt just kept on growing. "I'm sorry, I didn't mean to—"

"Stop," he said, putting his fingers in front of my lips. "Don't apologize."

"I just needed some time off, and—" *I'd taken too long.* I realized it now, and I wished I could take it back, but the whole day was already over.

Gods, the whole day...

"There's nothing to explain either," he told me and kissed my lips. "Nothing at all."

"I'm okay," I promised him, and again—only when I said those words, did I realize they were *true*.

I was okay. My memory worked, and I remembered everything I'd seen, and I was okay with it.

Or at least I knew for a fact that I would be. I trusted myself to handle it when the time was right.

"Are you sure?" he said, searching my face as if he were expecting to find a hint of a lie.

I rose on my tiptoes and kissed him. "I think you brought me back to life with all that fucking," I whispered, and his lips stretched under mine instantly. I was blushing bright scarlet—still shy to talk to him like that, but I wasn't going to let that stop me.

And I loved that he was flushed, too. "Well then, we'd better do a lot more of it every day, just to keep healthy and alive," he said, and I grinned.

"Deal."

"If you two are done being nauseating, I suggest we go talk to John," Rowan called from the bottom of the stairs.

But Lucien kissed me one more time. "Did I ever tell you that I have a very hard time tolerating my little brother?"

I burst out laughing. "I think I had a feeling." But it was just because they were very different and also much the same. "Let's get going. I do want to talk to John."

Finally, we all went to the kitchen together to find John playing chess with his Pops on the dining table.

~

HE LOOKED SO MUCH BETTER than I could have hoped—and his fuller cheeks made him so much like Jack, I wouldn't have been able to tell them apart if they dressed the same and kept their hair the same length. Almost completely identical—just Jack's eyes had a bit more green in them.

Their grandfather had gone to rest, and I'd even eaten some leftover chicken breasts that Jack's cousin had cooked for them, so I felt pretty great physically.

"Thank you," I told John when all of us sat around the table. "For letting me see your memory. I appreciate it."

"You're welcome," John said. "I was afraid that if I tried to explain, I'd do it wrong. I'd miss some things and misinterpret others. It was best if you saw it for yourself."

I nodded. "It...it was an accident." My father *had* killed me, but it had been an accident. I hadn't seen how it happened—John had been in a pretty bad shape, but Father had slammed onto Lucien, who was trying to get away with me, and we'd all been knocked to the ground. My father had had his talons and his wings out, so he must have cut my neck at some point. All that blood...and the way he'd tried to stop the bleeding, the way he'd roared at the skies...

"It's always an accident. Even when *I* died—it was just an accident. Imagine it—Jack shot me in the head."

"What the—" Jack jumped to his feet so fast, the chair fell to the floor.

John laughed, and gods, he looked more and more like his brother by the second. "Calm down, it's not like I didn't come back."

"You lying piece of shit—stop lying," Jack said, pointing

his finger at his brother. "I do hate your guts, but I would never shoot you."

"It was an accident—sit down," John said. "We were still outside of the manor that morning when you shot me. You were merely checking your gun and you must have pulled the trigger. You shot me right in the temple. I died on the spot."

"You're joking," I breathed, shaking my head.

"Yep. All those years gone, just like that. Everything was reset," John said.

"Liar. You're a damn liar," Jack insisted, then grabbed the chair and sat down again. "I know how to handle a damn gun."

"*Accident,* my brother. You didn't train in that life. You weren't the king's guard in that life. Just an accident, but I think it was meant to be. If I hadn't died, I wouldn't have remembered anything right now," John said, looking at me. "I wouldn't have been able to let you see."

I swallowed hard, looking down at Lucien's hand on mine. "I did see plenty. I also heard thoughts in your head, and I have questions."

John nodded. "I imagined you would."

"What thoughts?" Rowan asked, looking a bit curious for a moment. "*His* thoughts?" And he pointed at John.

"Yes. I could tell they were his—it was his voice." I looked at John again. "You said...you said *he'd* promised that my father wouldn't be able to shift. That you'd be safe from the dragon." John's eyes closed for a moment. "Was that...the Ether?"

I'd read an entry by Alexandra once—she'd claimed the Ether had the power to null our shifting. Every morning that I died I could never shift. My husbands, either, and now that I'd seen the whole thing from John's eyes, I knew that even my father shouldn't have been able to shift.

"Yes," John said reluctantly. I wasn't surprised at all. John had definitely seen the Ether.

Twenty-Seven

"You've seen him," Rowan said, looking at John now as if he were an alien. A very curious alien.

"I've merely spoken to him," John said. "He's come to me in my dreams in the past." He looked at me. "The same way you have."

I'd had no idea I'd gone to him—I always assumed that he came to mine. Willingly. Like he *chose* to.

Which, now that I thought about it, was ridiculous.

"What did he say to you?"

Did he have all the answers we were looking for? Was he *the answer* to a better world?

"He said that we needed you, that we could never defeat the king without you," John said, and my stomach rolled and rolled... "He said that as long as Archibald Azarius is alive, there would never be balance among the elements." My eyes closed, and I willed the tears away. "He said that he could grant us a moment, just a couple of hours where nobody, not even him, would be able to shift, just until we got you out of that manor."

"Except, he did." My father hadn't shifted all the way, but

he had shifted halfway. He'd had talons, and in the end, when he saw Lucien trying to run away with me, his wings had burst out his back, too.

John nodded. "He's stronger than the Ether anticipated, I think," John said.

"You said, *in the past*," Lucien said. "You said he came to your dreams in the past."

"In the lives I remember, yes."

"Not *this* life?" I asked, and John shook his head.

"No, not in this life. At least not yet."

I was only twenty now. I still had another two years to live before my end—if my past lives were anything to go by.

"So, the king has to die," Jack said, and his voice was like a knife right through my neck.

"You're only just figuring that out now?" Rowan mocked.

"Rowan," Lucien warned, but it was fine. I didn't take it personally.

"If I'd known..." Jack whispered. "I was his guard for three years. I could've..."

His eyes met mine as if he just remembered who I was. He turned pale as a sheet, and I'd never hated anyone so suddenly.

"You could've what?" I asked, though I knew the answer.

And I didn't understand why I became so defensive—it was my father. I knew he was a bad man. I knew that very well. But there was something inside me, a stranger, a force that rose from deep within that demanded I react—and it sounded an awful lot like my dragoness.

"He doesn't have to necessarily die," John said, before Jack could make up his mind to speak. "But he can no longer be a king."

"And he won't be," I told him. "He won't be king."

But they were *not* going to kill my father.

At least...not yet. Not until we saw the whole picture.

"He tried to kill my brother when he was thirteen years

old," Jack said, and it was all I could do not to throw something at his face.

"That was his soldiers—it wasn't the king himself," said John reluctantly. But my father's soldiers did his deeds—so it *was* the king. John could just tell by the look on my face that...*what,* exactly?

I didn't want to hear it?

I didn't want to admit it to myself?

That I was too much of a fool to believe it?

"You've killed people, too," I told Jack despite my better judgment, and my poor heart paid the price.

I didn't want to be mean, not to Jack. He was my friend. And the way he looked at me...

"We all have," Lucien said before he could answer, but if he only knew...

If he knew that Jack had helped my father kill his, what would he think?

My own mind was turning into my worst enemy.

"Regardless of the past," Lucien continued, squeezing my fingers, and I was thankful for the distraction. Thankful that I was reminded of who I was—not this bitter person who turned on her friends. It wasn't my place to tell Lucien—and Rowan—anything about that. It was Jack's business. I could trust him to handle it the way he thought was best.

"And what about *her*?" I said, breathing in deeply, trying to hold myself together. "In the memory, you said to Lucien, *we have to go before she can't keep the king back any longer.* Who were you talking about?"

Even though I hadn't seen anybody else alive at the manor that morning, I thought I had a good idea of who he'd meant.

"The wyrm," John said, and I let go of a sigh.

"She exists?" Lucien asked, not entirely convinced yet. "She really, really exists?"

"Oh, she does. If we all hadn't been here, the Ether

wouldn't have had the power to even speak to me in my dreams or null anyone in that manor from shifting when we went for Ella," John said, grabbing a small black horse figure from the chess board at the corner of the table to play with it.

"So, who is she?" Rowan asked, and he looked like he was actually believing what he heard. He'd been skeptical until now.

"I don't know," John said. "I don't remember her face or her name, just her eyes—blue. I didn't remember Lucien's face or name, either, until I saw him. Just Estella."

"I tried to do the trick—the Water trick you told me to do in that dream. It didn't work," I said, and John flinched.

"It would work—it works for the draca when it is done by us. That is how I found her in the past lives that I remember. That is how I found Lucien as well—though with plenty of difficulty," John said, then grabbed the edge of the table and stood up.

Jack stood with him. "Whoa, take it easy..."

"It's fine. I just want to get a glass of water. I can do it myself," John insisted, thought he could still barely walk. The cabinets were behind him, barely four feet away, though, so he managed, limping and going slowly. His legs were so thin compared to his upper body.

"Maybe it works for *you*? Because it wasn't doing anything for me. Or maybe..." I shrugged. "Maybe I did it wrong."

John grabbed a glass from the sink and filled it in the faucet—just a bit. Then he opened a cupboard and grabbed an empty plate, too.

"Yeah, that's how I did it, too," I said reluctantly.

Jack was at the ready to grab his brother if he fell while he came back to the table. He moved slowly, but he made it back with the glass of water and the plate intact, then sat down on the chair, smiling proudly. I would imagine this was a huge deal for him, and it spoke a lot about his character that he refused help.

"Our energy is different from that of other shifters. We both release and attract it differently. That's why I always got the old tricks to work for me—back in the old days, they used to work for everyone because everyone had energy to spare." Slowly, he poured the water on the plate, then put the glass in the middle, upside down just like I'd done all those times. "I found Lucien like this in just a few weeks, and the wyrm in a day." He put his hand over the bottom of the glass and closed his eyes. The drop of water rose inside the glass the exact same way, too.

Except when he pulled the glass aside, and the water hovered over his palm, it began to vibrate west.

My mouth opened and closed a couple of times.

"Mine *never* did that!" The drops of water had never moved for me, not a single time. "It always just stayed right there in the middle of my palm."

"Impossible," John said. "You're not Water."

"I'm telling you—it *never* moved! It always stayed right in its place." I would have remembered—I looked closely. I tried it so many times...

But then John met my eyes as the drop of water kept on trying to move west, but it hit some invisible wall that outlined John's hand.

"Where were you when you did it?" he asked me.

"Ohio. I did it in my aunt's house like a hundred times, and then again on the road to Vermont—two different places." When we stopped for gas, and then when we slept by the lake, too. That was the last time I tried.

John closed his fist around the hovering drop of water and lowered his hand before he said...

"Who were you with, Ella?"

Every single hair on my body stood at attention.

I couldn't find enough air to fill my lungs for a long moment. The entire world fell on my shoulders, and I didn't even see anything around me anymore...

"Mikhaila."

My eyes closed and a rush of tears came over me all of a sudden. It was all I could do not to throw up the bile that was rising in my throat.

Mikhaila.

My gods, she'd been right there with me...

"Mikhaila," John whispered, and when I opened my eyes, he was smiling, his eyes gleaming.

"Who the hell's Mikhaila?" asked Jack, and Lucien tugged at my hand.

"Little fox?"

I shook my head, still unable to believe my own thoughts. "I think she might be the wyrm."

Twenty-Eight

"You're joking," Jack said after I told them the story. "You were *with* her the whole time?!"

I nodded. "I met her at my aunt's place. She was sick. She could barely stand most of the time."

"Why?" Lucien said. "Was she wounded—like Jack?"

"No—my aunt said she had no idea what was wrong with her, she was just feverish, slept a lot, and was very pale." I remembered her—her blueish green eyes and her sick-looking skin. The way she always collapsed whenever she was up for too long... "Gods, she wasn't well at all," I whispered.

"It could be shifting pains. I remember they were bad at first," John said in wonder, shaking his head. I had no clue if he was right. I couldn't remember shifting pains from my other lives.

"I'm not sure if she's mated, though. All she said was that she's a tiger." And I hadn't even suspected anything.

"She doesn't know," Lucien said. "She probably has no idea."

John nodded. "She hasn't tried to shift. Or she has, but it

didn't work because she would need to be in water to shift—*if* she really is the wyrm."

Gods—and we'd been right by the lake! We'd slept there, too. I shook my head. "I don't know. No clue if she's mated, if she ever tried to shift. We never talked about any of that." Of course not—my mind was elsewhere. I was being ripped apart by the knowledge of who my mother had been, who my aunt was.

"Where is she now? Do you know?" John asked.

"She was going back to her ex-boyfriend to kick his ass and return his truck. He lives in Springfield—that's where she dropped me off at the bus station."

"Shit," Jack muttered.

"Did she say where she was going next?" Lucien asked.

I shook my head. "No. She said she didn't have a family. She had parents but she'd..." I closed my eyes, breathing deeply. How did I not see it? "She said she'd had to fake her own death at eleven years old to save her parents. Probably..." Probably from my father.

"Could be," John said. "That's how the king found me— the tricks. He must have done it for Water, too. And Air." He looked at Lucien.

"I live in possibly the most well protected town in the world. Aither is foolproof," Lucien said. "He couldn't have found me with a simple Air trick. It's a lot more magic that I've put around this place right now."

John nodded. "That's probably why I could never find you until you came out of the border. I was searching nonstop, every single hour of every day," he said in wonder, then shook his head. "We have to find the wyrm. Before we summon the Ether—we have to bring her here."

"We can go back to Springfield, see if maybe the Water will lead us to where she went next," I said.

"We can," Lucien said. "We will."

"It's too risky for us to go out there right now," John said. "The king is looking for us. Your magic and Jack's shields are the only thing keeping us invisible, and we have to keep it that way." And he turned to Rowan. "Maybe—"

"No." The word that left Rowan's mouth was so definite.

A second of silence followed.

"Rowan," Lucien said, but he shook his head.

"I am not your errand boy. I will not go looking for strangers—"

"I'll come with you," I said, and Lucien almost broke my fingers from how tightly he squeezed.

"You're safer here, Estella."

"No, *you're* safer here because if my father finds you, he'll kill you. If he finds me..." I looked at John.

My father *had* killed me in my past lives, maybe even in *all* of them, but they'd been accidents. He wouldn't kill me intentionally, would he?

"Absolutely not," Lucien said.

"It makes sense, actually. She knows you, right?" John said.

"She does," I said. I'd go so far as to say we were *friends* even.

"She could be persuaded by you to come talk to us, I assume."

I flinched. "I think so." Though I wasn't really sure. From what little I knew about Mikhaila, she could be pretty stubborn.

"Then I'm going with," said Lucien, but while Rowan rolled his eyes, he said nothing.

"No. If you leave, not only are *you* in danger, but Jack and John, too. They'll be unprotected—you said so yourself," I reminded him, and his jaws clenched hard.

"I am not letting you out of my sight," he said.

"I'll be with Rowan," I said. "We did just fine on our way

here, right? It's just Springfield. We'll get there and back in no time."

"Rowan can stay here with all of you then, and *I* can go search for her myself," Lucien insisted, and I loved him for it, but I also wanted to smack him upside the head for being so stubborn.

"You can't. I don't know how to keep anyone safe, and Mikhaila knows me. If you show up and tell her she's a wyrm, she's going to laugh in your face, and it won't be easy to kidnap her and bring her all the way here. But if I talk to her, there's a chance she'll believe me." Hopefully. Or maybe just because she wouldn't have a place to go...

"Rowan, what do you say?" said John, looking at Rowan, who had eyes only for me.

"C'mon, Rowan. It wasn't a bad ride, was it?" I said, forcing myself to smile. "It's just to Springfield and back." Though I had no clue how far Springfield was from here...

"On one condition," he said. "I bring you back, and I leave here." He turned to Lucien. "I leave right away."

Lucien's jaws clenched so tightly we all heard them. He looked at his brother as if he wanted to murder him on the spot.

I squeezed his fingers, trying to get his attention. We needed this. If Mikhaila was really the wyrm and she was here, we'd have no use for anyone else.

"Have it your way, brother," Lucien said. "I always knew you were a coward, anyway."

"Lucien," I whispered, but Rowan laughed.

"Coward? Oh, please. You think I'm going to keep fighting *his* fight for the rest of my life—like you?" He shook his head, and I knew he meant their father. "No, I am not going to sit around here and obey *your* orders, too."

He stood up. So did Lucien. So did I.

"Guys, please..."

"I am your older brother, your family," Lucien spit.

"You're just like Michael, for fucks' sake!" Rowan said. "I could do nothing against *him,* but *you?* You didn't raise me, Lucien. And I have a life to live."

The look in his eyes was murderous when he walked around the table and out the door.

I could tell that Lucien wanted to say something else, but he controlled himself and I was thankful. I didn't want them to fight right now.

Gods, I didn't want them to fight *ever.* They were brothers. They were all each other had—they could be so much better than this.

"It's okay," I whispered, pulling at his arm to get him to sit down, and by some miracle, he did.

He sat down and he continued to play with my fingers, even though he was pale as a sheet.

"I, for one, don't blame him," John said. "Who would want to be in our shoes, anyway?"

Nobody.

But at least none of us were alone anymore.

TWENTY-NINE

WE STAYED AT THE KITCHEN TABLE FOR A LITTLE
while longer, planning. As much as I yearned to release my
Fire and my dragoness, we decided that it was better if Lucien
and I didn't mate until I got back because my father would be
able to feel my dragoness clearly. He'd be able to find me in no
time while I was away. It was for the best, but that didn't mean
I liked it. Lucky for us, Springfield was only about two hours
away, so I was set to leave at three in the morning, hoping to be
back just after dawn.

Assuming I even found Mikhaila in the city, and she
agreed to come with me right away.

I was calm, though. Despite everything, I was perfectly
calm when we left the kitchen, but I didn't want to lie
down yet.

"Come outside with me," I whispered to Lucien, and he
still wasn't himself after what happened with Rowan, so he
eagerly accepted the chance for fresh air.

It was after ten p.m., and everybody in the small town was
already inside. The night was perfectly quiet, the air motionless, and the moon...

The full moon in the sky made everything better, just like that.

"Walk with me," I told Lucien, and he said nothing but let me guide him all around the houses.

I'd seen some of the townswomen sitting near a large willow tree during the day, sewing and having tea. I was hoping the old folding chairs were there still—and they were. Four of them were around the tree, and from there, the moon looked magnificent.

"Let's sit over there," I said, and again, he didn't hesitate. It helped him just to be outside with the cool air, I thought.

Ahead, we had the small mountain with the playground to our right, and the back of the town's houses was on our left, the small woods just behind them.

"Will you wait for me for just a second?"

Surprised, he sat up straight. "Why? Where are you going?"

"Back to the house. I'll be right out," I promised him, then gave him a quick kiss.

"Little fox," he called, but I was already rushing toward the house.

"I'll be right there! Don't go anywhere!"

There was a very good chance that this would backfire, but I had to try it anyway. Rowan was everything Lucien had—him and his sisters. If they could have a decent relationship, like Jack and John seemed to have, it would make both their lives easier. Better. So that's why I went back to the silent house, through the first floor and to the rooms at the other end where Rowan and Lucien's men were sleeping. Jack must have already taken John upstairs because all the lights were off in the kitchen and living room.

Taking in a deep breath, I knocked on Rowan's door.

A second later, he was in front of me, the sleeves of his shirt folded up, his hair still wet from the shower. The way he looked at me, you'd think he was shocked that I even dared to exist right now.

"I, erm..." I started, clearing my throat. "Something happened and I need you to come with me."

He narrowed his brows. "Find Lucien—I'm sure he'll want to help." And he was going to close the door on my face.

I put my foot forward and stopped him. The door bounced back on my sneaker. "It's just for a second, okay? It's important. *Very* important."

"For fuck's sake," he whispered, rubbing his face.

I grinned. "I'm not going to take no for an answer, so just...follow me."

Safe to say I was his least favorite person in the world tonight, but he still followed me outside the house, muttering under his breath things I didn't even want to know. Just as long as he kept walking.

I took him around the houses and to the willow tree—to Lucien sitting on the folding chair all by himself. He turned when he heard us approaching, and though I couldn't see his face clearly from the dark, I knew he was *shocked* to see Rowan behind me. He stood up instantly.

"What the hell is this?" Rowan said, more shocked than his brother, and he stopped ten feet away.

"We're watching the moon tonight," I told them, my voice shaking a little bit. Gods, I was so nervous so suddenly my palms were sweaty. "You, um...you don't even have to talk. We'll just sit there and think for a little while, and then we can go to bed."

Lucien looked at me like he couldn't decide whether to start shouting or burst into tears. I waited, heart in my throat, almost regretting the whole thing, but...

Seconds later, he fell back on the chair and turned his eyes to the sky again without a word.

And Rowan...

He was smiling, shaking his head, his wet hair glistening blue under the silver moon.

"Rowan, please," I said, waving for the chairs, but he took a step back instead.

"No, thanks. I'm good," he said bitterly.

"Rowan, come on!" I grabbed him by the arm. "Please, sit down. Just for a minute."

I don't know what he saw in my face, but I saw raw *pain* in his. My heart tripped all over itself. So much more about him that I didn't know.

"Please," I repeated, putting my whole heart into that word, sure that it wouldn't work. Rowan didn't seem like the type to be persuaded by pleading.

But by some miracle, he was. With a loud sigh, he lowered his shaking head as if in surrender, then walked around me, pissed as all hell, and went and sat on the chair farthest away from Lucien.

Good enough for me.

Stifling a smile, I sat next to Lucien and grabbed his hand, brought it to my lap. He didn't look at me at all, only slipped his hand between my thighs and squeezed a little bit, his eyes on the sky.

Meanwhile Rowan had his head back and his eyes closed, the light of the moon falling on his face. Like that, he looked unreal, a marble statue made by the hands of an incredibly skilled artist, not a man.

They hadn't started arguing yet. That had to be a good sign.

I rested my head on Lucien's shoulder and breathed deeply. I don't know why, but I hadn't felt more *whole*, more at peace, since my own mother was alive. Because right now, sitting with them in the dark, the air slightly cold, the silence perfectly comfortable, I felt like I was sitting with *their* mother, too. I felt like she was right there with us.

And I prayed to all gods that the boys felt it, too. That this moment made them feel closer to her.

"Would you mind a little company?"

We all turned toward the houses, to Jack holding John by the arm as they came to us slowly.

I shook my head, smiling. "I thought you two were in bed."

"We were curious to see what you were up to," Jack said.

"Of course," Lucien said. "Come and join us."

Jack helped John to sit on the last free chair, and then he sat on the ground and rested his back against his legs. They all turned their eyes to the sky, and even Rowan had his open now. He looked so much calmer already, though he refused to say a word.

"So, we're just going to sit here and stare at the sky now?" Jack said, making me chuckle.

"What could possibly be better?" said John, and he sounded completely in awe of the world around him. I imagined I would be, too, if I'd been asleep for the past six years.

I kissed Lucien's cheek and rested my head on his shoulder again.

We stayed like that for a long time.

THIRTY

I KEPT EXPECTING HIM TO STOP ME. I KEPT expecting him to say something—that it was a bad idea, that my father would find me, that he wouldn't let me go on my own, that either he came with or nobody went at all.

But Lucien knew exactly how important this was—sometimes, I thought, he knew it better than me, even if he didn't remember our past lives. He'd been preparing for this ever since he was a boy.

And he was *not* my Angel of Death. He had never killed me. He'd simply wanted to turn me against my father—before it was too late, before I became queen.

He had never killed me.

"I'll be okay," I promised him for the twentieth time. The truck was ready—Ezrail would drive, and Rowan and I would stay in the back until we arrived in Springfield. The sun wouldn't rise for another two hours, so the darkness would cover us. Everything was as we'd planned.

"I know," Lucien said. "I still want to be there with you."

I grabbed his face in my hands, rose on my tiptoes and

kissed him. "I'll be back before you know it. It's just a few hours."

His arms wrapped around my waist and he slammed me to his chest hard. "Be careful, little fox. There's only so much I can do to keep the monster on the inside."

I smiled, running my fingers through the ends of his hair. "Your animal is not a monster." It was a beautiful silvery white wyvern with wings and gorgeous eyes—*not* a monster.

"But *I* will be if you're not back in time..."

"Stay put," I said and kissed him again. "Don't do anything you'll regret later, okay? Just wait for us to get back."

But even so, I knew he'd be counting down the minutes.

Jack and John were there, too, with William and Riad, watching us. Rowan pulled the small metal stairs to the side of the truck out and we climbed in. I walked deeper into the trunk backward, eyes on Lucien, trying to smile for his sake.

"Be careful," John said, waving his hand—he could already stand much straighter on his feet.

I nodded to say that I would. I'd do my best to be back here—with Mikhaila—long before noon.

Rowan raised his hands and pulled the back doors of the truck closed with his magic, drenching us in darkness before the small blue lamps at the corners buzzed to life. I could no longer see Lucien.

The bad feeling in my gut was automatic.

"There, now, don't look so sad," Rowan said, and it was the first time he'd spoken to me since last night. He'd watched the moon with us for a while, and he'd been the first to go back inside.

Jack and John had left, too. Lucien and I stayed until almost midnight.

"I'm not sad," I said and went to sit at the end of the truck, in my small space under the beer cases.

I doubted they really helped—only Rowan's magic that

was slowly infusing the air would keep me invisible to my father.

Then again, I'd had my doubts about that, too, but it had worked perfectly on my way here from Aither.

"You wear your emotions all over your face, Princess," Rowan said as he came to sit down against the aluminum wall that separated the driver's cabin, just like last time.

For a moment, a strong sense of deja-vu took my breath away.

We'd been in this very place, Rowan and I, just a few days ago, but so much had changed since then. *Everything* had changed since then. And I had yet to confront all that I wanted to feel from everything I saw in John's memory.

"I've had to wear an artora my whole life," I told Rowan, watching him put down the empty plate, the small bottle of water and the glass he'd brought with for the Water trick. "I never really had to keep my face expressionless."

"Must have been difficult to grow up like that," he said. "In all that luxury, with servants and cooks and all those designer clothes..."

The instinct to tell him that he had no clue about how I grew up took over, blinding me for a moment, but I bit my tongue. Rowan was teasing me—he just wanted to fire me up. I was starting to think that this was his version of *fun,* and I played along.

"Mhmm. And the fancy cars, the horses, all those shoes and purses..." I said with a sigh.

"Did you have people clip your nails for you?"

"Oh, yes—separate crews for my manicure and pedicure. A person to comb my hair. One to trim each one of my brows...you know how it goes. It was a pretty tough life."

Through the corner of my eye, I could see him grinning. "So surprised you survived with a such a humble attitude."

"Believe me, it wasn't easy," I said, barely holding back a laugh.

"Did you use to do pointless things then, too?" he then said. "Like sit outside in the dark and stare at nothing?"

I flinched. "Never."

"Good for you," he said.

I knew he was being sarcastic, and I got the strange way he said things. I was pretty sure that he was trying to tell me that he enjoyed last night, but I also wanted to hear it in plain English.

"You left him alone. He let you down. You're still family," I said, expecting him to lash out, but I was going to say what was on my mind anyway. Now—before I chickened out.

Yeah, Rowan left. And, yeah, Lucien was too much like their father for his taste, but that didn't mean they were strangers.

"As if that means anything at this point," he said, but he turned his head to the other side.

"It means you're the first person he calls to watch after his home, to take care of the people he loves," I said. "It means you'll do things for him you'd never do for anyone else, even though you hate it."

The silence that followed made me think I might be deaf. I couldn't even hear him breathing, and I thought that was the end of it, but...

"He changed," Rowan whispered. "He changed so much when Mom died. He shut me out. I tried."

"And then you stopped."

At that, he turned to me. "What the hell else was I supposed to do?!" And he accused me.

I shook my head. "I don't know, I've never had siblings. But maybe you could have kept trying? Not all the time, but maybe once in a blue moon. Or maybe you could have *forced* him to not shut you out anymore?"

He burst out laughing. "You have no clue who you're talking about—there's no forcing my brother to do anything. Only my father could ever do that."

"Please don't think I'm blaming you," I said, shaking my head, because I got the feeling he was growing colder on me. "I'm not, Rowan. It's both your faults. It always takes two." I always knew that...in theory.

He sucked in a deep breath, his laughter echoing in my ears still. "It takes two," he repeated. "So, what did *you* do?"

I turned to him. "What do you mean?"

"With your father, Princess. How did *you* fuck up so much that you end up conspiring to kill him and take over his reign?"

If he'd have slapped me and stabbed me and burned me to a crisp, it would have been less shocking. Less hurtful.

Tears spilled from my eyes as if a button had been pushed. My throat tightened—I couldn't speak.

"I would imagine it takes a lot to end up in your position," Rowan continued.

"*Stop,*" I whispered, but he pretended not to hear me.

"I am very curious, though," he said. "If it takes two, what did you do to get here? Because fathers do what fathers do— that I understand." And he looked at me. "How did *you* let it get to this?"

He didn't listen, I wanted to say.

I tried.

He didn't care.

He never listened!

But my tongue was tied, and I couldn't speak. And I broke so much I could hardly breathe.

The guilt, my oldest nemesis. It came forth grinning like it had waited lifetimes for this moment. It had waited lifetimes to tell me that *it* was behind all of this madness. Because deep down...deep, *deep* down, the question I'd always ignored was still there: had I done all that I could have done? My father was a difficult man to speak to. I'd always known that. But hadn't he always told me that he didn't know how to speak to me, either?

"Estella, I didn't mean to—" Rowan said after a while.

"I resented him," I said, and my own voice surprised me. I looked at Rowan, at his wide eyes, the *sorry* written all over them—he hadn't expected me to break the way I did at his questions. He thought I could handle it.

I'd thought so, too.

"I saw him with my eyes and didn't care to look deeper. I hated him the most because I thought he didn't care about my mother." I thought he didn't care about *me*, either. "He put his work before me. He never knew how to talk to me. We're..." Oh, gods, I was going to die... "We're too much alike."

So little air in the truck.

"He was always the bad guy in my story. In my head." I had no idea how I kept talking, but those words were determined to come out of me. They'd waited lifetimes, and now that the dam was broken, they refused to stop. "I never knew who he was as a man—I just knew him as the villain. I never saw his pain, his regrets, his complete cluelessness in speaking to me as a kid, as a teenager, as a *woman,* and not the future queen who would take over his kingdom when he was gone..." I wiped my tears but more kept coming. "I didn't really want to, because..."

"You resented him," Rowan repeated, and I nodded.

It came down to that. It always came down to that.

"And you still wanted his approval more than anything in the world," Rowan said, and I nodded.

"And you still cared, and you hated yourself for it," Rowan said, and I nodded. Again and again and again.

"You just wanted him to see you. To understand."

Pieces of me all over the truck's floor, mixed in with pieces of him.

Rowan smiled and reached out his hand to touch my shoulder. "And that is why we watch the moon."

I turned to him. "To take a break?" From all those bad feelings, from all that misery...

But he shook his head. "To remind ourselves that there can be light in the deepest darkness—and usually, that's the most beautiful light of all."

I laughed though I was crying. "Thanks for that." I'd needed it, even though I had no idea.

"Thank *you*," he told me. "For reminding me of that last night."

"A day," I said, wiping my face—enough crying for today. Gods, *more* than enough.

"What?" he asked, brow narrowed.

"Give me one day. When we get back, don't leave right away. Just one day." I swallowed hard. "One more try."

He smiled. "And if it doesn't work?"

I shrugged. "We'll still have the moon every night."

He laughed, too. "Only because I like you," he said. "I hardly believe it myself—it's a matter of *despising* everything my brother likes. Always has been," he admitted, and I loved him a little bit for it. I laughed again.

"That's okay, though. He *loves* me, so you're safe."

He shook his head, smiling like he couldn't believe he was agreeing to this. "One day, Princess."

"One day." And I prayed with all my heart that by the end of it, they would both be a little less alone.

THIRTY-ONE

The sun had turned the sky a light grey, preparing to rise. We'd arrived faster than we expected.

And by the looks of the empty street where Ezrail parked the truck, we hadn't been followed.

"This is it," I said to Rowan, showing him the drop of water hovering over my palm. I'd done the Water trick—for the fourth time now, while Rowan instructed Ezrail by phone which turns to take.

This is where it stopped moving to the sides and just floated peacefully over my palm, like it used to when I was with Mikhaila.

I had yet to believe that this actually worked, though.

"She could be in any of these houses," Rowan said, raising his arms to the sides of the wide street—and he was right. On the left, two-story houses lined the sidewalk, and on the right, there were even a couple of apartment buildings.

Could any of these places be where Mikhaila's ex-boyfriend lived? I regretted not asking her for a specific address now.

"Let's just keep walking. We'll take this with," I said, holding the plate and the glass in my hand.

"Not very smart to be out in the open for long," Rowan said, and I could tell that he was nervous, but he followed me. So did Ezrail.

"We'll find her. She has to be here somewhere," I said, only pretending to believe in my own words.

The more we walked down the wide street, the lighter the sky, and the clearer we saw. I had no idea how big of an area that drop of water showed, but I was starting to think we'd have to go knocking on each one of those doors to find her, and that took time.

Time we didn't have.

My eyes constantly moved to the sky as if I really expected to find my father's dragon flying up there, watching me, which was ridiculous. If he were anywhere around me, I'd have known already. He wouldn't have cared about not being seen by other people.

"I think we should get back to the truck," Rowan said when we reached the end of the road. My hope fell in pieces to the ground. "It's not safe out here. I can't keep us shielded in the open so easily."

"You're right," I said, turning to look at the wide street one more time—two men walked side by side to the left, but they were the only ones out, and they weren't paying us any attention. Mikhaila was nowhere to be seen. "You're right, let's go," I said, and turned around, but...

Something about red.

Something about a rusty red truck parked on the street, right around the corner.

I froze, my eyes glued to the asphalt before I squeezed them shut for a moment.

"Ella?" Rowan said, but I didn't respond.

Please, please, please let it be real and not my imagination...

I turned, and a red truck was parked by the sidewalk on the other side of the street corner indeed, barely twenty feet away from me. And it was a red truck I knew well.

"Please hold this," I said to Rowan breathlessly, and put the plate and the glass in his hands before I started running.

It felt like hours before I was close enough to the truck to confirm to myself that it really was the same one Mikhaila and I had slept in. That it was the same cargo bed, the same navy blanket we'd been covered in near the lake, and...

Mikhaila was still in the back, sleeping.

Burning up. Grunting in pain.

We'd found her.

"By the Wind," Rowan said, stopping beside me near the truck. Tears in my eyes—another set of happy ones.

Mikhaila was right there, lying on her side in the cargo bed, clutching the thin navy-colored blanket tightly under her chin, brows narrowed and skin a sickening yellow hue, her curly hair as wild as always...

"That's her," I whispered, hoping that this wasn't just a dream. Praying I was really here.

Easy. Too easy—and I was so used to everything being *hard*.

"She's burning up," Ezrail said, reaching to touch Mikhaila's cheek, then flinching.

"She's just sick," I told them, then hopped on the cargo bed. Gods, she really was feverish—just like that night by the lake. She wore new clothes, but her skin was just the same, her big lips almost blue. "Mikhaila," I said, pushing the cover down just a bit with shaking hands. "Mikhaila, wake up."

She didn't.

Groaning still, she turned her head from one side to the other, and it was deja-vu all over again.

"Mikhaila..." I slapped her cheek lightly—gods, she was so warm. "Mikhaila, wake up!"

"We don't have time for this, Princess," Rowan spit, then jumped onto the bed. "Step aside. I'll carry her to the truck."

"But—"

"I can't keep any of you undetected for much longer—I am *not* my brother," he spit. "Step aside."

I did. Jumping off the bed, I gave him enough room to grab Mikhaila's body and pull her up. He carried her and jumped to the sidewalk like she weighed nothing, and then he started rushing back around the street corner to the white truck.

She was here. We'd gotten her—she was really here—why was that so hard to believe? As sick as always, but she hadn't changed one bit. It was Mikhaila, and when she woke up, I'd explain everything to her. It wasn't right to take her like that without her consent, but when she woke up, if she wanted to leave, then...

Then *what*? I would just let her walk away?

I would, I thought. I absolutely would—I'd been a prisoner once. And even though things worked out for Lucien and me, I would never do that to anyone else.

Except...

"They're here."

Ezrail's voice turned the blood in my veins to stone. We were already at the truck, the back doors open, and I was helping Rowan climb the tiny stairs to the back, and I spun around to look at the end of the street—right where we'd been just minutes ago.

I saw the three men, dressed in their silver armors, bows and arrows in their hands as they slowly walked to us.

It wasn't Trevor, but he'd be close. He'd be *really* close.

And my father wouldn't be far behind, either.

～

EZRAIL DROVE LIKE A LUNATIC. The beer bottles on the cases all around us sounded like they were about to break every time the truck took an unexpected turn or rode fast over a bump. I was with Mikhaila in the back, holding her to my chest, calling for her to wake up, while Rowan and Ezrail were in the driver's cabin. We'd gotten in as fast as we could once we saw my father's soldiers, but how far could we really make it before they caught up with us?

"Please, wake up," I said, slapping Mikhaila's cheek. She wasn't grunting in pain anymore—she was just sleeping. "Wake up, damn it. I don't need your blood on my hands, too!"

If she died here because she was unconscious and we'd basically kidnapped her, how was I ever going to sleep again?

"What the hell..."

My heart stopped beating altogether as I looked at her face and saw her eyes—half open.

"Mikhaila!" She was awake. My gods, she was awake.

"Ella? That you, or am I dreaming?" she mumbled, raising her hands to touch my face.

And I let her, laughing. "No, not a dream. But I really need you to wake up now, okay? Just...just wake up. I'll explain everything when you do."

She did. It took her a while, but she blinked her eyes and focused on my face, and her brows narrowed in confusion—until Ezrail turned left fast, and almost slammed us both against the aluminum wall.

"What the hell?!" she shouted, sitting up, looking around us. "What the hell is happening? Where am I? What—"

"You're in the back of a truck," I told her, rising to my knees. "You're okay, I promise. I took you."

"You *took* me?!" she shrieked. "What the hell does that mean—how did you *take* me?"

"I carried you, okay? I found you sleeping on the bed of

your truck, and I tried to wake you up, but you wouldn't, and I carried you—"

"Bullshit—you're tiny. You could never carry *me!*" she hissed. "What the hell is happening, Ella?!"

Ezrail hit the brakes so hard, we both slid on the floor and slammed against the aluminum wall this time.

"Listen to me, Mikhaila," I said, the fear shaking every inch of my body. "I need you to calm down, okay? I'll explain everything once we're safe, but right now, I just need you to listen to what I say."

She shook her head, already scared out of her mind. "What do you mean, *safe*? Why wouldn't I be safe? What—"

The truck doors opened with a loud groan and both of us jumped to our feet.

We saw the highway we'd been driving on, the cars in the distance. Nobody came to talk to us—not Rowan, not Ezrail.

And I knew why.

Rowan had opened the doors with his magic to tell us to get out.

"We have to go," I said to Mikhaila. *"Now."*

"Wait, hold on, just—"

I grabbed her hand and ran. "I'll explain everything later," I said, heart in my throat. "Just *run!*"

And I pulled her to jump off the truck and onto the ground with me.

By some miracle, neither of us lost balance, and we immediately saw why we'd stopped.

"*Who the hell are they*?!" Mikhaila shouted when we moved to the right of the truck and saw Rowan looking ahead and Ezrail already taking his shirt off.

We were at the edge of a large bridge with eight lanes, what must have been the Connecticut River underneath us and large trees on either side of it that would have been perfect for hiding if we could just get to them. There were cars coming and going, but the two large SUVs parked at the end of the bridge, and the nine soldiers that had formed a line twenty feet away from us, didn't really care about them.

Neither did we.

"Ella," Rowan called, turning his head to me for just a moment. He saw Mikhaila and was almost surprised to find her standing. "I need you to go back. Hide. Wait for me to find you."

I shook my head. "We can all run. C'mon, let's just go!" I said and moved back with Mikhaila's hand still in mine, but she jerked away from me and stepped aside.

"What have you done?" she whispered, looking behind us, right where we came from, so scared she looked even paler than normal.

When I turned around, I realized why.

More SUVs, too many to count, had stopped right at the mouth of the bridge. The doors of the first one opened, and Trevor stepped out of the passenger seat.

He didn't wear his armor, but all the soldiers did. So many of them—at least thirty. A small army was at his back.

"They found me," Mikhaila choked. "They...they found me..."

I turned back to Rowan, angry tears blurring my vision for a moment. This couldn't be it. This couldn't be how it ended, not when we were so close.

Damn it, we were so close!

"Ella!" Rowan shouted, his hands already in front of him, his leather jacket on the ground.

Ezrail roared when his shifting pain started, filling my head completely before black and orange fur sprouted from his skin. His jeans were ripped to shreds seconds before he shifted into a large, terrifying tiger, whose roar was ten times as loud and menacing.

"Enough with the games, Estella!"

My eyes moved forward again—to Trevor. He was coming closer, eyes bloodshot, shoulders expanding as he came—he was going to shift, too.

Gods, no. Please, no...

It couldn't end here. I *wouldn't* let it end here—Lucien was waiting for me. They couldn't take me back to my father, not now.

I shook my head, moving backward until I hit the door of the truck, whispering, "No, no, no..."

"It's over, Princess. I'm taking you home now," Trevor said, stopping ten feet away from me.

I'm not going anywhere with you! I shouted in my head, but the words refused to come out of my mouth.

I just kept thinking, *it can't be...*

"Princess?" Mikhaila's high-pitched voice pierced my ears. She was shaking from head to toe as she moved farther away from me, to the edge of the bridge, her eyes darting from me to Trevor and back again.

"*Princess?* Are you fucking kidding me?!"

But my head was already buzzing.

Something stood out in my own chaotic mind.

A thought I'd had just now—two words: *shifting pain.*

We were in Springfield, and it was morning, cars driving by on the other side of the bridge. A *bridge*—below which was a river, and what was it that John had said yesterday?

She'd need to be in water to shift.

Trevor shouted something else—I couldn't hear it because I couldn't stop looking at Mikhaila. Ezrail's tiger roared—he was ready to attack, but we wouldn't make it. Even if Rowan shifted, too, we'd *never* make it against all these soldiers, unless...

Unless I did something about it.

It was a second's decision, one half of me was certain I'd regret. But what other choice did I have? If I let Trevor take me away now, all of it would have been for nothing. The others couldn't summon the Ether on their own without me —they needed my Fire.

Rowan called my name again.

I moved.

I'd never forget the look on Mikhaila's face when I slammed my hands on her chest and pushed her with all my strength. If she hadn't been so sick, if she'd had any strength at all in those long limbs of hers, she'd have stopped me easily.

As it was, she stumbled back, as shocked as I was to find myself moving.

One step, two...the back of her legs caught on the low railing at the edge of the bridge.

I'm sorry.

She screamed, arms spinning at her sides as she tried to keep her balance.

She fell.

I ran to the railing, and I could have sworn that the world moved in slow motion as I watched her falling. Her hands reached up—for me—and the look in her eyes was that of a woman who still refused to believe what she knew to be true. She kept falling and falling and falling for what felt like *days* to me, until she reached the surface of the water, and...

She disappeared.

A splash. The sound of her cries was cut off abruptly. My heart all but broke right out of my ribcage.

Hands on my arms, trying to pull me back, but I gripped the metal of the railing so tightly, they'd have to cut my hands to get me to let go.

Please, please, please...

The bubbles in the water where she fell disappeared completely. The green of the river was calm again. Mikhaila was gone.

I'd killed her.

"Do not make me carry you, Princess," Trevor hissed in my ear, but I couldn't look away, couldn't blink, couldn't *breathe* yet. I refused to believe, just like Mikhaila had, because it was absurd. Impossible. Utterly ridiculous that I'd killed her.

Oh gods.

I'd *killed* a person. I'd killed Mikhaila.

The scream that tore from me made even Trevor flinch. He wrapped his arms around my waist and pulled, and my fingers had no choice but to let go of the railing.

My mind was still stuck in a state of disbelief, my own thoughts mocking me—*you killed a person!*

Then the bridge underneath our feet groaned.

Everybody stopped screaming and shouting and talking and trying to pull me back. Trevor's arms around me loosened.

Mikhaila.

I didn't think—I just pushed Trevor aside, hopped onto the railing and jumped, ready to swim every inch of this river until I found her, pulled her out of the water, apologized.

I'm sorry. I thought I knew what I was doing—I was desperate. I'm sorry.

But my feet were barely off the railing when strong hands pulled me back and I slammed onto a chest hard. I thought I screamed again, but I couldn't be sure.

And then it happened, right before my eyes.

The creature jumped out of the surface of the water upright, straight as a pin. Dark blue and green scales made her body, shimmering silver as the fresh sunlight fell on them. She roared, then spun into a perfect *U*, and slipped into the water again, almost completely soundlessly.

Every person on the bridge with me held their breaths for a long moment.

"What have you done?" Trevor whispered somewhere close by, but he was no longer holding me back. Instead, when I made for the railing to see the water better, he joined me.

And there she was again, coming out with a loud roar that shook me to my core.

I smiled, body light as air. I hadn't killed her.

And Mikhaila was definitely the wyrm.

"Get back!" Trevor shouted, and he moved back himself when it was obvious that the wyrm was aiming to land atop the bridge now.

Cars honked. People screamed.

The asphalt broke to pieces when she landed in the middle of the lanes. She wasn't big—not half as big as my father, even a bit smaller than Lucien. But she was fierce.

Four crystal blue eyes. Fins at the end of her long pointy tail, spikes all over it, and her back, and her large head. Her teeth were just as big as Lucien's, and the way she moved was mesmerizing. She had no wings and no limbs, but her body knew exactly how to move out of water, on the surface of the bridge—almost exactly like a snake, but faster.

I could have been dreaming, but I saw it when she swooshed her long tail and slammed it against the soldiers, against the SUVs parked behind our truck.

Bullets and arrows flew at her.

Trevor, who'd been on the ground and was trying to sit up, met my eyes. I was kneeling on the ground, hands around my head, watching in awe—and he saw it.

I shook my head at him. *I won't be going anywhere with you right now.*

He understood.

Thirty men were not enough to fight against a wyrm, not without a plan, and he knew it. I had no clue if he knew wyrms even existed, that it was possible, that they ever had, but he knew he couldn't win this fight when the wyrm roared again, shaking the entire bridge. She slammed her tail onto another group of soldiers who were trying to take their armor off to shift, while others shot their arrows at her. No matter.

Even if they got through her scales, I'd be there with all my blood to heal her.

Trevor moved.

He called for his men to retreat, and slowly, eyes on the wyrm, he moved back to the last two SUVs, the only ones that hadn't been ruined completely yet.

Hands on my shoulders, pulling me to my feet. Rowan was beside me, and Ezrail, completely naked, was right behind him. We all stared at the wyrm—so incredibly beautiful and terrifying as it roared, moving from one side of the large bridge to the other, watching, restless.

Trevor and the guards were driving back, most running away on foot.

And then the wyrm jumped off the bridge and into the water again.

"My gods," Rowan breathed. "She's *real.*"

I smiled so big my cheeks hurt. I cried so hard I could barely see.

But I saw enough when the wyrm jumped out of the water and onto the bridge again.

Her roar this time was different, *painful.* The SUVs and all the soldiers who'd been about to attack us were gone. Plenty of cars, possibly all of them human, stopped on both sides of the bridge, watching, recording with their phones.

There was no way my father wouldn't see this, if he hadn't already.

He was coming to find me. We only had *hours,* and that's counting on Lucien's magic to keep us shielded, before we all ended up dead—or worse.

It was time to summon the Ether.

"She's shifting back," Ezrail said, his voice barely a whisper as we moved back and watched the wyrm thrashing to the sides, her tail slamming against the asphalt over and over again, restlessly.

And she was getting smaller.

We watched in awe as she shrank and shrank, and her scales bled out of color, and her eyes turned to *two*. We watched until she was no longer a creature of myth come to life, but simply a woman, wet and naked and unconscious, lying on the asphalt.

"*Move!*" Rowan shouted, and he ran for her, took her in his arms, then turned to the truck.

Ezrail, butt-naked still, ran for the driver's door—still open.

There were cars all around us, but it no longer even mattered. We were done hiding.

It was time to act.

So, I climbed in the truck and pulled the doors closed even as Ezrail took us forward.

THIRTY-TWO

INCREDIBLE HOW MUCH COURAGE I'D GATHERED from the moment I saw Mikhaila shifted into a wyrm and on the ride back to Albany.

Incredibly how much *love* was in my heart as I watched Rowan hold her on his lap, his shirt on her body—his jacket probably lost somewhere back at that bridge.

It was over.

We'd all seen that—it had been real.

The dragoness. The wyvern. The drake.

And now the wyrm.

All draca, alive, about to change the world.

Until we arrived at Jack and John's town, and the doors opened, and Rowan carried a still unconscious Mikhaila in his arms.

I could barely hold back the tears, searching for Lucien's face, telling myself, *just keep going until you're in his arms. Then, you can break down and cry as much as you want.*

But Lucien wasn't there.

Instead, we were met by Jack's cousins, William and Riad, who looked...not well.

Blood on their torn clothes. Guns in their hands.

I almost passed out when Rowan and I jumped out of the truck.

"What happened?" he asked as Ezrail approached, wearing a pair of grey sweatpants and nothing else.

"Come see," Riad said, nodding toward the houses.

Rowan didn't let go of Mikhaila even when William offered to carry her. "I got it," he said and kept walking beside me, never daring to look at me, or I at him.

He was okay. Lucien was okay—I didn't care what had happened. He'd made it because he could take care of himself. No matter how many people had attacked here, he could handle it. He knew what to do.

I had to keep my faith in that; otherwise, I'd have collapsed the moment I was out of that truck.

I don't even remember how I made it to the first row of single-story houses or to Jack and John's house—but William and Riad didn't stop there.

They took us behind it, and to the willow tree where we'd hung out the night before, and the folding chairs were gone, and...

Lucien.

I ran so fast it was a miracle my legs carried me. I jumped in his arms, so relieved that he was standing, awake, *breathing*, I would have cried out if I had the energy.

"You're okay," I said over and over again, allowing myself to believe it.

"I'm okay," he said, his voice hushed, and he leaned back to look at me, smoothing my hair behind my ears.

His pale face was splattered with blood, his hair disheveled, his shirt dirty and torn, his hands bloody.

"What...what happened?" I asked, heart in my throat, trying to search the rest of him for any wounds, but...

"I'm sorry, little fox," Lucien said, and I stopped breathing, as if my body already knew things I didn't. "We had no choice."

"What?" I asked, shaking my head, trying to smile just to get him to smile, too, so that I knew that it was okay. Whatever it was—it wasn't *bad*. It would be okay if he was smiling.

But...he wasn't. He wasn't smiling at all. Instead, he looked like he was in pain.

"I'm sorry," he repeated in a whisper and let go of me to step to the side.

To show me what his body had been hiding.

To show me what was in the distance, at the edge of the small mountain where the playground was, a large chunk of it missing, like someone had taken a large spoonful out of it.

The people disappeared. The voices, the sounds—even Lucien. It was quiet in my head, too quiet, but the view in front of me still made no sense.

My father was buried halfway in the ground, his arms to the sides held by a million chains that went into the mountain behind him. He was bloody, his beard all over the place, his hair, too. His torso was naked, and there were cuts on him— swords coming out of the ground, the tips of them *inside* his body, in his ribs, in his stomach, and he was just *bleed, bleed, bleeding* on them. All over them. Dripping.

His eyes were open and right on me, green and piercing and *full*.

He saw me.

I saw him.

My legs gave up, and I hit the ground on my knees hard. The world shook from the weight of me—I was so, so heavy. With every new breath that left my lips, pieces of me spread out into the world, gone forever.

Hands on me. Words in my ear. Knives in my heart.

The tears tried so hard to wash away the colors of the world, to change the image ahead, just alter it, make it into something different, but they failed. I blinked and he was still there, watching me, chained and bleeding.

Calling my name with his eyes, so disappointed I felt it in my bones.

"I'm sorry," Lucien kept saying, holding me in his arms.

It was too much. My mind shut down even before my body knew to let go.

THIRTY-THREE

I WOKE UP BARELY TEN MINUTES LATER, BUT MY father was unconscious by then.

Still chained to a mountain, hip deep into the ground. Still with all those swords in his body as he slowly bled all over them.

And the fire I hadn't noticed at first was there, too, a small river all around him, five feet wide, the lava burning bright orange inside it. Flames danced on the surface, and they looked like they were waving at me.

But nothing compared to the sight of the creature walking in circles around the river of fire.

A body just as large as Mikhaila's wyrm. Brown scales that didn't look like scales, but like dry land, cracked all over. Massive paws the size of my head, with claws bigger than my fingers.

Two heads, one set of eyes green, the other brown. Large jaws and spikes all over the heads, almost identical to my father's dragon. No wings—and he held himself like Ezrail's tiger had, like he thought he was just an ordinary animal, not a draca.

John and Jack. They'd shifted—and they were looking right at me.

"Let's just go rest for a bit first," Lucien was telling me, trying to stop me from going closer, trying to stop me from seeing my father.

I didn't speak—couldn't if I tried. I just kept on walking, closer and closer, expecting my legs to give up on me again, but they somehow didn't. He walked with me.

"We had no choice," he was saying, as if he heard the silent questions in my mind. "If his body is constantly bleeding, he'll spend all his energy to try to heal and won't be able to shift with mine and the twins' magic holding him back. We have to keep him bleeding, little fox. We have no other choice; otherwise..."

We're all dead, he wanted to say but he didn't. He didn't have to—I knew.

"Who?" I thought I asked when we reached the river of lava and I realized I couldn't jump as high as I needed to get to the other side.

"My father's theory. *Plan,* really. But me and the twins... implemented it," Lucien said, and I could hear the guilt in his voice so clearly it made me flinch.

I looked at him for a moment. "Why didn't you kill him?" My voice sounded like it was somebody else's.

"I didn't let them," he said, his eyes dark and full of clouds. "I couldn't...not without you knowing about it."

Was I thankful to him?

Was I mad, was I sad, relieved, or even resentful?

I nodded—it was the best I knew how to do. "I need to get to the other side."

"Little fox, you—"

"Just me, Lucien. I'll be fine," I said, and he must have realized that my voice sounded like a stranger's, too, because he stepped back instantly, and looked at the two-headed creature that was a set of twins, coming closer to us now.

The drake. Jack and John together.

He looked even bigger from closer up, just as beautiful as Mikhaila. Just as terrifying.

"I need to get to the other side," I told him, as if I was sure he could understand me. Could he—*they*?

It didn't really matter. There were plenty of trees around us—I could make my own bridge if needed across the river of lava.

But I didn't have to.

The drake came closer, walking slowly, all his eyes focused on my face. I wasn't scared—I was curious. I was curious to know what it would feel like to touch those scales.

The ground shook a little bit, and then it rose just in front of me, two feet wide. It climbed over the lava until it connected with the ground on the other side. I didn't hesitate —I stepped onto the tiny makeshift bridge and I jumped to the other side.

The drake's shoulders were level with the top of my head. He growled lowly, two different voices at once, and he lowered his heads as if to tell me not to be afraid. I wasn't.

"Leave me alone with him," I said, and I turned to my father. My curiosity would have to wait. If I wanted to analyze the creature better later, I would.

Right now, I just want to...*be here.*

The drake growled again but stepped back. I only saw it through the corner of my eye when he jumped over the lava like it was just a tiny puddle on the ground. I kept going until I was ten feet away from the side of the mountain, to the missing piece of it where they'd half buried my father. They had chained his arms—four different chains each— then had stuck five swords all over his body to keep him bleeding.

It's funny that *he* was the monster in this scenario, chained up and half buried and bleeding like that.

I sat on the ground, hugged my knees to my chest and I looked at him. My father. My flesh and blood. Technically the only family I had—Annabelle was pretty clear that she didn't want to have anything to do with me.

And a question popped into my head as I watched him barely breathing, bleeding his life down those swords: what would my mother say if she saw us right now?

I FELT it when she sat next to me, but I couldn't even turn my head. It had been...how long since I'd sat here, watching my father die?

I had no idea, but I was exhausted.

"Hey, girl," Mikhaila said, resting her elbows on her knees, head turned to me. "I knew there was something about you. The *princess*, no less." She snorted. "Good thing I didn't know; otherwise, I'd have killed you."

That made me smile. "You couldn't even raise your hand," I reminded her. "I literally saved your life."

"You also almost got me killed," she said. "I can't believe you pushed me off a bridge. *Seriously.*"

I laughed. "Out of everything, *that's* what you find unbelievable? That I would push you off a bridge?"

"Well, yeah. I mean, being a wingless dragon is cool and all, but you literally pushed me into a river. That's just...a bit much, don't you think?"

A bit much. I shook my head, smiling. "How about watching your father chained to a mountain, half buried and bleeding to death right in front of your eyes? Is that *a bit much*?"

"Oh, we're comparing pain now? Because I've got some

cards up my sleeves, girl. You won't be able to compete," she said, grinning.

"I assure you, I have more." So many, my sleeves were full.

And Mikhaila sighed. "Yeah, they told me the crazy story. Which is *crazy,* by the way. Seven lives?"

I looked at her. "*A bit much,* right?"

She burst out laughing. "You can say that again."

"You're not sick anymore." She looked perfect, actually, her cheeks flushed and her eyes sparkling.

"I'm not. I feel great. Turns out, it was just my animal trying to force me to shift and I was locking her in unconsciously," Mikhaila said. "So crazy. I was so sure the mating ritual didn't work—I didn't really love Torin. Far from it. But he said, *let's mate,* and I said, *why the hell not?* And I did the whole thing, and I thought it didn't work because tigers mate when they're in love—how was I to know I was a dragon?"

"A wyrm," I corrected her.

"Whatever. They're all dragons to me," she said with a shrug. "I thought that's why Torin left me at Annabelle's door. That the mating didn't work and he got pissed so he bailed."

"So, what happened?"

"I don't know. His father said he hasn't been back. I was waiting for him to return from wherever the fuck he is," Mikhaila said, then flinched. "I guess it's a good thing you found me first."

"Good thing." And I *knew* it was.

So, why didn't it feel like it?

"Makes sense," I said, more to distract myself. "We don't have to be in love to mate, either. Just do the ritual. Makes sense that it worked for you, even though you weren't in love with the guy." I'd done it six other times with my husbands in my other lives, had never been in love with any of them, but I still mated with them.

"I guess so," Mikhaila said, then looked up at my father. "He came after me, you know. I was eleven. He sent his people after me and they followed me everywhere, tried to charge me with theft so that they'd have reason to take me away, then do whatever they wanted with me. I didn't know why then, but I know now."

I swallowed hard but couldn't say anything yet.

"I left my parents because of him. Stayed away from my magic, thinking he would find me easier if I used it. I stayed away from water altogether. I've been on the run my whole life because of him."

"I'm sorry, Mikhaila." And I was.

So, why didn't I sound like it?

"Don't be. Not your fault. Who woulda thunk the princess herself would save the day, huh?" And she nudged me with her elbow.

I wanted to rip it off her.

Closing my eyes, I breathed in deeply, trying to control these urges that came at me so suddenly lately.

My dragoness. The same animal I was going to unleash into the world—*tonight*.

"I know you love him," Mikhaila said. "He's your father." My eyes closed again. "But he's a bad man, Ella."

What did it say that I was part of him, though?

And I really—I *really* wanted to know, what would my mother say if she were sitting here with me right now? If she saw me watching him bleeding like this—what would she think of me?

I had no idea because I had no idea who my mother was as a person. I'd only ever known her as my mother.

The dream I'd had days ago came to mind—the one where she told me that I needed to kill my father. I'd known it wasn't her, as fucked up as it sounded. That had not been my mother, I was sure of it, but...what if she was?

"There's something I don't get, though," Mikhaila said after a while. She wouldn't leave—she just sat there with me, and now she had more to say.

"Your great-great-great-whatever," she said. "Alexandra, the chick who helped you out of the basement—so she just happened to *know* where I was, and she just...grabbed you and brought you to me?"

I stopped breathing for a moment, then turned to her.

No, I wanted to say. *No—Alexandra knew my blood. She took me to my blood—to my aunt. She took me to Annabelle because she was my only other relative out there except my father.*

Except...

My eyes squeezed shut and I reminded myself to draw in air.

Alexandra hadn't taken me to Annabelle because she was my family. She'd taken me to Annabelle because Mikhaila had been there.

"I mean, it's fishy as hell. She's an Azarius—why would she take you to *me*? It's like she wanted you to find me, and I can't trust that. Can *you* trust that?" Mikhaila continued.

"No," I said, shaking my head. I could not trust that, even less when I knew who Alexandra was.

How did I not see it? My gods, it was right there—how did I not see that she'd taken me straight to Mikhaila?

My eyes closed. My thoughts were rioting in my head, answers colliding with questions, truths posing as lies. Nothing made much sense, except the fact that Alexandra knew exactly what she was doing.

And she'd *wanted* me to summon the Ether. It's why she'd showed me that spell, and why she'd saved me and Lucien and Jack—because I told her that I was going to summon the Ether.

Why? She was an Azarius and proud as hell to be one—

why would she want me to summon the Ether and threaten the reign of dragons?

"Exactly," Mikhaila said. "It just feels wrong, is all I'm saying. It feels off."

"It feels off," I repeated. It *was* off.

And just the thought that Alexandra wanted me to summon the Ether made me want to abandon the idea completely.

"Ella."

I turned to the side to find Rowan standing there next to where Mikhaila was sitting, a plate in his hand. A piece of meat on it and some mashed potatoes.

"Thanks, I'm not hungry," I said automatically.

"You need to eat," he insisted, squatting in front of us.

"While I watch my father bleed to death?" Was that what he was saying?

Rowan flinched, lowering his head as he rubbed the back of his neck.

"Then come inside. You're going to mate in a bit. You need the energy," he said, and the look in his eyes was earnest, as if he *cared* about me. As if he understood exactly what I was feeling.

And I remembered...*he did*.

And I remembered, I did need the energy—I was going to mate with Lucien before sundown, and then I was going to release my Fire and my dragoness, and then together, the five of us, we were going to summon the Ether and put an end to the world's madness while my father bled on those swords.

So simple.

So very, *very* simple.

"My knight in shining armor," Mikhaila said to him. "Who woulda thunk they make them like this anymore? Tall, dark, handsome—*and* perfect, kissable lips? I mean, *come on*."

I thought Rowan was going to lash out at her, tell her he

was too good for her or something, but instead he grinned, and I could have sworn a bit of pink touched his cheeks.

"You haven't seen anything yet," he said in a whisper, as if he were hoping I wouldn't hear.

My, my.

I stood up, taking the plate from his hand. "I'll find my way back myself," I told them, then turned around and walked back to the twins' house. These two apparently needed a bit more time together.

Lucien was waiting for me on the porch.

"You want to go inside?" he said, looking at me with those eyes, and it took all I had to fight the urge to curl into a ball in a corner somewhere and cry my life away.

I nodded.

Taking the plate from my hand, he led me inside the house, up the stairs and to the room we were sleeping in. He sat me down on the bed and took my sneakers off, then sat down with me and began to feed me.

It was strangely...comfortable.

"He's going to hate me forever," I said after a bit, the food in my mouth tasteless.

"He won't," Lucien said.

"Oh, he will." I was going to mate with Lucien—not the man he chose for me. And I was going to put an end to the reign of dragons—how very *un-Azarius* of me. "And that should be okay," I said. It should—I knew who that man was.

"He's your father, little fox. Of course, it's not okay," he said, then brought the fork to my mouth again. "But he'll have time to think. Eventually, I think he'll come around."

I nodded, hope spilling like candle wax over the cracks of my heart, as if trying to glue the pieces back together.

It worked—for a moment.

But the truth was that I knew my father. Yeah, it would have been the best-case scenario if we summoned the Ether, and he returned the balance of the elements to the world, and my father saw that it was for the best, and he went on his own for a while to think, like they do in movies, and then he came back. He hugged me and kissed me and told me that he loved me, that he was sorry for everything, and that he was proud of me for doing the right thing.

What a beautiful dream.

A *dream*—not reality. Because my father's name was Archibald Azarius—and he was not a man who apologized. Not a man who would ever be proud of anything I did.

I was crying before I knew it, resting on Lucien's shoulder. I'd eaten half the plate, though, so I had strength. I could do the ritual. Despite the guilt and the fear and the pain—so much godsdamn pain—I could do this. I could let my father, half buried and chained and bleeding, watch me summon the very thing he'd spent his whole life trying to keep away, and I could sleep at night. I could eat and I could breathe and I could be happy when it was over.

I *could*.

I would.

THIRTY-FOUR

THE FIRE MATING RITUAL WAS DIFFERENT FROM THE rest of the elements—it required blood and words and real fire to seal the flesh of my mated to mine. It would burn him, and he would carry the scar forever. The mark of the dragon, my father used to call it.

And funny because he'd never shared the details of the ritual with me before my weddings, not in any lives, but I'd already done it six times, so I knew it by memory. It was simple enough, anyway.

We were in the twins' living room—I'd wanted to be inside for this, and I'd never tell them why, but I wanted to be away from my father's eyes, just in case he'd wake up and see me.

I felt guilty. Like I was betraying him. Like I had never truly been worthy of his love and acceptance, and that's why he'd never loved me and accepted me in the first place.

Too much—so I was just going to stay inside.

"This is for you," Rowan said, putting a small knife in my hand as we waited for Lucien to come downstairs. I'd showered first. He'd said he'd be right down.

"Thanks," I said, looking at his face, feeling more like

myself now that I'd cried and I'd eaten and I'd showered and I'd dressed in somebody else's clothes. I didn't even ask Jack who the jeans and the red shirt belonged to—I just put them on.

And Rowan looked...good. He didn't look pissed. Instead, he seemed relaxed.

"One day, remember?" I reminded him. He'd promised me he'd be here for one more day, and I'd planned this whole thing very differently. I was going to want to celebrate my mating to Lucien tonight, and I was going to want to dance with him, and I was going to want to talk to him and Rowan, and try to get them to see past their differences...

Everything had changed, though, when I saw my father. *Half buried and chained and bleeding.*

Stop, I said to myself.

But Rowan smiled. "Make that two."

My brows rose—was he serious? And his eyes, as if to answer my unspoken question, darted left quickly—to where Mikhaila was sitting on one of the couches, looking down at her phone.

I held back a laugh, shaking my head. "She'll bite your head off," I whispered to him.

"Oh, Princess, don't tempt me like that," he said with a wicked grin that was so much like Lucien it made my stomach turn.

I could hardly believe it myself, but he meant it. He actually meant it.

"She's older than you, you know," I said, though I already knew it didn't matter.

"And stronger than me," Rowan said, sneaking looks Mikhaila's way every few seconds. "I'm not saying I'll ask her to marry me. I'll just...play it by ear."

Except the way he looked at her right now said very differently. He wasn't going to play anything by ear.

But the footsteps coming from the top of the stairs distracted all of us. Lucien was coming—showered and dressed in old clean clothes that could have been Jack's. And Jack was behind him, too,

"We're all here," John said as he entered the living room, and Mikhaila stood up. "Good." He looked so different—so much more like Jack with every new hour. His cheeks were fuller and his eyes brighter, his legs stronger now that he'd shifted.

And Jack, too—the wrinkles on his face were gone, and there was no more silver hair on his head, either. They'd shifted, and it's like they'd both become better versions of themselves.

But Lucien...

That man tugged at all the pieces of my heart at the same time. He was clean-shaven, a small smile playing on his lips, the white shirt bringing out the colors of him—his dark hair and perfect blue eyes. He was worried about me, I could see it even now, but half of it was lost as he analyzed my face, my body, and his smile widened.

"Try not to fall on your face," Rowan told him, offering him his own small knife, identical to the one he'd given me.

But Lucien took the knife and didn't even look at him. Instead, he came to me, put his hand on my waist and kissed my cheek.

Gods, he smelled good. Clean. All *Lucien.*

"Is this okay?" I whispered in his ear.

"More than okay—you're breathtaking, Estella. Red was made for you," he said, and I smiled.

"I mean *this.* That we're doing this inside and without... without..." Any celebration or anything. I don't know, it just felt like so *little.*

But Lucien grinned widely. "I'm about to become your

mate. How can anything else matter?" he asked, then kissed me.

The others burst out laughing.

My cheeks must have been as red as the shirt I was wearing by the time we stepped away from one another, just a little.

"Alright, people. Let's do this. Let's finish this thing," John said, coming closer to us as he cleared his throat. "First of all, I'm honored to be part of this."

Lucien looked at him. "You're literally just going to burn my hand."

And John grinned—he looked so different like that. So carefree and so *young*. It suited him, that look.

"Exactly," he said, patting Lucien's shoulders.

"Let's just get it done," he said, trying to stifle his smile.

And for a moment, I was awestruck, in disbelief that this was even happening. I was actually going to mate to someone that I loved this time. After six times, I was going to come alive with the blood and the touch of a man I lived for.

"Ready?" John said, and I nodded, rushing as if I was suddenly in a hurry.

I grabbed Lucien's hand and stabbed the middle of his palm with my knife. I did it with such ease, you'd think I'd been rehearsing this all my life. Lucien didn't flinch, like he didn't even feel the cut. He eagerly took my hand in his, then stabbed it with his knife the same way, in the same spot.

I didn't feel it, either.

We were both smiling, eyes locked as we raised our hands and brought our palms against one another, connecting our blood.

It occurred to me that we'd already done this once—when he was wounded and I healed him from the arrow's poison. Our blood had been connected then, too.

Now, we would do it properly.

"May our blood be our bond, and my flames yours forever. May our magic be our seal, and your Air mine until the end of times," I solemnly said. Those were the words that my father had told me to say on my wedding days to my husbands. But this time, I wanted to say just a bit more because Lucien was smiling at me, and my heart sang with the words he'd said to me, the same ones I yearned to say back to him so that he would know beyond a shadow of doubt, "If I live another thousand lives, I'll be yours in every single one of them."

Someone cheered. Someone clapped. Lucien squeezed my fingers, his eyes boring into mine, owning me even before his hand began to buzz lightly. His magic slipped from his skin and onto mine, spreading fast over my fingers and to my wrist, up my arm, *exploding* in my chest before I could blink. My breath caught in my throat and Lucien's magic consumed every inch of me the way it had never done before. I felt it merging with my every cell, infusing it, completing me in a way I never knew I could be complete.

The moment lasted an eternity, our eyes locked and our bodies one, hearts perfectly still when he whispered, "*Carpe anima.*"

Everything came back at once—air and sight and sound and heartbeat. I was enveloped by magic, buzzing with it, just like him. Lucien smiled brightly. "Seize the breath of life," he whispered.

And his Air mating ritual was complete.

I was his—officially, the way I'd never been before.

Now, it was time to complete the Fire ritual, too.

John came closer to us and raised the little torch he'd made for the occasion—just a stick with a piece of cotton cloth wrapped around the tip that he set on fire with a match. He then brought the new flames between us, and said exactly what I told him to say, what my father had always said to me and my husbands in my past lives. I wasn't entirely sure it was part of the ritual, but it was my favorite line:

"May Fire keep you warm and ablaze your whole lives."

We pulled our bloodied hands apart, Lucien's Air magic remaining inside me, then closed them around the flames dancing eagerly on the tip of the torch.

Everything changed instantly. I was no longer light with Air.

The fire burned. It burned so beautifully. My skin came alive.

Lucien hissed—it did not feel good for him, I imagined, but to me, it was so freeing to feel those flames licking my skin. It was so freeing to feel them burning my blood, burning Lucien's blood, merging it together, linking us forever, until our dying breath.

I *felt* it, felt my own body suck in the flames under my skin, every cell inside of me desperate to ignite. The Fire set me ablaze, merging with my magic, rushing throughout me, lighting up every little corner of my body from the inside. It was different from what I remembered in my other lives. It was faster, much more intense, and the colors that burst inside my closed lids were mesmerizing. I felt Lucien, too, as if he was a part of me, as if the brand new—and at the same time familiar —element that had claimed me knew him in detail. We were truly connected to one another in heart and blood and magic.

I burned.

I was finally whole.

And my dragoness was free.

"HOW DOES IT FEEL?"

I looked at Lucien. His voice was strange. The sight of him

moved, as if someone was pulling and pushing the fabric of reality around me. I couldn't stop smiling.

It feels like power.

It feels like I've unlocked a different dimension.

It hurts.

It burns.

"Intense," I said, touching my chest for a moment—I feared it would split wide open any second. The way my heart was beating...

"You're smiling. That's good," Lucien said. I took his left hand in mine and looked at his palm. His skin was burned and raw red still—that had to hurt. And the scar would remain on him forever. It was proof that he belonged to Fire now.

He belonged to *me.* Forever. For real.

"Does it hurt?" I asked him, fingers hovering over the wound.

"Not too much," he lied, then raised my chin with his other hand, looking at me like he couldn't believe his own eyes. "You're *glowing*, little fox."

His face turned to a blur for a moment, and my knees shook.

"I'm...I..."

My chest stung now, my body weak—like I had five swords in me and I was bleeding on them—and the roar that filled my head was merciless. "Lucien," I thought I said because I was losing sight of the world around me, and I was losing sound, too. There'd been whispers in my ears just five seconds ago, and now there was nothing but that blaring roar, piercing my ears, my brain, every cell of my body.

My dragoness wanted out.

I remembered the other times I'd mated. Six other times— I remembered all of them. I remembered the burn and I remembered the sting, but nothing had ever—*ever* felt the way it did now. My dragoness had been calm, had had to be *lured* to come out with nightfall in my other lives. She'd had to be persuaded by me, by my father, to take over and release herself from the inside of my mind.

Not now.

Cold air in my nostrils, and I blinked and blinked but I still couldn't see. I still couldn't hear anything but the sound of my bones breaking, the sound of my flesh tearing, the sound of my pieces falling to the ground.

She wanted out, and I had no hope of controlling her.

I let go.

The world returned to me full force—sound and sight and smell. Lucien was calling my name. We were outside, in front of the house, and Jack and John and Rowan and Mikhaila were around me, arms at the ready as if they were thinking about containing me, horrified looks on their faces.

The sky was dark over my head. The air was free. Fire coursed through my veins, more powerful than I'd ever felt it before.

"*Get back!*" I thought I said, and the others slowly moved away from me, gave me space.

Gods, it hurt. It hurt so much I couldn't breathe. I was really shifting.

My own screams filled my head, but I wasn't sure if I screamed out loud, too. I was breaking to a million pieces, rearranging into something else. I'd never remembered the shifting pains, not like this, and if I had any control of this at all, any way of stopping it, I would—consequences be damned.

As it was, the shifting burned every inch of the human part of me for what felt like hours, and left way for the drag-oness, who clawed her way out until the air was hers to breathe and the world was hers to conquer.

Just like that, it was over. The pain retreated to a faded memory within seconds.

The dragoness roared, and even the highest mountain heard it.

I was shoved somewhere in the back of her mind, surrounded by darkness, no body to control.

But I *felt* hers.

I felt her legs and her arms, the tip of her claws. Her chest and her back, the long tail barbed with spikes. Her thick neck and her head, every little inch of her wings.

Eventually, all that she was would be *mine,* too.

Right now, her wings spread, and she took us up in the air. I saw clearer by the second, saw Lucien—who *glowed* to our eyes now, too—and the others, stepping even farther away from us as we rose in the air. The cry that left my dragoness's mouth was almost identical to my father's.

She still hadn't properly mastered coordinating her wings and her body, but she would be a pro before the hour was over. It was fascinating to *ride* in her mind, to see the way she saw—to see Lucien, who took up half her attention like he always did mine, like none of my husbands in my past lives had done. My dragoness had never cared about them, but she cared about Lucien. There was an incredible need inside her that I felt as if it were my own that yearned to *protect him*. Against all, everything, whatever the cost—his life was more valuable than ours, and we would protect it with our everything.

But that wasn't all.

It was so beautiful to see the edges of her wings as she flapped them, growing stronger by the second, moving higher and higher still; to see the tip of her tail, full of spikes, her scales a red so intense it could have been paint. I was dying to see the rest of her, but she had other plans in mind, and once we were high enough to see beyond the houses around us, beyond the trees...

Her eyes zeroed in on him.

My father...*half buried, chained, bleeding.*

Her roar was that of a monster. She cried out so loud, the dead could have heard her, too.

My father certainly did. And he raised his head to see her. To see me.

That's when I realized that all of this was *wrong*.

I was supposed to have more time. This wasn't what happened—I had hours after I mated to convince the dragoness to come out of me—*hours!* I was not prepared for her to burst out of me just like that. I had no control over her, I hadn't even considered training because I thought I'd have time!

And now she was flying in circles, getting used to her wings, inching closer to that mountain, to him, *dying* on the inside to see him like that, carrying twice as much pain as my body had the capacity to feel at the sight of his blood.

He was *ours*, too. He was our blood, our responsibility.

And we had to save him before it was too late.

No! I shouted at the top of my lungs, but the sound of me was a mere whisper compared to her roars. Fear suffocated me even though I didn't have a body of my own because my dragoness's mind was made up. She didn't care about what *I* thought on the matter—she was going to fly to that mountain and save my father—*right now.*

But before she launched herself toward the ground, something else caught our eyes.

The two-headed creature jumping over the river of lava, then walking in circles around my father.

Irritated.

My dragoness was *irritated* at the sight of the drake, and she saw him so clearly. My gods, her eyes saw so much more than mine. There was much more detail to the world than I'd ever realized. She saw every single scale on the drake's body, every color in his eyes, every sharp edge of his teeth. She heard his growl even high up in the air, and she wasn't afraid. She wasn't worried.

Instead, in her mind she had already planned the best way to kill him, and the image was shoved in front of my eyes as if on purpose—she would grip both his heads in her hands and pull them aside, ripping the drake in half.

Easy. Fast. Plenty of blood.

Stop! I shouted, and for a second I was terrified because I was a prisoner here. I had no control over this massive body—which was still *small* compared to my father's dragon. To what my dragoness would become in a year. I had no clue how to stop her, and I was freaking out. The panic wouldn't even let me remember the tips my father had given me in my other lives, but...

Then we felt it.

We both felt the strong wings and the wind they commanded, and we felt his presence like it was connected to us—like a limb—rising up in the sky.

My father and the drake forgotten, we turned to the trees, to the houses, and we saw the wyvern rising up to meet us, high in the air, so majestic even my dragoness was *shocked* at the sight of him.

Time stood perfectly still for a long moment as our eyes locked.

She saw him so much better than I ever would. The white scales and the silver shimmer on them—right now, with the black sky behind him, he shone brighter than the moon. His eyes had so many more shapes and depth than even I knew, and the horns on his head and the large white wings that were also his arms, his long tail swirling behind him...

Her heart all but burst in her ribcage as she shot forward with all her speed, which wasn't much.

And the wyvern cried out, then took flight toward us, too, meeting us halfway.

We collided in the air, wings flapping and claws against scales. The smell of him, the sight of him, the feel of him against my dragoness's body was exactly *right*. He was bigger than us right now because we were just born—and when was *he* born, my dragoness wondered?—but he was *perfect, perfect, perfect,* and he purred like a cat.

We liked it. We *loved* it. And we slammed onto him, tackling him to the ground.

We fell against trees somewhere, and I couldn't keep track of all the emotions running through my dragoness right now, but one thing I felt above all else—she was *happy*.

How strange. She had never been happy before. She was roaring, but it was a different kind of roar, and she was *licking* the wyvern as he purred, licking his jaw, his head, his wings, savoring the metallic taste of him.

The wyvern grabbed us and threw us against the ground, a different roar coming from him as well. My dragoness recognized it as if she'd heard it a million times before—he was *happy*, too. We were rolling together, slamming onto tree trunks on the way, and it was so *ticklish* to feel the branches against her scales and to feel the wyvern's claws locked around her that I laughed.

I laughed like I had never laughed before because even though they clawed each other and pushed and shoved one another against the ground, they were only playing.

The dragoness and the wyvern, playing, tasting one other, getting to know each other under the open sky.

It was the strangest, most beautiful thing I had ever seen in my lives.

THIRTY-FIVE

I KNEW I WASN'T *ME* EVEN BEFORE MY EYES OPENED, but I thought I was shifted into my dragoness still.

She'd come out, all right. She'd clawed her way out of me, taking me by surprise, taking control like she'd never done before. She'd *felt* so much it had shocked me, and when she'd seen the wyvern...

Shivers washed down the length of me at the reminder of how she'd felt about him, and I thought we were still there, playing in the forest, slamming against trees, but...

It was *bright* in the world, and when I opened my eyes, the sun was shining right over my head.

And I was...I was *small*.

Roses. Cherry trees. Cobblestones that looked like large snakes, but they didn't scare me anymore...

No—they didn't scare the person I was inside right now because I was not my dragoness.

I was not *me,* either, though I faintly remembered this place. I could have sworn I'd been here before.

And then...

"Lucien, look!"

My head moved the side, following the voice of the woman, and I looked where she was pointing—the blue butterfly floating over the large red roses to my left.

A cry escaped me, but nobody heard the sound, and I knew exactly why: I wasn't really there. Realization kicked in, shaking me to my core. I was inside a mind, the same way I'd been inside John's mind, except this was different. So, so different.

I was *Lucien* when Lucien was a little boy, playing in his mother's garden.

I was crying, *sobbing* but nobody could hear me, thank the gods. Nobody could see me, but I could see through the eyes of little Lucien. I could faintly hear his thoughts, too, and as he watched that butterfly his mother had showed him, he decided that it was the most beautiful thing to have ever existed in the world.

And he wanted it.

I *felt* the way his body moved, his steady feet, his steps almost soundless as he went between the roses. The sound of laughter behind him made his little heart flutter like the wings of that butterfly—his mother. That was his favorite sound.

And he slowed down, moving carefully as to not scare the butterfly away.

I just want to touch you, he thought in a voice that belonged to a little boy, but I heard Lucien in it. I all but melted wherever I was as I watched him moving closer, eyes never blinking, so excited you'd think he was looking at the biggest treasure of the world.

"Use your magic, son," a voice said from behind him. "Use the air beneath its wings to bring it to you—you can do it!"

His father. It had to be his father, and I was desperate to look back, to see his face, but...

Little Lucien didn't want to use his magic. He didn't want to scare the butterfly—he just wanted to touch her. And she was so beautiful, so blue, such pretty wings. Maybe he could take her to his mother—she would love her. She loved butterflies and flowers. She would take care of her the way she took care of him.

Yes, she will, he decided, and his mind was made up. Such strong conviction, I laughed among my nonexistent tears.

But the butterfly was flying up, higher and higher, beyond his reach. His mother and father were saying something to him, but he didn't hear them at all.

He wanted that butterfly. It would make his mother so happy.

He really, really wanted that butterfly. And when she climbed too high in the air, he knew he could never reach her, but he jumped for her anyway.

That's when it happened.

It wasn't painful, at least not that little Lucien felt. It was just strange to him how his body was suddenly light as air, and it changed. It changed fast, and he had no clue what was happening. He didn't really care—he just wanted that pretty blue butterfly.

Now, he could suddenly catch it no matter how high she was because he had wings, too. They were small, but they were working, and if he just kept pushing them up and down and up and down, they would work even better.

Screams behind him, but little Lucien didn't turn. The butterfly was getting away and he *had* to have it. He had to reach it, right now, before it disappeared completely.

And he did.

He flew just as high as her, and suddenly he panicked —*where are my hands?*

He had no hands, only wings, and the butterfly was

getting away again, so he opened his mouth as wide as he could and caught it between his jaws.

The tiny wings flapped against his tongue and it was ticklish. It made him want to throw up.

Don't throw up—it's nasty!

He stopped moving his wings and the next second, he fell fast and slammed onto the ground hard.

The butterfly—*are you okay*? he tried to ask her. Actually *ask* her with words, but instead strange sounds came out of him, and the moment his mouth opened to speak, the butterfly escaped. She flew out and she flapped her wings faster and faster and she rushed away, over the flowers...

But little Lucien's attention was on his parents now because they were acting really strange. They surprised him.

His father was on his knees at the beginning of the wide pathway, looking at him with weird eyes—full of tears, but little Lucien couldn't tell—and he was saying, *"My son. My boy. My little boy..."* And he was completely in awe.

But it was his mother who made him freeze in place—she was crying and she was also smiling, standing near the bench where she'd been sitting, holding her hands to her chest.

My gods, she was beautiful. Lucien had taken after her so much—the blue of her eyes and the color of her hair and her smooth, fair skin.

But in those moments, little Lucien could only think that she was crying and smiling, and it confused him so much it made me laugh. He didn't understand what was happening.

"Come to me, my boy," his father said, and little Lucien tried to walk to him, but he realized something was different about his feet. They were bigger. They were *naked*—he could feel the soil underneath like he wasn't wearing his shoes at all.

And he wasn't.

One look down and he saw his feet—they weren't feet at

all. They were paws and they had claws and his skin was white now. Completely white.

His parents kept called him to them. The panic that rose in him nearly suffocated him, just like it usually did with me.

Little Lucien screamed.

MY EYES OPENED.

THIRTY-SIX

I WAS ALONE IN THE GUEST ROOM OF THE TWINS' house when I woke up, overwhelmed with emotions, crying and smiling and just being ripped apart by feelings that weren't even mine.

My dragoness.

Little Lucien.

I'd felt all of it to my bones, and it both gave me incredible energy and drained me completely.

I was naked under the covers, and the sun was shining outside the window, which meant...

How long had I been asleep?

New old clothes at the foot of the bed. The way I'd shifted the night before, I imagined I tore the old ones Jack had brought me, which was a shame. Lucien had liked the red shirt on me, and the new one was baby blue.

And... "Oh, gods," I whispered, looking at my left hand. I was mated.

I was *mated* to Lucien, and my dragoness had already merged with me, and my skin would now be immune to fire, and...

I brought my hand closer to my lips.

"*Burn,*" I whispered to my palm.

A surge of power went through me. A single flame came into existence right over my skin. A cry escaped me—it was Fire. It was *my* Fire.

I smiled so big my cheeks hurt. I felt the heat of it, the power, and it was like I'd had it right there with me every single day of my life—I just hadn't realized it. And when I closed my fist, the fire just *slipped* under my skin painlessly, already impatient to come out again.

My gods, it was really done.

I had to tell Lucien. He had to see this. Magic was in my veins, and my Fire was everywhere—I felt it. My skin had become thicker, and I almost felt completely invincible. I had to show Lucien everything I could do, right now.

So, I put on the clothes within the minute, ran down the stairs and outside the house, ignoring the way the people looked at me, the way they stepped away instantly to make way for me—it didn't matter. I was mated, I had my Fire and my dragoness. I was—

I stopped dead in my tracks when I reached the side of the house and took in the view in front of me.

My father, *half buried, chained, bleeding* on the side of the mountain, his head down, his eyes closed, his skin white.

And the forest to the other side, almost completely ruined, while people pulled pieces of the trees to the sides, trying to clean up the mess.

"Good morning, Your Highness."

I jumped, barely holding back a scream to see Mikhaila standing there with her hands on her hips, grinning at me.

"Just don't go all dragon on me, okay?"

"What the hell happened?" I breathed, turning back to the forest and the people—Lucien, Jack and John among them, dragging pieces of broken trees to the sides.

"*You* happened, that's what," Mikhaila said, coming to stand next to me. "A bit of a heads-up would have been nice, you know. I made this plan to throw you in fire first, just to get even, but then you just shifted out of the blue."

Gods, the way she was still caught up on that made me want to smile.

"I had no other choice but to push you off the bridge," I reminded her. Trevor and a small army had been about to get us, and if I hadn't pushed Mikhaila into that river, she wouldn't have shifted. We wouldn't be here right now at all.

"Yeah, yeah, whatever," she said and showed me her phone. "Look at this. I caught most of it on camera."

And she pressed the play button in the middle of the screen without warning.

My heart tripped all over itself instantly—it was *me*. It was my dragoness, flapping her wings and trying to rise up in the air for the first time.

I took the phone from her hand and went to the back of the house and sat on the ground, a hand in front of my open mouth.

My gods, she was *gorgeous*. Her head was different from my father's—longer, the spikes more curved and sort of pulled back behind her head. Her eyes were a brilliant blue that I saw even on the camera—the same shade as mine. She was less than half the size of my father's dragon, and it took her a good few minutes to rise in the air—that to me had felt like seconds.

She cried out and roared and reached for the sky as if she was trying to claw out the stars until she finally steadied herself, looking around, searching...

"*Holy motherfucking shit, this is nuts,*" Mikhaila was whispering to her phone, while Lucien called my name.

My dragoness stopped and looked at him for a moment, suspended on air, red wings spread wide. Even the red of her scales was different from my father's, so much brighter.

And then she flew higher and higher, moving closer to the small mountain and the forest.

The view was disrupted while Mikhaila probably ran with her phone in her hand, and when it cleared up again, the drake was already there, running to my father as if to *protect* him.

When the dragoness saw it, she roared at the top of her voice, a roar I hadn't even felt, too consumed with what went on inside my dragoness in those moments, focused on her feelings. She'd been irritated at the sight of the drake. She'd even imagined exactly how she'd kill him—rip him in half by the heads.

Goose bumps rose on my forearms. I'd never known her to be so violent before. The way she *felt* everything was different from my other lives. The way she thought—in sentences that I understood and in images that I could see—was incredible.

And then Lucien.

His wyvern rose in the air to the right of the dragoness, over fifty feet away. Lucien must have shifted right in front of the twins' house.

When she saw him, she froze. I'd felt that second, too—even her wings hadn't moved, yet somehow the air had held her up anyway.

And then she moved.

The wyvern moved, too, and they both flew toward one another lightning fast.

People screamed. Mikhaila sounded *terrified*, and I understood why. From down here, it had looked like the dragoness and the wyvern were *attacking* each other.

And then they collided in the air, wings and arms wrapped around each other as they spun around.

More screams—it really, *really* looked like they were fighting, trying to bite each other's heads off. I found myself smiling at the video as the dragoness and the wyvern roared and purred and tasted each other, explored each other with their teeth and claws and tongue—and then they were spinning and spinning again, pushing and pulling at each other, until they were right over the forest.

Then they hit the ground with a loud thud that shook the ground.

Mikhaila kept cursing under her breath as she moved again, running to get closer.

The dragoness and the wyvern were *playing*. I could see it, understood why the people watching were so terrified—it didn't look like a game. It looked like they were fighting as they slammed each other onto the ground and against trees, bit each other and roared—that was *laughter,* I could tell, even though it sounded bad. It sounded like the end of the damn world.

"Yeah, yeah, keep smiling," Mikhaila said as she stood over me, watching the video, too. "You almost gave us a godsdamn heart attack."

"They were just playing," I said, then flinched when I saw how the draca had ruined the forest completely—slamming onto trees like they weren't even there. I hadn't even noticed —gods, I thought we'd just bumped a couple trees on the way.

"Of course. Just playing—two big ass dragons, *playing*," Mikhaila said, shaking her head, and the video ended.

"What happened then?"

She took her phone back. "Then both of you flew away, and then the white dragon came back with you in his claws— as a girl. Naked ass girl."

"The wyvern," I corrected, but she rolled her eyes.

"They're all dragons to me."

I stood up again, looking at the forest, at Lucien, who was looking my way, too, even though he was still dragging pieces of wood toward the piles near the houses.

In my head, I saw little Lucien chasing that blue butterfly, catching it with the wyvern's mouth, and my dragoness roared in my head.

It scared me so much I jumped. It was a roar—a real roar, even though the world couldn't hear it.

My gods, she was really here.

And my father was, too.

I tried not to look at him, tried to focus on Lucien coming my way, a small smile on his face.

Just don't look...

"There he comes," Mikhaila said. "Come eat with me after you're done—and *do not* shift again, you hear me?"

"Sure," I said, trying to smile for her sake, before she turned around and went back to the houses.

Suddenly, as I waited for Lucien, I was perfectly aware of all the people watching me—the fear in their eyes, the way they kept a bigger distance than usual from me.

They'd seen. Gods, the show I'd given these poor people last night. They'd seen all of it.

"Hey, beautiful," Lucien said, taking his hand in mine, bringing my knuckles to his lips to kiss them.

"Hey," I said, already breathless. "Can we go somewhere?"

He grinned, like that was exactly what he'd wanted to hear, then pulled me to the side, toward the other end of the houses.

I kept my head down as I followed him, not wanting to see the looks in people's eyes just yet—I was embarrassed. Ashamed that I'd lost control so easily, until Lucien pulled me into a narrow space between two houses, the grass so long it reached my knees.

Then he pushed me against the wall and pressed onto me, taking my face in his hands.

Everything else came to a halt just like that, and a sigh escaped me—I hoped it never stopped feeling like this to be touched by him.

"My dragoness is madly in love with your wyvern," I said,

and his lips were hovering right over mine, so I felt them stretching into a wide smile.

"My wyvern is worse," he said. "He won't shut up about it. It's like he's not even mine anymore." He kissed my lips gently. "He'll follow you anywhere now..." His tongue slid over my lower lip. "I'll follow you anywhere."

He kissed me again, this time almost violently, just like I needed. I wrapped my arms around him, and he pulled me up until my ankles locked around his hips. I was already panting, so wet it was uncomfortable, and my dragoness's roar was in my head, too, igniting me even more than Lucien's kiss usually did.

Gods, I was *burning* and his tongue in my mouth, his hands on my ass, his hard cock against my center suddenly became the whole world for me.

I wanted our clothes off, and I wanted him to be inside me, deep and hard and fast, and I wanted to ride him until I couldn't move anymore.

I wanted his cum inside me, filling me up, and I wanted—

My eyes popped open. The heat on my skin burned in the best possible way, and the need gnawing at my insides was driving me insane, but it was different from what Lucien usually felt like.

So different—and I knew why.

I'd *mated*—and my dragoness wanted a little baby dragon already.

"Lucien," I breathed, and he was worse than me—eyes bloodshot, biting my lips so hard he drew blood, grinding his hard cock against my center like he couldn't even imagine stopping for a second to take my clothes off.

"Lucien, stop," I breathed, though I was kissing him, touching him, moving against him, my hands under his shirt, scratching his skin.

But we needed to stop soon because I *would* get pregnant.

Right away, on the first try—I would. And I thought I understood why it had never happened in my other lives—my dragoness had never *wanted* to breed before. She'd never even
made her presence known when I was with my husbands in
my past lives. I'd never felt her there, and now she was
everywhere.

"I can't," Lucien breathed. "Fuck, little fox, I can't stop.
Do you have any idea how you taste?" He bit my lip again and
moaned, and my back arched all the way as I tried to melt onto
him. "I want to tear your clothes off and fuck you until
sundown. I want to fill your beautiful pussy with my cum
until it drips out of you. I want to own each one of your holes,
and make you come so many times you'll—"

"*Stop!*" I choked, putting my hand over his mouth.

Gods, I was so wet I couldn't breathe. I pushed him back
and jumped to the ground.

He fell against the wall of the house on the opposite side,
eyes completely red, breathing as heavily as me, looking at me
like he wanted to *eat* me raw.

"Little fox," he said, and it was a growl, low and animalis-
tic, and I was dripping so hard even my jeans were wet.

"Stop—don't come near me," I warned him when he
made an attempt to move.

"I *need* you," he breathed—and gods, he'd never looked
sexier to me than he did right now.

It was our animals. *They* were doing this to us—they
wanted us to mate and to fuck and to make baby dragons—
and like a fool I'd asked to be alone with him.

Run, my mind screamed at me. *Just get away from him!*

Lucien reached both hands to grab me.

I ran back behind the houses like he was about to rip my
heart out.

People. I squeezed my eyes shut and breathed—people all

around us. They could all see us—the men working in the forest, and the women going about their business.

My father—*focus on Father!*

Gods, I couldn't even see.

None of this was supposed to happen—I wasn't prepared for this. Not this clawing urge, not these all-consuming feelings—I'd never had them before, not in any life.

"It's okay," Lucien said, and I blinked the black dots away from my vision until I saw him.

He'd stepped away from the houses, too, his eyes on the ground, breathing in deeply.

"It's okay, little fox. We're in control," he said—but we weren't. We couldn't be allowed to be alone with one another right now—too dangerous.

"Just...just don't come close enough to touch me," I said, and he nodded.

"I won't," he said. "I won't. It's just the animals. They'll settle down."

"*When*? Because this has never happened before with my husbands. I've mated six other times, and never did my dragoness lose her mind like this, and—"

"*Don't* say that word," Lucien suddenly hissed.

I blink. "What?"

He looked *mad* all of a sudden. "Don't say that word in front of me, little fox. Because then I want to kill something."

I raised my brows. "*Husbands*?" Was that the word he meant?

Yep—it was. His eyes closed and his jaws clenched so hard I saw it.

"It's fine—I won't. I won't say it again, okay? I just mean..." My voice trailed off. I didn't know what the hell I was saying. My eyes squeezed shut. "The *Ether*, Lucien. We need to summon the Ether."

And my dragoness cried out in my head again, this time a different sound.

"Yes," Lucien said. "We will. Tonight—we will."

I nodded. "Good. Good." I moved back a couple of steps. "Until then, let's just keep some distance between us."

He looked like I'd stabbed him. "Okay."

"Okay," I whispered. We could do this. We had this—it wouldn't be that hard.

There were people around us and they were watching us, and...

"I saw you," I whispered, suddenly smiling when the memory came back to me in a rush. My gods, I'd *seen* him! "I was in your mind, Lucien. I saw it when you were chasing that butterfly. I saw you when you first shifted!"

I'd seen his mother and his father, and the garden he'd built for her to watch the moon from. The roses, the trees, the way his parents had looked at Lucien—so lovingly, like he was their whole world.

"I was six years old," Lucien said. Only six years old. Tears in my eyes.

"They were so proud of you," I said with barely any voice.

Lucien met my eyes. "I saw you, too."

My heart skipped a beat. He'd been inside my mind, too. "Really? When I shifted?"

But Lucien shook his head. "No—another memory."

"Which one?" Because I'd seen what my dragoness had been so desperate to know about. The moment she'd laid eyes on Lucien's wyvern, she'd wanted to know how he was born, too. That's why I figured whichever memory Lucien had seen was something he'd really wanted to know about.

"When you came back," Lucien said, and he didn't look very happy anymore. Instead, he looked...regretful. "When you came back with Mikhaila." My smile dropped. "When you saw your father."

"Oh." Words got stuck in my throat. Every good feeling that had consumed me until now let go all at once.

"I'm sorry, little fox," he said and tried to come closer. I moved back on instinct. "If I'd known, I'd have—"

"What?" I cut him off. My voice was back to sounding like a stranger's. "You'd have let him kill you?"

Lucien looked like I'd stabbed him *and* set him on fire. He lowered his shaking head—he had nothing to say.

Neither did I.

"I'm gonna go eat with Mikhaila, then we'll prepare to summon the Ether," I said, and he nodded, so I turned to leave, but...

"Estella." I only turned my head, knowing whatever he was going to say to me was going to hurt.

I was right.

"It's not your fault," Lucien whispered. "He's your father. It's not your fault."

He meant it wasn't my fault that I cared.

He was a liar.

THIRTY-SEVEN

BARELY AN HOUR UNTIL SUNDOWN.

John had learned Alexandra's spell by memory. Mikhaila was practicing Water magic with Rowan. Lucien and Jack had been working on the forest all day with the other men from town, and they'd already cleaned up the whole mess.

My father still hadn't opened his eyes.

He was still bleeding, though slowly. So slowly.

As slowly as I was dying, sitting there looking at him.

And my dragoness had stopped screaming in my head a long time ago. It had been...how many hours since I sat here?

I didn't know, but we'd be summoning the Ether soon. We'd put an end to this madness and go back to normal, soon.

I'm sorry, Lucien had said because he'd been in my head, had seen the memory of the moment I saw my father like this —had probably felt my feelings and heard some of my thoughts, too, just like I did his.

But was that *it?* Or was Lucien sorry for something else?

I raised my hand—I hadn't showed him my Fire at all. Better that we didn't go close to one another, or I forgot reason and succumbed to my dragoness's most primal needs.

Burn, I thought in my head, and the Fire heard. It sparked to life in the middle of my palm, dancing slowly to the rhythm of my heartbeat, warming me to my core. I couldn't wait to train, to learn how to expand that little flame into a blazing inferno...

I'm sorry.

Not just because of what he'd seen in my head, but because he knew that it was only going to get worse. So much worse.

I fisted my hand and the Fire disappeared. The question remained, though—would I keep lying to myself? Would I keep telling myself that my father would survive this?

Or would I actually admit to myself that the moment the Ether was here, he would kill him?

As long as Archibald Azarius is still alive, there will be no balance among the elements. That is what the Ether told John.

And my father was still alive.

Closing my eyes for a moment, I tried to breathe in deeply. Secrets inside me—once again, I was full of them. And I couldn't bring myself to speak about them. Not just about my father—but about Alexandra, too. I hadn't had the guts to even mention to Lucien or the others what I'd talked about with Mikhaila.

How had Alexandra known where Mikhaila was?

Why did she want me to summon the Ether?

Later. I would have to talk about all of it with him later, just as soon as this was done.

"Hey."

I turned to find John walking over the narrow bridge he and Jack had made for me yesterday to cross over the river of lava they'd called around my father. An extra measure of security, just in case.

"Hey," I said, suddenly feeling like I was sitting on needles.

"You okay?" he asked, squatting by my side, ignoring my father like he wasn't still chained right there.

"Peachy," I said, and he could hear the sarcasm in my voice just fine.

"We're almost ready," he said. "As soon as the sun starts to set."

I nodded. "Okay."

"Okay," he repeated. "You don't want to come inside, maybe rest—"

"I'm good," I cut him off.

"Good," he repeated.

The air between us was thick and heavy with tension like it had never been before. He stayed there for a moment longer, as if he wanted to say something, but then he changed his mind, and just stood up to leave.

But I changed my mind, too, when a memory came back to me.

"What did he say to you?"

John stopped walking again. The memory wasn't even my own—it was my dragoness's. Last night, my father had been awake when I shifted, though only for a little while, and he'd said something. My dragoness had seen—her eyes were so much better than mine. She'd seen him saying something, but she'd been too far up in the air to hear.

Not Jack and John, though. They—their drake—had been right here with him, *protecting* him from my dragoness.

John said nothing for a long time, so I turned to see if he was still there. And when I met his eyes, I knew what went on in his head—he wanted to lie to me.

He *wanted* to.

"Ella," he said, but I needed to know.

"Tell me the truth. I'm just curious," I insisted. So very curious, like a stranger under my skin.

John closed his eyes, hands fisted at his sides. "*That's my daughter,*" he whispered reluctantly. "He said, *that's my daughter.*"

I nodded, turned back to my father.

John walked away.

There was never a time when I hadn't wanted my father's approval, no matter in how many ways I hated myself for it.

"You seem surprised."

I looked up, the view blurry—I had tears in my eyes, and I hadn't even noticed.

But when I blinked them away, I realized my father's eyes were open, though his head was down still.

Half buried. Chained. Bleeding.

Alive.

"I'm not," I said, pretending my heart didn't want to fly out of my chest. Pretending my stomach wasn't twisting and turning and threatening to swallow me whole. Pretending my dragoness wasn't screaming her guts out in my head. "Not really. You love that dragoness," I forced myself to finish.

And Father raised his head a bit. "Of course, I do—she is going to make sure you're safe for the rest of your life," he had the audacity to say.

But I was pretending, wasn't I? I could pretend a bit more.

So, I raised my brows. "What—like *you* are now?" He had a dragon, too—one bigger, stronger, faster than mine. And look at how he'd ended up.

Father sighed. "I let my guard down," was what he said, and that curiosity in me turned to a monster again—*how*? How had they managed to trap him like this?

Why hadn't I asked Lucien?

Why had I been so terrified of the answer?

I still was...

"A wyvern *and* a drake," Father said, and he made an attempt to laugh. "And you mated with him, too." If he was accusing me, I didn't hear it.

"Do you know who he is?" I asked instead, and Father met my eyes. His were so dull. No more green in them, just a muddy brown, completely spent. "Blood Blade's son."

He hadn't known. Of course, he hadn't known—and now I told him and I saw his pain. I felt it all over me.

"Lucien Di Laurier is his name," I continued, and I had no idea why it was important that he knew that.

He thought about it for a second, eyes on the ground again. "I guess it makes sense in a twisted way..."

It would—to him, it absolutely would. The way he'd killed Lucien's father, the way he'd tried to kill John and Mikhaila, too. He'd known. All this time, he'd known, and he'd made me think I was insane.

And it just pissed me off—*so so so much!*—that I wanted to claw my eyes out, because....

"Why don't I hate you?" How dare I not despise this man? What kind of a monster was *I*?

But I knew the answer to that question: I was a very specific kind—an Azarius.

"Of course, you do," Father said, and he sounded so sure of it. "You hate me almost as much as I hate myself."

Did I, though? Because I knew how much he hated himself. I'd seen it in that mirror in the library with my own eyes, right before he burned it.

"We're going to summon the Ether tonight," I said, and at that, my Father raised his head all the way.

His strength was incredible—he'd been bleeding for days, never eating or drinking, buried in a shitload of magic, both Air and Earth, and he was still conscious. I'd never seen him look worse, but he was awake. He was talking to me.

"There's so much you don't understand yet, my daughter," he said, and he suddenly sounded exhausted.

"I've tried telling you that, you know. I've tried talking to you." And I wanted the pain so much that I hurt him the best way I knew how. "See, I tricked you, Father. I was never at the tournament—Greta was under that artora, pretending to be me. I ran away." I could tell by the look in his eyes that this was news to him. "I was in Lucien's town, very close to the castle, but you can't see it because it's invisible. I was there for twelve days." I'd made a home out of it. "And then I found my way into one of the Moving Forests, too."

"Ella," my father said, but I'd started now and I couldn't stop. I couldn't let myself stop because I would never say this again—and I needed him to know.

"They confirmed that what you called *fantasies* were actually true—I have really lived six lives before this. And I've already died six times. Every time I die or one of the draca dies, time resets and we go back. We start over. To try again—to overthrow you and bring the balance back to the world."

"No," he said, trying to shake his head, which then made him move a little bit, and the tips of those swords went in deeper, and he bled more, and I was crying just as fast as he was bleeding.

"Yes," I said. "Yes—and I finally did it. I finally had the courage to do something with my pathetic lives, and I put a stop to you." I sank my fingernails into the ground so hard they bled. "I put a stop to you, Father."

"You don't know..." he whispered, and I didn't stop.

"I ran away. I ran from Trevor. I made a difference—I changed something. After six lives, I changed something." So why did it feel like I made everything *worse*?

"So many things I need to tell you," Father said, but I was done listening to him now.

"You made me think I was crazy. You never believed me, Father. And you...you kill children? How can you... how do you..." I couldn't speak.

Too many heavy words, I couldn't carry them all on my own. I buckled under their weight.

Father raised his head again. "I would never kill children," he had the audacity to say, so I laughed. "I would *never* kill children, my daughter."

"Of course, you would—you tried. You almost killed John. You almost killed Mikhaila."

And he shook his head, moving again—*stop moving!*—and the swords went deeper. All that blood. So much blood.

"No. I would never. I never wanted to kill them," he said. "I never...I never..."

"You did!" I thought I shouted. "John has been asleep for six years because your men shot him with a poisoned arrow on his leg. Mikhaila had to fake her own death at eleven just to keep her parents safe from *you*!"

He looked surprised. The guts on this man. The courage in him to look surprised, and say, "No."

"How *dare* you."

"You don't know what you're talking about, Estella," he said. "You don't know what you're saying."

"You're a liar," I spit, but he kept shaking his head— moving, moving, moving.

"There's so much you don't understand," he whispered. "The Ether...it's not what you think."

I laughed again—gods, it sounded so awful.

"You can't summon him, my daughter," he said. "If you do, unspeakable things will happen."

I dug the heels of my hands in my eyes like I wanted to stop seeing him forever.

"No, Father," I said then. "It's just that the reign of dragons will end."

Finally.

"Do you know what that means?" I looked at him, at his pale face and blue lips and dull eyes. "Do you know why the reign of dragons exists?"

Blood dripped out of his lips. He tried to talk, but he couldn't.

And it was for the best.

"I know why the reign of dragons exist," I told him. "To keep the power for ourselves."

No more.

"Yes," he choked. "And...and to save the world as we know it."

Lies, lies, lies. Everything around me was always a lie.

Everything around me was always confusing.

And he could barely keep his eyes open while he spit out blood.

"I'm tired," I thought I said. "I'm just so tired, Father. I want this to end. I don't want to go back."

Seven times.

My soul was old. It wanted to rest.

Father couldn't say anything for a while, and I thought maybe he'd fallen unconscious again.

I stared at the darkening sky, at the white clouds over us.

"I met Annabelle, you know," I whispered, watching them floating in the sky. "She told me about Mom, about her plans to *change the world*. Why did she change her mind?" I wondered, though I didn't expect an answer. "What did you do to her?"

A second ticked by.

"I'm tired, too, Estella," Father whispered so low I barely heard him. "I'm tired of being here without her..." He said more, words slurred together that I couldn't understand, and then... "Maybe this is for the best."

Maybe.

"She was taken from me," I said, watching the blood coming out of him again—so much more color than the sky could offer me. So much more pain. His was mine to feel, no matter that I didn't understand why. He hurt, and so did I.

"Why did you say that, Father? On the night of my engagement party, why did you say, *she was taken from me?*"

He didn't speak.

For a long time, Father didn't move at all, but then he said...

"Because she was."

Lies, lies, lies.

"Who took her from you?" My voice was eerily calm.

Father tried to raise his head but couldn't—I saw the muscles on his neck straining. "The Ether."

That old noise went on in my head—white noise that spread all over me, under my skin, taking me away for a second.

But when I blinked the darkness away and I focused on the sounds of the world around me, nothing had changed. My father was still there. My father still spoke.

"There's so much wrong I've done in my life. I wish we knew better, your mother and I. I wish we knew better..."

"Knew better about what?" I asked, my voice completely dry.

But he said, "Don't trust the Ether, Estella. Remember who you are."

It was like he was pulling me apart with his own hands all over again.

"*Ella!*"

People were calling my name. I couldn't turn. I couldn't stop staring at my father.

Why would he do this to me now? How could he lie to me in this way?!

Gods, I knew why—he would do *anything* at all to stop me from doing what was right, from summoning the Ether, from putting an end to his life. He would do anything to continue the reign of dragons, even lie to me about my mother.

Even raise his head a little—just a little so he could see me, see the way I'd frozen on the ground, worse than a statue—because I *felt*. Statues didn't.

"I'm sorry, my daughter. I'm sorry I didn't know how to be a father. I was only ever taught how to be a king."

Blood on his lips.

Hands on my shoulders.

"Estella, we need to go."

John, Jack, Lucien around me. My father didn't move, his head down, his eyes closed.

He didn't speak again.

Thirty-Eight

Liar.

He was a liar, the best of them, the biggest of them, the smartest of them.

He knew exactly how to get to me. He knew exactly how to make me second guess everything.

He knew how to infiltrate my thoughts and turn them against one another.

Liar, liar, liar.

Lucien was in front of me, his hands on my face. I was standing now—had I moved? Because I couldn't remember. But I was standing, and he was in front of me, and he was asking me if I was okay.

Yes, I thought I said. *I'm fine.*

I was a liar, too.

I would never believe him. Of course, I didn't—I knew who he was. I knew exactly who my father was.

I would not fall prey to his manipulations. Never.

Because that's what this was—his last attempt at manipulating me, so he threw lies at my face and tried to disguise them as truths. He spit blood out of his mouth to say them to me because he was afraid.

He was terrified that it was over.

He wasn't tired. He didn't think this was for the best—he was just *terrified* that it was over!

...wasn't he?

I looked up at the moon, almost full, reigning over the dark sky—*he's just a liar, isn't he? He just lied!*

And the moon asked me, "*What if he didn't?*"

"We're going to start now. I think the whole thing is pretty straightforward. We need the elements, manipulated by our magic, and then I say the words within ten seconds, and it's done. Are we ready?"

John—that was his voice. It was different from Jack's, though they were more identical now than they'd ever been.

"Estella?"

I blinked, then focused on his face, only to realize that they'd all moved.

We were standing in a circle near the willow tree, with an audience of at least fifty people around us. Jack and John, sitting across from me, held up a ball of dirt inches over the grass with their magic. Mikhaila, sitting to my left, held up a ball of water, eyes stuck on it and teeth gritted, as if she was having trouble keeping focus. And Lucien, sitting to my right, swirled air around his fingers, and I could almost *see* how fast it moved.

They were all looking at me.

I didn't speak at all, I just pressed my palm to the ground and thought, *burn*. My skin caught Fire, and so did the grass and the ground underneath it.

Nobody made a single sound.

I looked at the flames, at the way they lit up the dark, a stranger in my own skin.

What am I doing? I thought I asked myself.

I knew the answer to that.

I was sitting here, ready to summon the Ether.

I was sitting here, ready to return the balance of the elements to the world and save the people from the reign of dragons.

I was sitting here, watching my father, *half buried, chained, bleeding,* until the Ether came here and killed him.

And then, I would sit here and watch that, too, until it was over.

Until I existed no more.

A hand over my forearm squeezing me. I looked to the side, to Lucien, eyes wide and perfectly blue, perfectly concerned.

He raised his brows: *What are you doing?* he asked me, too.

I am killing my father.

Was that the *right* thing to do—or the Azarius thing to do?

"Are we ready?" John asked, and I couldn't look way from Lucien. He couldn't look away from me.

My dragoness cried out in my head—it could have been his name. She wanted to reach out and touch him.

She wanted to apologize because she was coming.

And Lucien smiled as if he heard her. Then he nodded, too, as if to say, *it's okay, little fox. It's okay.*

I was beginning to think there would never come a time when I *wouldn't* be crying my eyes out because right now, I couldn't stop the tears. They were relentless, rushing out of my eyes like they were in a race.

John called my name, called Lucien, but neither of us looked away from one another.

The dragoness was coming, and I knew I wouldn't be strong enough to stop her.

Gods help me, I didn't want to.

I'm sorry, I said to him with my eyes, and with my mind, and he understood. I liked to think he heard that, too.

He squeezed my forearm again, and I broke a little more. If I'd been a mountain when this first began, I was reduced to tiny rock on the ground by now.

My dragoness took over before I'd finished taking in a full breath.

Half of me was surprised, and the other half expected it. Since she'd taken over right after I completed mating with Lucien, I knew. There was a reason why she'd wanted out —*right away*—and there was a reason why she'd taken flight immediately, when her wings hadn't even been properly stretched yet.

I'd felt it in her, and I'd chosen to ignore it because she got so easily distracted by Lucien's wyvern. She'd looked at Father, and she'd lost sense of everything else, but that didn't mean she'd forgotten.

Especially now, when I'd admitted to myself beyond a shadow of doubt that my father wouldn't survive this night, not once the Ether was here.

She hadn't forgotten at all, and she would not accept that. She simply refused to let him die on her watch.

I refused to let him die on my watch.

And now we were flying.

The pain of the shifting barely reached me. My skin stretched and my bones broke, and I felt them rearranging themselves as my body expanded, but I hardly felt the pain that came with it because of the fear. Because of the excitement.

Because of this incredible relief that I'd decided to do something, that I could stop trying to pretend—I had decided to take action.

We were *flying*.

I looked down at the others, all of them standing now,

John and Jack shouting at me to get down, while Mikhaila refused to even stand up. Maybe she just couldn't—she seemed to have frozen in place.

Lucien just looked at me. He didn't smile, didn't nod, didn't do anything other than look at me.

I roared at him to tell him how much I loved him—both my dragoness and I did.

And then, we turned for my father.

He had his eyes open, and his head up—somehow he was still conscious. And when we flew over the river of lava and landed in front of him, he smiled. Gods, the way I saw his paper-thin skin, so white it made me sick. The way I saw the colors leaking from his eyes, so fast it made me want to break the whole mountain that held him back.

I went closer, and my dragoness cried out—she was in pain. She was angry. She was outraged.

Father threw his head back and closed his eyes. He was surrendering. He thought my dragoness was there to kill him. And wouldn't that have been the right, smart, *better* thing to do?

Claws against chains, breaking them apart. My dragoness jumped in the air before the chains hit the ground and wrapped her talons around my father's arms. His eyes were closed, his head moving to the sides without any control —unconscious.

Then, she took us up.

Screams and shouts, people calling my name, Lucien watching me without an ounce of disappointment or judgment or accusation.

He understood. That's all I truly cared about.

My father's body came out of the ground where the twins had half buried him, and where they'd kept his magic under lock. The swords that had been cutting him in five places, bleeding him out, remained on the ground as we flew up. They could no longer hurt him.

My father was heavy, but my dragoness didn't care. She rose higher and higher, holding on tightly to his arms.

Then she let out a heart-wrenching sound that was meant as a warning to the whole world. And with another look at Lucien, so small, feet stuck to the ground, she took us away.

Thirty-Nine

Lucien Di Laurier

SHE'D GROWN A BIT, my animal said. He knew her already —knew every inch of her body, every scale and every claw, every shade of red that made her. And he was trying to shred me to pieces, demanding I let him out so he could follow her.

Anywhere in the world, he'd follow her. He didn't care about anything anymore as long as she was close. One look— that's all it had taken. One look at the dragoness, and he found his purpose. To serve her—that's what he was here for.

And I wanted to agree. She felt unlike anything else I could have possibly imagined. I'd gone through life unenthusiastically, never really expecting to find the beauty poets wrote about. I thought that was simply fiction, and real life was *real,* and I had myself to sacrifice for the greater good. That's all I ever knew. That's all I accepted.

Until Estella.

So, I understood my animal and his needs, and I understood mine, too, now as we watched her fly away with her father. I knew she would do this the moment I connected to her and went through to her mind.

That morning when she and Rowan came back with Mikhaila, I'd never forget the look on her face when she saw her father. When she fell to her knees and cried in silence, she'd looked like the world had ended right before her eyes.

I'd thought about what it must have been like *inside* her, and maybe that's why I saw it. However, this connection we had worked—that's what I saw. The moment she took in her father chained to the mountain and the way it killed her.

I had never felt pain more raw in my life.

I'd lost both my parents, but never had I felt even half of what she felt in that short minute before she collapsed. It was a miracle she hadn't fallen apart physically, too, because her soul had. I'd felt it. That she was able to contain all of that inside her told me just how strong she was—so much more than I had given her credit for until then.

And I'd known she would never let her father die. After feeling all that she felt, I was glad she hadn't. As much as it killed me to admit it, what would be left of her would never be my Estella again.

"What the hell, what the hell—*what the hell*—" John was shouting, and Jack was trying to calm him down, and somehow Rowan was right beside me, looking up at the small dot that Estella had become in the sky before she disappeared completely in the dark of the night.

Gone.

I looked at Rowan. He looked at me.

And he smiled, as if he was glad she'd gotten away, too.

He must have been just as insane as I was.

Slowly, I took my magic back, feeling it spread under my skin, finally at home. There would be no need to keep this place shielded anymore. The king was not going to come find us. Nobody was.

"Lucien, this is insane! What the hell—did she talk to you about this? Did she—"

"Calm down, John," I said, turning to him. "Calm down."

"I can't calm down—we were so close! We can't—"

"We still are," I said, and took my place on the ground again, around the fire burning the grass, the fire that had come right out of Estella's hand—true Fire that had already connected Mikhaila's Water, the twins' Earth, and my Air.

A full circle.

I looked up at John, who stared at the Fire like he was seeing it for the first time.

"It will work without the princess?" Jack asked, and I nodded.

"We need the elements. We have the elements. I suggest we hurry before the Fire goes out," I said, and the twins sat down so fast, I almost laughed.

I was in good spirits—for what, I had no idea. My little fox, who was a gorgeous, terrifying red dragoness, was gone, and I had no idea when she'd be back.

But I knew she would. And that was why I was calm.

"I don't know, guys," Mikhaila said, hands shaking as she looked at us. "Without her, it feels wrong."

"It doesn't have to feel right," I promised her, words my father had said to me a thousand times. "And it's okay that Estella left. She knew we'd be able to summon the Ether without her, put an end to this."

"Yeah," Jack said, nodding. "I think she knew. She *wants* us to go ahead—she just didn't want her father to die."

John nodded, already convinced. Sometimes I wondered if he wanted this more than the rest of us did. More than *me*—and I'd been raised with this purpose in mind since I was a six-year-old boy chasing butterflies.

Taking in a deep breath, he said, "I'm ready."

Mikhaila sat down on the ground again next to me.

Rowan stayed close, too, watching, more curious than I'd ever seen him before about anything.

"Do it," Jack said, and John grinned, looking at all of us.

"I'll see you in a better world," he said.

Then he began to chant.

Forty

It doesn't have to feel right.

That's what my father said to me when he first shared with me his plan. We were in his office, and I must have been no older than sixteen when he said, "We can't do this alone. We need her."

And I said, "Who?" thinking maybe he meant Taylor or Nina, my sisters.

"The princess," my father said. "We need her to kill the king."

I remembered that day clearly because I thought for a moment, what would I say if I ever found out that someone, somewhere, wanted to use me to kill my father?

The question remained with me. Every time I tried to tell my father that there had to be another way, that it felt so wrong to turn a daughter against her father, he said, "*It doesn't have to feel right, Lucien. It just has to* be *right.*"

And I believed him. For the longest time, my whole life, I believed him. As long as it was right, I could do it. I could get to the other end of this.

Right now, with every breath I took, I proved myself right.

I'd done it. I'd gotten to the end of it. I'd done what my father had spent his whole life trying to do. I'd fulfilled his dream, the dream of my ancestors, of a better world.

It was the *right* thing to do.

And it still felt so wrong my wyvern drove me nuts with the growls. His instincts were much more enhanced than mine.

I should have listened.

Instead, John finished speaking the words he'd memorized, words Alexandra Azarius had written herself on that book page, and I stayed put, watched the flames dancing on the ground, burning the grass.

I felt the hum on my skin, like the pressure from my Air magic, even though I wasn't using it right now. I wasn't shielding anything anymore, yet the pressure was right there.

And it began to rise in the air as I watched.

The Fire burning between us was put out at once.

The entire town held their breath as we watched the tendrils of smoke gather up in a ball a few inches away from the ground.

And then we saw the shimmer.

It came to life out of thin air, charging it with so much energy, it shocked me. The shape of a man, his head and his shoulders, came together slowly, and I realized that up until that moment, I hadn't really believed that this was possible. I hadn't truly thought we could actually do this, summon the Ether, bring him back.

But it was happening right in front of my eyes.

And my wyvern was relentless.

"My gods," John whispered, reaching out his hand to touch the shimmer that kept gaining more and more color as the seconds ticked by.

The sound of laughter came from somewhere far away or from the inside of my head.

Then, all sound was *absorbed* from the world completely, as if someone had put me inside a bubble. The shimmer grew bigger, and it sucked me in, and I lost control of my body completely. It felt like I was moving, but I was frozen in place instead, and the shimmer grew bigger and bigger and bigger...

It doesn't feel right, Dad.

That's because it never was.

The explosion took me by surprise, the sheer energy and heat coming from the shimmer that had *burst* into fireworks, picking me up and throwing me in the air, so high all I saw was the dark of the sky.

No sound yet—I was still stuck in that bubble that separated me from the world, and my body was still frozen, unable to move, and I was falling, slow, then faster...

I hit the ground on my back so hard, the earth cracked and groaned under my weight. Every bone in my body felt completely broken, and my lungs refused to expand.

Estella.

My mind shut down and turned on again, as if someone was playing with its remote. On and off. Loud, then completely silent.

My wyvern couldn't reach me, and my mind couldn't reach my limbs. My body was foreign, no order of mine registering or obeyed.

Raise your head.

Sit up.

Stand!

I must have ordered myself a thousand times before I was able to move my hands, before I was able to blink the blur and the bright stars away from my vision and move, only slightly, to see better.

To find out what had happened. What had exploded.

Where the others were...*Rowan.*

Nobody moved. Nobody spoke or made a single sound—

except the hiss in the air, coming off the naked man lying on the grass at the heart of it all, at the exact point where the explosion had happened and had pushed every blade of grass away, every person, had broken every window in the nearest houses and every branch on the willow tree.

Estella.

I pushed myself up, searching the inside of my mind for my wyvern to find comfort in his growl, to know I could let him loose any second, but my animal refused to make a single sound, like he wasn't even there.

And the man began to move.

To my right, I could faintly see Jack sitting up, and then Mikhaila. Their noses were bleeding, and I thought I felt blood on my upper lip, too, but I was too distracted by the view to check.

Too distracted by the man who was slowly rising to his feet, and his skin was *buzzing*. I felt it in the air, felt the way it vibrated with energy, as if it contained it, as if one touch could blast you, reduce you to ashes.

He was as tall as me, skinnier but ripped, dark blond hair, bags under his eyes as dark as the hollows of his cheeks. The smile on his face raised the hairs on my forearms. His eyes, dark and gleaming, searched the bodies of each one of us, and they skimmed over my face as if I wasn't even there.

He turned around, slowly, searching, watching, and his back...

On his back was a large tattoo of black wings, like a bat's, like my wyvern's, and electricity jolts jumped on his skin. I felt the magic in them, felt the way they charged the air, and they were coming right from his body.

Impossible, my mind insisted. It wasn't possible.

And then he turned to me again, making a full circle. His eyes finally stopped on my face. He *saw* me and I saw him. I saw his magic buzzing and slipping out of his pores—pure, raw electricity.

It doesn't feel right because it isn't.

"Where..."

His voice was like smoke, dark and cold, sneaky, just like the rest of him.

And he closed his eyes, inhaled deeply.

"Are you...are you the Ether?"

Jack.

He was sitting up now, same as me, and he was shaking. John was still down, and Mikhaila was still trying to keep her head up, but Jack was smiling.

He was smiling and he shouldn't have been.

"Yes," the man said, long fingers fisted as small jolts of electricity flashed all around his knuckles. "Yes, I am."

Jack laughed. "We did it," he said, reaching for his brother, shaking his arm. "Wake up, John. We did it! *We did it*!"

The man moved.

Like a charge of electricity, he disappeared from where he was standing and appeared crouching right next to Jack, his hand wrapped around his neck.

"Where. Is. My. *Fire?*"

He merely whispered, but the words were in my head.

Jack couldn't breathe. Electricity slipped into his skin and his eyes rolled in his skull.

"She's gone!" Mikhaila shouted, and she was on her feet, crying, rushing to the Ether. "Let him go—she left!"

The Ether let go of Jack and stood up, smiling so widely as he turned to Mikhaila.

"What are you doing?!" she demanded. "You're supposed to be the good guy—you were *hurting* him!"

Jack was breathing, but he was unconscious now, same as John.

I pushed myself up—my animal. Where was my animal?

He had been with me every day since I was six. Where was he now?

The laughter echoed in my head, making me look at him. The Ether.

The biggest mistake I'd ever made.

"The *good* guy?" he asked in a slight British accent, laughing some more. "What do you know about *good*, wyrm?"

Mikhaila moved—picked up as if by the air itself and thrown on her back a few feet away.

My blood boiled. My magic unleashed from me, aimed without my even having to think about it, but everything changed so absurdly fast yet again.

"I'll find her," he said, his dark eyes on me—and he ceased to exist as my Air went through to where he had been standing.

He was gone.

My body let go of me, and I fell back, barely breathing. My eyes closed, and the roar of my wyvern broke me open. The relief, the guilt, the fear took over me, shaking me to my core.

My animal was here. He was back. He was okay.

"What the hell, what the hell, what the..."

John must have been up, and I heard his voice growing closer and closer.

"Lucien," he said, and I had no choice but to sit up. No choice but to search for Rowan with my magic, make sure his lungs were full of air. They were. He was just unconscious, however far he'd landed from that blast.

Mikhaila was helping Jack to stand while John fell to his knees in front of me, eyes wide, tears streaming down his cheeks.

"What...what have we done?" he asked me.

I said, "We summoned the Ether."

He shook his head. He opened his mouth and tried to speak but couldn't find words.

It was okay—I couldn't find words, either. But I had to get up and find my brother. Find my mate.

Protect her at all costs. Because that man was coming back. He'd called her *my Fire,* and he would be back. I'd have to be ready and show him that Estella belonged to me. She was *mine*, even if he was a fucking god.

I found Rowan near a tree trunk, looking so peaceful with his eyes closed, breathing even. I kneeled in front of him and touched his face, his skin cold.

Rowan had told me about shifters once, different kinds that used to exist back in the old days but didn't anymore. They died out, he said, because they were few and far between.

One in particular I'd told my little fox about, back when we were in my home, in my bed, oblivious to what the future had in store for us. Back when I didn't even know who she really was.

Electricity shifters—who could manipulate electricity and could upload themselves into anything with an electricity charge. They could make blasts so powerful they would knock down anything in their path for miles. They could alter the electricity waves in one's body, basically altering their entire anatomy if strong enough. They could *change* you...make you less than what you were. Connect you or *disconnect* you from other parts of you.

From your animal.

Impossible, impossible, impossible, my mind said, but it wasn't.

We'd done what the world had thought impossible, too— we'd summoned the Ether.

I just had no clue that he was a shifter. I had no clue that he was really a man—like me.

I had no clue that he could be anything less than the answer to all our prayers.

"What the hell happened, Luc?"

Rowan had opened his eyes and had been watching me while I sat near him and looked at the sky, the moon, all the stars.

"He came," I said.

Rowan sat up. "And?"

"I don't think he's going to save the world, brother."

His hand fell on my forearm. "Luc." I met his eyes. He looked so much like my mother, like *me,* that it made my heart skip one too many beats. "What do you mean?"

I didn't want to tell him, but I did anyway. "I mean, Estella might have just given us a small chance when she took the king away from here." Every hair on his body stood at attention, and I felt it in the air about him. Maybe because he was thinking what I was thinking, what the Ether had told John in his dreams: *as long as Archibald Azarius is alive, there will never be balance among the elements.*

The others were there, all around us—Mikhaila checking Rowan for wounds, John trying to rip his hair from his head, Jack keeping his eyes closed as if he hoped to change the view about him if he prayed hard enough.

"This is bad," one said.

"So bad—how is the Ether like *that*?"

"What the hell happened? That *is* the Ether, right?"

"It should be—so why was he not...I don't know, *friendly*?" Jack. "He almost killed me!"

"We fucked up. We fucked up bad." Mikhaila.

"He's going to kill us. He will—I know it." Jack again.

"It's over. If *that* is the Ether, then it's already over—it's *over!*" John.

That's when I said words I never imagined I could possibly say and mean with my whole heart.

"Not everything is lost yet. The king is still alive."

≈

—THE END

*Thank you for reading **Warden of Water!***
I hope you enjoyed the continuation of Ella and Lucien's story.
*The 4th and final book in this series, **Queen of Fire**, comes out*
May 23rd, 2023! To be notified, you can follow me on Amazon,
social media, or visit www.dnhoxa.com

Sincerely,
Dori Hoxa

More by D.N. Hoxa: The Hidden Realm Series

Savage Ax (The Hidden Realm, Book 1)

I heard the stories about Savage Ax. They're whispered among vampires everywhere in the Hidden Realm.

He's dangerous, merciless, a predator even among monsters...but nobody told me that he was dangerously sexy, too.

Now, on top of having to go searching for a vampire out there in the human world infested with sorcerers, I have to do it with *him* by my side.

Handling Savage Ax didn't seem like a big deal—despite his looks, our covens are sworn enemies. Despite his reputation, I have the green light to get rid of him if needed. And it's all fun and games, empty threats and dirty words at first...

But there's a spark of madness in his eyes that draws me in. Something about the way he takes what he wants, even from me, and gives no explanation in return. Something about the rough touch of his hand that melts all the ice I've spent years layering around me.

The farther away from home we go, the easier it gets to forget who he is. Who I am. Where we are.

And that's exactly where my real troubles will begin...

Savage Ax is the first book in The Hidden Realm series, written in 2 POVs, packed with magic, mayhem, and explicit romantic scenes intended for mature audiences.

PIXIE PINK SERIES

Werewolves Like Pink Too (Pixie Pink, Book 1)

What's worse than a pink pixie living all alone in the Big City, eight thousand miles away from home?

A pink pixie who's stuck behind a desk all day, taking calls and managing monster-fighting crews without ever seeing the light of day herself. *That's* what.

For two years, I worked my ass off to prove myself to my boss, and prayed for a chance to do the work I left my family behind for.

And I'm finally about to catch my break. I've got an undercover mission with my name on it, and it's everything I've been dreaming of since I got here.

Until I find out that Dominic Dane will be my partner. That self absorbed, narcissistic werewolf who humiliated me in front of all my coworkers on day one, and loves to pretend that I don't even exist.

It's bad enough that he tried to kick me out of my mission. It's even worse that he's sinfully hot and fries braincells with a single look of those gorgeous green eyes.

Now, on top of having to kick ass on my first mission, I have to pretend to be his *girlfriend* for three days, and keep my ridiculous attraction to him under control, too. So much for catching a break.

Lucky for me, I've got a secret weapon that's going to help me handle Dominic Dane, and it's God's best gift to mankind: chocolate. Armed with as many bars as my purse can fit, and with my wits about me, I'm going to survive the gorgeous wolf-ass one way or the other—and *win*.

THE NEW YORK SHADE SERIES

Magic Thief (The New York Shade, Book 1)

Welcome to the New York Shade!

My name is Sin Montero--hellbeast mercenary, professional liar, and
I'll happily be your guide.

Supernaturals are free to be who they are in the Shade. That's the
point of its existence--just not for me. I've spent my whole life lying
about what I am, until it all comes crashing down on me with a
single bite. Turns out, my blood can't tell lies, not to a vampire.

Damian Reed is achingly beautiful the way a lion is breathtaking--
right until he rips your throat out. He claims my baby brother is in
trouble...

THE NEW ORLEANS SHADE SERIES

Pain Seeker (The New Orleans Shade, Book 1)

Betrayed. Defeated. Chained.

I used to be a sister, a friend, a ruler of the elflands that belonged to my family's House. Now, I am a prisoner of the fae, my kind's sworn enemy since the beginning of time.

They put chains around me, thinking they can keep me from breaking free and taking their lives. They can't.

The only reason I stay is because I no longer need a life. My home, my family, my dignity were all taken away from me.

But I have the fae. My captor. He is every bit the man I was taught to hate long before I knew how to love...

The Dark Shade Series

Shadow Born (The Dark Shade, Book 1)

They call me Kallista Nix, but that is not my real name. *My past was taken from me, and though I search for it every day for the past five years, all I find are dead ends.*

Though I search for the Dark Shade, everyone keeps telling me that it doesn't exist. The darkness, the monsters, the fear—they're all in my head. I'm tempted to believe them. The Shades are magical safe havens where everyone can be who they truly are without having to hide. Supernaturals of all kinds love them. They're not supposed to be *dark*. But how can I argue with my own memories? Everything changes when I steal a magical artifact...

SMOKE & ASHES SERIES

Firestorm (Smoke & Ashes, Book 1)

Having no soul definitely has its perks.

After all, I can kill as many magical beasts as I want and not have to worry about the blood on my hands. But no matter how hard I try to run, I can never escape where I came from: the pits of Hell. Now Hell's elite have a job for me, a job I can't refuse. A nocturnal witch is on the loose and those are never up to anything good. She's hiding in my city, so they've decided I'm the best person for the job— together with Lexar Dagon'an. He's Hell's very own Golden Boy, my archnemesis, and he's sexy as the sins he makes me want to commit when I look at him. Like *murder*, obviously...

Also by D.N. Hoxa

Winter Wayne Series (Completed)

Bone Witch

Bone Coven

Bone Magic

Bone Spell

Bone Prison

Bone Fairy

Scarlet Jones Series (Completed)

Storm Witch

Storm Power

Storm Legacy

Storm Secrets

Storm Vengeance

Storm Dragon

Victoria Brigham Series (Completed)

Wolf Witch

Wolf Uncovered

Wolf Unleashed

Wolf's Rise

The Marked Series (Completed)

Blood and Fire

Deadly Secrets

Death Marked

Starlight Series (Completed)

Assassin

Villain

Sinner

Savior

Morta Fox Series (Completed)

Heartbeat

Reclaimed

Unchanged